SCOT'S EGGS

Catriona McPherson

**SEVERN
HOUSE**

First world edition published in Great Britain and the USA in 2025
by Severn House, an imprint of Canongate Books Ltd,
14 High Street, Edinburgh EH1 1TE.

severnhouse.com

Cover and jacket design by Jem Butcher Design

British Library Cataloguing-in-Publication Data
A CIP catalogue record for this title is available from the British Library.

ISBN-13: 978-1-4483-1286-3 (cased)
ISBN-13: 978-1-4483-1883-4 (paper)
ISBN-13: 978-1-4483-1287-0 (e-book)

All Severn House titles are printed on acid-free paper.

Typeset by Palimpsest Book Production Ltd., Falkirk, Stirlingshire, Scotland.
Printed and bound in Great Britain by TJ Books, Padstow, Cornwall.

The manufacturer's authorised representative in the EU for product safety is
Authorised Rep Compliance Ltd, 71 Lower Baggot Street, Dublin D02 P593
Ireland (arccompliance.com)

Praise for the Last Ditch Mysteries

'Plot twists . . . quirky characters, humor,
and the introspective Lexy . . . add up to a
successful entry in the series'
Booklist on *Scotzilla*

'An engaging plot, eccentric characters, plenty of humor'
Booklist on *Scot in a Trap*

'Wildly funny'
Kirkus Reviews on *Scot in a Trap*

'Clever turns of phrase and witty observations fuel
this fast and funny novel'
Publishers Weekly on *Scot Mist*

'The banter among the various characters
will draw Janet Evanovich fans to this engaging,
not-quite-a-locked-room mystery'
Booklist on *Scot Mist*

About the author

Born and raised in West Lothian, **Catriona McPherson** left Edinburgh University with a PhD in Linguistics and worked in academia, as well as banking and public libraries, before taking up full-time writing in 2001. For the last fifteen years she has lived in Northern California with frequent visits home. Among numerous prizes, she has won two of Left Coast Crime's coveted Humorous Lefty Awards for the Last Ditch comedies.

www.catrionamcpherson.com

This is for
Dru Ann Love
with my love and thanks

Acknowledgements

I would like to thank, as ever: Lisa Moylett, Zoë Apostolides, Elena Langtry and Jamie Maclean at the agency; everyone at Severn House, especially Sara Porter, Jo Grant, Martin Brown, Lucy Page, Penny Isaac, Sianna King, Lianne Slavin, Laurie Johnson and Jem Butcher; so many other friends and family that I can't dream of listing them (which isn't much of a plight, as plights go), and every single bookseller, librarian, reviewer, blogger and reader who's ever worked not just to keep my books afloat, but who's ever worked to keep people reading instead of not.

Also this time I'd like to thank Glenn 'Vegas' Villegas for help with Mexican Spanish and everyone at the University of California Washington Center, where I was given an office I had no right to and made to feel very welcome. So that's Clifton, Debbie, Dione, Eugene – we hardly knew you, Gloria – love and hugs, Jeanne, Jimmy, Kim, Mac – big thanks, Marc, Mary – for so much, Michael N, Michael S, Marlee, Narine, Santos – muchas grazias, Sherdera, Steven, Tanya, Tiara next door, Tiara in the lobby and Tyler. If my American characters sound a wee bit more DC than they do CA in *Scot's Eggs*, it's because I wrote their dialogue with my office door open and the sounds of the South wafting in and cuddling me.

ONE

At least it was raining.

I lay in bed listening to the drops as they hit the roof of the boat, the deck, the surface of the slough and my heart. Then, embarrassed by all that melodrama – or was it mawkishness? What's bathos? – even inside my thoughts, I prodded Taylor to get out the way, save me clambering over him. Our bedroom is too small to have the marital bed sticking out into the middle of the floor with space on both sides, such as is required for a hotel to jump from one star to two. Or maybe that's bedside tables. We've only got one of those as well, obviously.

Taylor didn't get out and let me emerge with grace and ease, or squiggle himself to one side to allow me to scoot out that way, or even tuck his legs up so I could burrow under the blankets and pop out at the bottom. He grabbed me and manhandled me up on to his chest, then kissed me, morning breath and all.

'It's raining,' I said, with my own morning breath, and I was the one who ended up on the schnapps last night. He blinked but didn't recoil. It's hard to recoil into a firm pillow when someone's lying on top of you. 'The egg-hunt's going to be a wash-out.'

'Another way Passover beats Easter,' Taylor said. 'Eggs made of chocolate aren't weatherproof. Eggs made of egg can take all the rain that's coming.'

'Coffee?' I said, slithering off him and plucking my dressing gown from the hook on the back of the door as I stood. Small bedrooms are efficient that way.

'I'll get it,' Taylor said, swinging his legs out of bed. 'Are you definitely . . .?'

'Yeah.'

'Baby,' said Taylor.

'Poor choice of words,' I muttered, then hoped he hadn't heard me. I'd have been able to tell from his face, so I didn't look back as I made my way to our minuscule shower room, where last night's fancy knickers were soaking in a bucket of cold, salty water and a big box of super-plus tampons with one missing was waiting on the narrow shelf, along with the rest of our pared-to-the-bone toiletries.

The boat dipped as one of my nearest-and-dearest friends-so-close-they're-family came aboard. If the window in here wasn't as titchy as everything else, I would have climbed out and swum away. I couldn't decide which one of them I wanted to see least.

There's Todd: always most likely to barge in first thing, with his unquestioned expectation of universal welcome and his boundary-free and rock-solid belief that he knows best. I genuinely couldn't face Todd this morning.

Maybe it was his husband, Roger: quieter (not difficult), more measured (inevitable), but a paediatric doctor and far too good at soulful eyes and sympathy. He would wreck me.

Noleen, the co-owner of this here motel that my houseboat is moored behind, has flinty eyes and the sympathy of a jackal with a migraine, but one of her brusque one-liners would wreck me in a different way. True, she doesn't talk much before ten, but she wears very forthright slogan sweatshirts.

Or it might have been Kathi. She's Noleen's wife, the other owner of the Last Ditch Motel as well as sole owner of the attached Skweeky-Kleen Laundromat, and just as silent in the morning, with text-free clothes too. But Kathi is so unnerved by displays of emotion that you kind of have to can it for her or her neck goes blotchy. I wasn't willing to be that kind right now.

If I wanted *incoming* kindness, Della would fit the bill. She's the third of my best friends after Kathi and Todd and she's got the biggest heart ever squashed into a human chest. But her kindness would be based in sympathy so she was as useless to me as Roger, this morning.

There's no way it was Della's husband, Devin. He'd already be at the coalface, working hard to get his family into a house, a condo, or even a little flat somewhere. Anything but the pair of motel rooms that have been their home for years, since even before Chihiro was born, back when Diego was a tiny little chubby toddler with eyes like soup plates and a piping helium voice, saying hello to his brand-new sister, with her little strawberry birthmark and her little rosebud mouth and her ears like tiny crumpled petals and her seed-pearl fingernails.

I stood up to wash my hands and to say that – the gist of it – out loud into the mirror. 'Baby Chihiro, hours old, perfect and welcome and loved and Della's. Nothing to do with me.' It was true. Della and Devin's good fortune was unrelated to . . . my current situation . . . and I refused to become one of those women who gets dreary and weird about other people's children. No way.

I only realised I was still speaking out loud when, on the other side of the bathroom door, I heard a stranger clear their throat. 'Mr and Mrs Aaronovitch? Can I have a word?'

Just like that, I was handed the only thing – instant rage – that could stop me feeling a spiral of misery, shame about it, self-pity about the shame, humiliation about the self-pity, shame about *that*, and regret that I still shopped for dream-me every time I filled my fridge, instead of inhabiting real-me, which meant that I had to face this hangover with fat-free yoghurt and blueberries, instead of bacon as God intended.

I blatted open the door.

'First,' I said, 'Mrs Aaronovitch, my dear mother-in-law, is dead. Next, neither one of *us* changed our names when we got married because it's 2025. Plus, if you heard two voices in here you need to get your lugholes syringed and, finally, get off my boat and spend some time learning the phrase "permission to come aboard". Capiche?'

I've been in America long enough to say things like 'capiche' now. I also say 'buck' for dollar sometimes, so long as none of my friends are around to mock me and I'm working up to 'bougie'. Of course, the corollary of that is I've been out of Scotland so long my entire rant came out fuck-free.

The guy, the stowaway as he would be called if this boat was mobile, took a step back and banged against the opposite wall of our narrow corridor. Good. It was only when the impact made various clanking noises that I realised he was a uniformed copper with all that stuff hanging off his belt as usual. So not just a stowaway. A violator of my right to be secure in my home against unreasonable search and seizure.

'Are you in hot pursuit of a fleeing suspect?' I asked him.

'Uhhh.'

'Are you concerned about the destruction of evidence?'

'I'm—'

'Is there an immediate threat to someone's life or safety?'

'It's—'

'Or do you have a warrant?'

Truly, it's a terrible idea to mess with a pissed-off, hungover, menstruating woman who's studying hard for her citizenship test. This idiot had cheered me up completely.

'Plocky?' came a voice I recognised, from the bank near the porch end. 'Did you enter this residence without knocking?' It was Molly Rankinson, of the Cuento PD, my almost-pal but for the fact that she thinks I'm a thorn in her side and won't admit that she's more often one in mine.

'There's no front door, Sarge!' the idiot said.

'What do you call the piece of wood and glass in the hole at the end of my living room?' I said, squeezing past him and marching along there. 'You see it? This thing attached with hinges and held in place by a latch and a lock?'

'The owner gave me permission to interview the guests,' the idiot chose to say next.

'Don't whine, Plocky,' said Molly, still on the bank. 'It suits you down to the ground but it grates on *me*. Ms Campbell? Permission to come aboard.'

'Granted,' I shouted. The deck tipped as Molly started to climb the porch steps. 'I am the owner of this vessel,' I said to the idiot. Plocky? I had no idea about the spelling, but I'd have ditched it for Aaronovitch, 2025 or not. 'There are no guests here. You're not making any sense.'

'Mrs Muntz – Mrs Noleen Muntz, this is – gave her permission for us to interview the motel guests,' Molly said, arriving at our side. My eyebrows went up, dammit. Molly is an eyebrow ninja. Each one has about five settings, independent of the other and so, while she's around, I try to keep mine still, so's not to be outclassed. 'Yeah, that's what I thought,' she went on, answering my entry-level brow work. 'Turns out no one's in, otherwise she'd have tried to make me come back with a separate warrant for every door.'

I said nothing. My studies hadn't taken me as far as the rules on searching rented rooms.

'This is a separate property, Plocky,' Molly said. 'Not a great start for you.'

'Is it your first day?' I asked, wondering if I could make it his last. He swallowed hard, his Adam's apple dipping down behind his collar and taking a good long time to reappear. I felt my resolve start to soften. 'What's up anyway?' I asked Molly, telling myself that if it was a big straightforward deal – kidnap, domestic violence, gun running, organised crime – I'd look past the idiot's idiocy and not slow them down. But if it was murkier than that – a brown guy annoying the cops, a homeless lady annoying the cops, a black kid annoying the cops (not that I'm cynical or anything) – then the idiot was about to get his idiotic arse handed to him.

'Murder,' said Molly.

It's quite a window on my years in Cuento that my first thought was: not again!

TWO

'Who died?' I asked and felt pretty proud of myself. What I wanted to ask was why they were sniffing round the Last Ditch, because I knew for a fact that no one had died here. Noleen is not dramatic but corpses in her renting rooms or floating in her swimming pool would definitely strike her as news worth sharing.

'Tourists,' said Molly. 'Name of Bill and Billie Miller.'

'That sounds made up,' I said.

'Right?' said Molly. 'It's not, though. William Whitstable Miller and Sybil Winifred Miller, née Tiller.'

'That's not helping.'

'You're not telling me anything I don't know,' Molly said. 'But those are their names. Found their ID and everything.'

'Here?' I flicked a glance at the idiot. He was trying to blend into the wall behind him which, considering he was wearing head-to-toe black and the wall is tongue-and-groove panelling, varnished like a toffee apple, wasn't going too well for him.

'We want to rule out the possibility that they stayed here,' Molly said. 'Which we reckon they might have. While they were still alive.' She too threw a quick glance her colleague's way. 'In the motel, though. Not on your boat.'

'So ask Noleen,' I suggested.

'Last weekend,' said Molly.

'Ahhh,' I said. 'Gotcha.'

The previous weekend, you see, had been Noleen and Kathi's fifteenth wedding anniversary and they had taken off on a three-day camping trip, a thing that struck them as a way to celebrate. Also Taylor and I had been down in San Francisco on the Friday night, trying to 'relax and let things take their course', like all the articles tell you. Todd and Roger had been hanging out with some of their gay friends in Sacramento on Saturday night, in that borderline-offensive way they say they need to sometimes, when the rest of us start to bug them. Not including Kathi and Nolly, I assume. Then Della and Devin had off-loaded the kids – on to a pair of pals who presumably didn't say no quick enough – and gone to Napa for Sunday.

All in all, it was a bit of a service-industry conundrum, until Roger, Dr Deep Pockets, sprang for stand-in motel managers for three days. He might as well have ripped up the constitution and billeted soldiers in the place, to drink rum and shoot holes in the walls. Noleen still hadn't stopped griping about the state they'd left the desk, the computer, the bookings and the takings and I suppose if they'd let a couple of tourists get murdered she might have had a point.

'Can't you ask the locums?' I said.

'The who?'

'The rent-a-pulse people who ran the Ditch last weekend.'

'Can't find them. But that's not our biggest worry. Look, can we do this sitting down? I can meet you out front in twenty minutes. Do you want to get dressed?'

'Do what?' I asked. 'Meet for what purpose? Dressed for what occasion?' The last question was pure arsery, but the other two were sincere.

'Twenty minutes,' Molly said. 'I'll get you a coffee from Swiss Sisters and see you poolside. You,' she added, turning to the idiot. 'Two large black Americanos.'

'And a cinnamon bun,' I added. I had no idea why Molly wanted to question me but I was going to find out without the taste of zero-fat yoghurt clagging up my uvula. Small victories.

'Bring Taylor and don't speak to the rest of them beforehand,' Molly said.

'I'll have a latte,' Taylor said, from behind the kitchen door where he had been lurking. It's not that he's unsupportive, more that he was bollock-naked. 'And an almond croissant.'

'I love you,' I told him, once Molly and the idiot were on dry land again. He had said crrrr-*wass*-ong, specially for me, instead of cruh-*sawnt*, which always makes me want to punch someone.

* * *

Twenty-five minutes later, we joined Molly and the idiot by the pool, at the best table. There's not much in it, but this one doesn't wobble, isn't rusty and has got an umbrella with twelve working spokes.

'So what do you want to know?' I asked, after I'd taken a noisy draught of foam off the top of Taylor's latte. It's an arrangement we've come to that suits both of us, no matter what anyone thinks, like all of a working marriage really. And our marriage, despite everything, *is* still working. 'Also, why were we not to talk to the others?'

'Tell me who you remember being at the motel last weekend, while you were here too,' Molly said. 'Because I didn't want you all comparing notes.'

'Why not just show us a pic of the Millers and see if we recognise them?' I asked.

Molly flicked a glance at the rookie.

'Wait, is this some kind of training deal, for *him*?' I said.

'With free coffee and baked goods,' said Molly. A fair point.

'I'll go first,' Taylor said, and added, 'I like trained cops better than the other kind, so I'm happy to help.'

Molly looked hard at that for an insult, then nodded.

'There were all the permanent residents, of course,' Taylor began.

'Never not going to be weird,' Molly said.

I've explained how come the Ditch had so many permanent residents to her numerous times but she prefers judging. Besides, there was nothing weird or even remarkable about Della and Diego living at the motel while she was undocumented. Barely more strange was Devin moving in to escape flatmate bullies on the college campus. And they've been broke since they got together. It's a story that's playing out all across the country every day.

And what could be more normal than Noleen and Kathi living right here at the motel they own, handy for the laundro-mat too? Yes, they might be expected to live in the owners' apartment, rather than in one of the rooms, with another one held in reserve in case of emergency evacuations, but . . . Actually there are no buts. That's weird.

Admittedly, Todd and Roger are another matter. Two doctors, even with one on long-term sick leave for a mental-health issue, shouldn't live in a motel. They should live in their own palatial house, instead of the tenants who've been there for years now. But Todd has an insect phobia like no other and Kathi's *germ*aphobia, which is what makes her clean her flat and live in a room instead, with a spare room to use if she needs it, also makes her keep the rest of the Ditch cleaner than a dentist's office at NASA. Plus, her cousin in Costa Rica sends her insecticide that could dissolve teeth and disable rockets if sprayed undiluted, so this is the only place in Cuento Todd's ever happy. Especially since he's got a key to the spare room too, in case of sudden infestations. Roger, it has to be said, is a saint. Or perhaps just really busy and happier when Todd's not in meltdown. Because although he's a saint, he's also a guy and guys, in general, kind of suck.

Take Taylor, for instance. When I zoned back in to the conversation he was nearly done. 'The stand-in motel managers were . . . regular, I guess. And there was only one guest that I saw. Right, Lexy? On Sunday or maybe Saturday? A man.'

'Describe him,' Molly said.

'A kind of regular kind of a man,' said Taylor. 'Middle-aged, I guess. I think he was alone. Right, Lexy? Did you see that guy?'

'I did,' I said, nodding. 'I did see him.'

Molly finished writing, turned over a page and gave me an expectant look.

I opened my pastry bag and frowned.

'Yeah,' she said. 'Swiss Sisters went nuts for the holiday.'

Because my cinnamon bun had a dent in the middle and three little eggs sitting in there on a puff of toasted coconut. Taylor opened his bag and pulled out a croissant with its ends joined together and a dent/puff/egg combo jammed into the hole.

'That's annoying,' he said.

'Tcha. Don't go downtown,' Molly said. 'And you,' she pointed at the idiot, 'should be taking more notes, or else you'll be on chick and bunny control at the bonnet parade.'

'Chicks?' said Taylor, coming alive. I considered how much I loved him for the second time this morning, which counts double during menstruation, I'd say. First he dug in with that pronunciation and then there was the fact that his immediate interest in chicks was based in ornithology and not sleaze-bucketry.

'Stand down, Bob Stroud,' said Molly. 'Little kids dressed *up* as chicks. You won that one years ago. Lexy?'

'Who won what one?' I said. 'Who's Bob Stroud?'

'When the Audubon Society—' Taylor began. That's usually enough to get me groaning, but in pursuit of citizenship I was trying to be as American as John Wayne's face in an apple pie crust, so I was prepared to listen.

'Lexy?' said Molly again, cutting him off.

I finished knocking the embellishments out of my breakfast order and took a big bite. 'I saw quite a few people last weekend,' I said, when I'd finished chewing. 'There was the guy who's working on the levée. You know? The construction guy? He was still here when we left on Friday.'

'Got him,' Molly said.

'Oh yeah,' said Taylor.

'Then on Saturday there were two sets of UCC parents come to pick up their kids for spring break. But they weren't your dead tourists, I don't think, because they've been here before and also I saw them leave on Sunday.'

'Forgot about them,' Taylor said.

'Yeah, we spoke with them too,' said Molly.

'And a huge family stopped off late on Sunday and left early on Monday: granny and grandad, parents, and it sounded like seven children. They had four rooms but the stand-in managers only charged them for three, Noleen said.'

'Was that last weekend?' said Taylor. 'I could have sworn . . . But you saw the guy too, right? The one I saw?'

'The middle-aged, regular guy?' I said.

'Yep, that's the one.'

'I saw *a* guy. I think he must have been a . . . Well, I don't know what he was, if I'm honest, but there had to be an explanation. I mean he could have been average height, but he was dead skinny and he seemed to have very long legs. I thought he might even have stilts on, mad as that sounds.'

'Anything else?' Molly said, in a cold voice.

'And he was bald as a beachball, with this wild frizz of bright ginger hair sticking out all round. Like a sea anemone. It was kind of mesmerising, when he stood in a breeze.'

'Oh . . . yeah,' said Taylor. 'I forgot that part.'

'He was dressed in a candy-cane striped blazer, a bowtie with a spiral pattern, and he had a straw boater in his hand. White trousers with a shiny stripe down the outside of the legs. And spats.'

'Yeah,' Taylor said. 'Definitely . . . spats.'

Molly clicked her pen closed and folded her arms. 'Two people are dead,' she said. 'Do you think you're being cute?'

'See?' I said, rounding on Taylor. '*See?*'

'See what?' Taylor and Molly said, in perfect unison.

'I'm not kidding,' I told Molly. 'Blazer, bowtie, boater, stripe on his trousers, spats over his shoes, possibly on stilts. And Taylor's not kidding either. He remembered a "regular, middle-aged" guy and agreed with the rest when I reminded him. You,' I said, rounding on my beloved, 'are not normal.' I turned back to Molly. 'Ask him what birds he saw here last weekend.'

She didn't need to; Taylor was off. 'Well, wrens, swallows and tri-coloured blackbirds,' he said, waving at the trees around the edge of the car park. 'Still a few white-crowned sparrows obviously. There was a sandhill crane in the slough and a white-breasted nuthatch, although I never saw its mate. Barry saw a pair of oak titmice, he said on the group, but that was Friday and we were down in the city.'

'Wow,' Molly said. 'Anyway, where did you see this oh-so-inexplicably-dressed individual, Lexy? And you?' She turned to the idiot again. 'Don't write any of this up, OK?'

'Coming out of Room 204 and clumping down the stairs,' I told her. 'Very awkwardly, as you can imagine, if he really was wearing stilts on those metal steps. I might have guessed cowboy boots from the sound alone because I've seen guys get into trouble that way before, but he definitely had spats on. How weird is that?'

'And what time would you say this was? Sunday?'

'Saturday,' I said. 'At about . . . it was when we got back. Check-out was noon and we drove straight home, so probably two-ish? Taylor?'

'Hm?' He had reminded himself of the trees by mentioning them and was laser-focussed on a twittering little flock high in the topmost branches.

'OK,' Molly said, standing. 'Thank you for the information. Barbershop singer, by the way.'

'What?' I said. 'Bob Stroud is?'

'Put down the constitution and watch some TV,' she said, shaking her head as she walked away. Which was probably treason, for a uniformed officer.

'Tay?' I said. 'Is Bob Stroud a singer in a hairdresser's?'

'Bob Stroud discovered a cure for haemorrhagic septicaemia in canaries,' Taylor told me.

'And how the hell would Molly know that?'

'While in Alcatraz,' Taylor added.

I blinked a couple of times. 'You are not normal,' I said again.

'What do you want to do today?' he asked me. 'To take your mind off . . . everything.'

That was actually quite sweet and I'm a cow for not telling the truth, which was I wanted to curl up and eat chocolate so he might as well go down to the wetlands like he wanted to. What I actually said was, 'Let's go to the parade.'

THREE

He took it pretty well. There was just one gusty sigh and I only heard that because he delivered it in the underpass that connects the Ditch and self-storage bit of town to the letter and number streets where parades take place.

'Did it strike you that Molly never even gave us a description of these dead tourists?' I asked him.

'Not hard,' Taylor said.

I grinned. He was hopeless in new ways every day but he was honest and he was funny. My brief first marriage had been to a deadly earnest dentist who lied with the same grim focus as he recommended water picks. I had traded up and no mistake.

'Asked us who we'd seen and never even told us who we were supposed to be looking for. I get the training angle, but still.'

'Not just training the kid though,' Taylor said. 'She probably wouldn't ever say straight off, "Did you see Bob and Barb Milligan last weekend?" and describe them. In case she implanted a false memory.'

'That's not even at the right stop to catch a *bus* to true,' I said. 'Police show photographs of murder victims to potential witnesses all the time. On their phones. Driver's licence photos if they can't get a family snap. Or even post-mortem photos. Why on earth wouldn't Molly?'

'If,' Taylor said, 'they didn't have driver's licences. Or any family. And if the corpses are too mutilated to help.'

'Glad I asked,' I said. 'How the hell could you be a tourist in this country if you couldn't drive?'

'Amtrak, Greyhound, chartered coach . . . loads of ways.'

'Name three more,' I said. It would sound like bickering to a bystander.

'OK,' said Taylor. 'Union Pacific, BNSF, Central Pacific.'

'Union Pacific only carries freight,' I said, softly – which is the best way to deliver knock-out blows to Taylor, I've found.

He whistled through his teeth. 'You are going to ace this citizenship, babe. But no one's ever going to play Trivial Pursuit with you again.' Taylor's mother, the late and much-lamented Amaranth, had been pretty elderly when she adopted him, and some of his references, as well as his wardrobe, were on the boomer-end of normal. He put his arm round me. 'And Central Pacific has been closed for years.' Like I said, as honest as the day is long.

We were passing the police station by this time. 'Will we stop in and ask to see Bill and Billie's photos?' I said. 'If they're pre-mortem, anyway. I'm pretty sure they didn't stay at the Ditch when we were around but we might have passed them in town somewhere.'

Taylor was scrolling on his phone. He held it out to me, showing the landing page of the *Cuento Voyager*. Half of it was taken up with a picture of the downtown block we were headed to right now, pastel-coloured ribbons wound round the shade trees and wicker baskets covered in cellophane lined up on trestle tables outside the businesses, all ready for creed to slam up against commerce in the usual way.

The other half of the front page was dominated by a second jaunty snap. A middle-aged couple were seated one behind the other in a bright blue kayak, clutching their crash helmets and grinning into the camera from under identical, flattened-down, sweaty hairdos. They were both lean and neat, not an ounce of flab stretching a single stitch of their outdoorsy, if not actually technical, clothing. They both wore close to identical sensible spectacles too.

Bill and Billie Miller, in happier times, said the caption. *Full story on page 3.*

'I thought they'd be fat,' I said. 'Their names sound chubby. Plus why would adventure tourists be in Cuento?'

'Same as all the other tourists,' said Taylor. 'Passing through.'

Then I heard the unmistakable sound of Todd, my three-way-first-equal best friend, squealing my name. He was at the corner of F and 2nd Steet, standing in a pool of sunlight and looking as perfect as ever, although not particularly Easter-themed. As we got closer, I did spot a tiny sparkling cowboy hat perched just off-centre on his head, white to match the rest of his ensemble.

'I'm so glad you decided to come!' he said, when we were beside him. 'Is that what you're wearing? Oh well. Like I say, glad you're here. It's all so unbelievably off-brand for me, but it's too good an opportunity to miss. I snagged us half the table at the Casual Browser—'

'How the hell did you man—'

'Puh-lease! It's a bookstore, Lexy. What kids want books on Easter?'

'Cuento kids, the poor wee souls,' I said. Which was true.

'And I told them you'd need a chair so don't worry about being tired.'

'How did you know I'd need a chair?'

'OMG! I was trying to smoke you out. OMG! You need a chair?'

'Oh Christ,' said Taylor. 'Todd—'

'I mean I knew when you went off to the city together last Friday,' Todd said. 'Instead of doing whatever sad-sack thing you usually do for fun at the weekend.' That was rich, considering most Friday nights Roger was working, Todd would be right there doing it with us.

'Todd—' Taylor said, trying again.

'So make the most of raking in business, as God intended, this year,' Todd said. 'Next year, you'll be at home covered in baby sick and for over a decade after that you'll be one of them.' He flicked a hand towards a gaggle of mostly women, with be-costumed toddlers either in strollers or in those little wagons that are such a brilliant idea that it always puzzles me why they only exist in America. Maybe because British kids would be unconscious from the traffic fumes before they could get soaked through with muddy splashes from the kerb puddles. Although at least the water would put out the cigarette stubs that would have fallen on them and, if it was cold enough, start to harden the spat-out chewing gum stuck to their clothes.

Yeah actually there's no mystery why parents back home don't give their kids brain damage from rattling wagons over the cobbles, crumbling tarmac and assorted potholes.

Todd was still talking.

'Todd—' Taylor was still trying to stop him.

'How did you persuade the Browser to give up half their table?' I said, during a breath.

'Oh! Oh!' said Todd. 'You're going to be one of those NBD mamas, are you? Well, knock yourself out. I, as godfather of final authority, am going to enjoy the next nine months.'

'She's not pregnant!' Taylor said. It was very loud and it fell into one of those moments of sudden silence that can occur anytime and anywhere. Right now, four Priuses were stopped at the intersection waiting for pedestrians to cross, so there was no traffic noise, and the wagon mums were in the middle of a prayer. So, all in all, probably about seventeen total strangers heard my non-news. A couple of the praying mums opened their eyes a slit, to check me out.

'Why did you go to the city?' Todd cried.

'To take our minds off waiting to see if I was pregnant!' I cried back. There was no point in lowering voices now, I reckoned.

'But you said you needed a chair!' Todd cried, a bit louder. He might have been genuinely upset for me or he might have been enjoying the drama.

'*You* said I needed a chair!' I pointed out. 'And I do. I feel like scunge because my period started.'

I was prepared for him to make a sudden move, but I was expecting it to be a huge leap backwards, away from me. I even kind of hoped he might jump into the traffic, not that any Cuento Prius driver would mow him down. What I wasn't expecting was for him to lunge *forward* and throw his arms around me, him in his head-to-toe white.

'Sweetheart,' he said, right in my ear. 'You have so much time it's making me want a nap. Have you never heard of pacing? How are we supposed to keep caring when there's so much time, stretching out to the horizon? Yawning eons of time?'

'How did you get half the Browser table, you gibbering maniac?' I asked his shoulder, which was muffling me.

He let me go and I was touched and kind of astonished to see tears standing in his eyes.

'I flirted,' he said. 'Duh.'

I would have known when we got there even if he hadn't told me. The look on the face of the young woman tasked to stand behind this year's treat table for the downtown bookstore was somewhere between Bugs Bunny when he's just been hit on the back of the head with a frying pan and Joe Biden at that last debate. Pole-axed, you know. Gone. And it made no difference that Todd, as well as being married and old enough to be her father (in a soap opera anyway) was gayer than a Bichon Frisé in a Mariah Carey costume, coming on to do a cameo in the *Drag Race Halloween Special*. He's a full spectrum flirter and very good at it.

'Thank you, angel,' Todd said. 'We'll take it from here and if you need to step away for any reason we can talk about books as well, you know.'

'What are we going to talk about the rest of the time, by the way?' I said. It was hard to see how any bit of our shared, four-pronged business could find a happy home at an Easter bonnet parade.

'Ahem,' said Todd, and nodded at the trestle table.

The Browser's end was floored in a drift of give-away stickers and backed by a mountain range of propped-up picture books, while the bulk of its real estate was two hefty buckets of miniature chocolate eggs. Halfway along, though, there was a little white picket fence, stolen from a toy farmyard it looked to me, and on its other side a lemon and lavender gingham tablecloth bore a tasteful array of white linen bags, tied shut with matching gingham bows. This end of the table was decorated only with drifts of primroses and violets, snipped off at the head for easier strewing.

'What's in the bags?' I said, as if I didn't know. I opened one and confirmed it for myself. There was a little bottle of 'reviving eye serum', a card with an exhortation to 'live your power and all will come to you', a lemon-yellow macaron, with lavender filling, inside a cellophane packet, and a twenty-five-per-cent-off voucher for the first consultation with Trinity.

'You must have been up all night opening fortune cookies to get this many bits of claptrap,' I said, holding up the little card. 'Why not "Live your all and power will come to you"? Why not "Power your come and all will live to you"?'

'Ew,' said Todd. 'That doesn't make any sense.'

'None of it makes any sense,' I howled. 'How many times do I have to tell you I don't want my counselling practice – my therapy practice – associated with the idea that having a separate kind of lotion for every square inch of your body is a treat, rather than a tool of the patriarchy? And I know Kathi hates it too. What's eye serum got to do with de-cluttering? Have any of these little handmaid packs got a stain stick in them, at least? Gahhhh.'

Then I turned round and saw that one of the moppets had clambered out of his wagon and toddled along to see what was cooking. He was looking up at me from under his bunny ears, with a fat teardrop wobbling on the lower lashes of each eye.

A shriek sounded from the wagon circle. 'Dutton? Dutton! Where *are* you?'

'He's here,' I shouted back. 'A bit less praying might be an idea, eh?'

'Jesus Christ, Lexy, it's Easter,' said Taylor, which at least made all of us at our shared table laugh again.

The problem, in essence, was this. Todd, Kathi and I collectively run a business called Trinity. Todd's Trinity for You does makeovers; Kathi's Trinity for Home does de-cluttering; my Trinity for Life is a counselling service. Then's there's the fourth bit that came later and thank God none of us has OCD among our various diagnoses. (I mean their various diagnoses; I'm being kind. And actually it's only one diagnosis each. It just feels like more.) Anyway, Trinity for Trouble is a private detective agency with Kathi as the licensed gumshoe – a term she, incidentally, objects to because of gum and shoes and germaphobia – and Todd and I as willing lackeys. Increasingly, in recent years, it's begun to feel as if the original three prongs of Trinity only exist to deliver customers to Trouble. And that's fine too. What isn't fine and never will be is that Todd has a blithe disregard for boundaries, as I believe I've mentioned, and brands Kathi's down-and-dirty cleaning enterprise as well as her further down-and-even-dirtier investigation gig, not to mention my stuff – higher ground, higher purpose, deeper meaning and all that shit – as if we belong in the back room of his non-existent spa.

Although, to be fair, a stainstick would be a pathetic gift. And what would I give away anyway? A packet of hankies, since by the time someone gets to me it's usually too late for anything but sobbing?

Still. 'You are not in charge,' I reminded him, once again. 'Trinity is a collective.'

'Never mind the naturalisation, Lexy,' said Taylor. 'That kind of talk will lose you your green card.'

'Trinity needs strong leadership,' Todd said. 'And, as Shakespeare knew: cometh the hour, cometh the man.'

'I think that was the Bible,' I said. 'Or Winston Churchill maybe, but' – I gave him a smile I hoped was smug – 'if you say you're the top dog, I suppose Kathi's next in line and I just have to accept it.' He frowned. He knows me. 'And if Kathi tries to remove you from office and assume top doggery pro tem, I need to decide – as the only other principal officer of the executive body – how I'm going to vote.'

'Is she on a cancellation list at the courthouse in case someone else drops out?' Todd asked Taylor. 'Because I don't know how much more of this I can stand.'

'But,' I said, addressing Todd while ignoring him, a very necessary skill, 'it does look pretty.'

'I've invoiced the business account,' he replied. He is such hard work sometimes.

And then the parade started: women and men in such enormous hats they had to support the brims with upheld ski poles, enough bunnies to wipe out an entire eco-system once they started breeding, a chicken that was really the turkey from the Thanksgiving parade with some different coloured bits stuck on, and the usual suspects: Oddfellows, bikers, vintage cars, jugglers and that one guy that walks around town all year lugging a full-size wooden cross. At least today he fitted right in with the theme instead of just unnerving UCC parents and asking strangers to help him dig splinters out.

Then I saw him.

In a parade of adults, children and dogs all dressed up in real feathers, tissue-paper feathers, clods of papier-mâché aimed at making you think 'feather', and real petals, tissue-paper petals, and yes, some weirdly bulky papier-mâché objects supposed to bring daffodils to mind, not to mention the various ways these time-to-spare weirdos had thought up to become eggs for the day – and this is besides the bonnets, mind – you'd think one oddly dressed individual would slide right by me.

But Easter is pastel-coloured as a general rule. Some people had overdone it with the yellow dye, it's true, but the blue was sky, the green was mint, the purple was mauve, and the pink was skelped arse, so the sudden appearance of red and white in my field of vision made me blink. Then I sprang into action.

'That's him!' I said, looking wildly to one side of the table and the other, briefly considering vaulting over it, then plunging under it, rolling once, and leaping to my feet in a way I have never done in a fitness class in my life. I hopped and skipped my way through a bunch of Brownies with decorated paper plates on their heads and laid a firm hand on the striped arm of our mystery guest from the Ditch on murder weekend. It was definitely him: he had the boater on his head, stuffed with blossoms from band to brim but still unmistakable, he had the shiny bit on the side seam of his trousers, he had the spats, and he had that dazzling striped jacket, totally wrong for Easter, only good at Christmas and on barbers' poles. The sole thing missing was the bowtie. Maybe it was too hot when he was bearing the weight of all the crap on his hat.

Also, it did occur to me that I was looking straight across into his eyes. I glanced down at the crooked hem of his trousers and the shoes that definitely had real human feet in them.

'No stilts today?' I said. 'They'd have been perfect for a parade.'

'St–Stilts? I've never . . . Ohhhhhh. Are you . . .?' He shook his head. 'Who are you? What's going on?'

The parade was going on, for one thing. It was flowing past us on either side while we stood in the middle like a pair of rocks in a stream. A Scottish parade would have had us whacked in the back with a majorette's baton by now, or whacked on the head by a beer can thrown from the crowd. But this was Cuento, where neighbours give each other garden gluts, and put stuff they don't need out on the street corner with a sign saying FREE STUFF, and pay for an extra coffee in Swiss Sisters in case a homeless person needs one. The chicks, eggs and bunnies split and reformed while we stood there.

'The cops are looking for you,' I said. 'Pretty bold of you to be right here instead of hiding.'

'Me? Why? What . . .? Who *are* . . .? The cops are looking for me?' He was shaking hard enough to wobble his hat. As I watched it teeter, my eye was caught by the neat dark sideburns in front of his ears and the sculpted dark edge of his hair on his neck.

'Uh, no,' I said, letting go of his arm and stepping back. 'Sorry. Not you. No. Easy mistake to make, given your . . .' I waved a hand at his get-up. 'And, actually, I'm wrong anyway. You're a witness, not a suspect. Not even you, I mean. The other one. And not even a witness. Just a potential witness to something that hap— Wait. Didn't even happen where you – not you – were staying. You know?'

'I can't say I do,' the man said. He looked over my shoulder and spoke to someone behind me. 'Are you supposed to be looking after her?'

'Lexy, what's happening?' It was Kathi's voice. News to me that Kathi was attending this open-air (but still close-quarters) disease-fest.

'I thought I recognised this guy as one of the Last Ditch guests from the weekend of the murder and—'

The man took a huge step back, a thing that river rocks never do, and caused a pile-up of ten-year-old eggs behind him. They were foam though so they didn't crack, although their limbs got tangled and one of them started to cry.

'I live right here in Cuento,' the man said. 'I have no need for hotel accommodation and, if I did, I wouldn't choose that perfectly named fleapit' – I felt Kathi bristle – 'where I'm only right now finding out there has been yet *another* murder?' He bristled too, hard enough to tip his hat over one eye. He righted it, glared at us and rejoined the parade, no longer enjoying it but grimly determined that a maniac and her carer from a flophouse weren't going to derail his day.

'He's wearing exactly the same clothes as the guy I described to Molly,' I said.

'That,' said Kathi, 'is the universal costume of members of barbershop quartets.'

'Ohhhhh,' I said. A couple of things had just become clear.

'You seriously never heard of barbershop quartets? I mean, there's usually four but—'

'Morris men,' I said.

'Huh?'

'Exactly. Leave me alone.'

'Can't do that,' Kathi said. 'Come on, Lex. Swim to the side and let's get out of this. You're needed at home. You'll never guess who just turned up?'

'Bill and Billie Miller?' I said. 'Please God, not in the slough, after a week.'

'What is *wrong* with you?' Kathi said. 'No, but close. Their kids have arrived and they need our help. They might not know that yet, but they do.'

FOUR

'I don't know how I'm supposed to know stuff if no one ever tells me.' I was still grumbling as Taylor, Todd, Kathi and I went back into the dark of the underpass headed south again.

(Why were we free to leave the spot that Todd had flirted out of the Browser girl? Because all his bags were gone already. He hadn't rammed this point home. Yet. I knew it was coming. He had prepared to leave by working his no-longer-needed tablecloth under the books, corralling the Browser's stickers inside a picket-fence paddock, strewing blossoms around the whole table and telling the girl she had a lovely smile and should share it more widely. Right enough, she had been reading a John Scalzi paperback with the cover bent right back in a way that surprised me in a bookseller and also meant no one could strike up a conversation even about her choice of novel. Instead of scowling like I would if some guy told me to smile, she had given Todd a grin so wide it nearly met round the back and then gazed after him until he was out of sight.)

'Molly told you,' said Taylor, here in the underpass.

'Molly said two words unrelated to anything else,' I reminded him. 'You knew I thought she meant the Birdman of Alcatraz.'

'Wut?' said Kathi. 'Never mind.'

'And Todd?' I said. 'Are you going back to pick up that cloth and midget fence later, or will I? I don't mind which. I *do* mind you ever charging another set to the business account, having donated the first lot to the Browser.'

'Huh?' said Kathi. 'Could we concentrate here, please? Not you, Taylor.' We were out in the sunshine again with mere minutes to go till we got to the motel forecourt. 'Son and daughter of Bill and Billie Miller,' Kathi said. 'Phil, early twenties, looks military but I haven't asked yet, and Jilly, maybe twenty, dressed like a student. Both in town to . . . Well, you know . . . and staying at the Ditch for budgetary reasons. Don't tell Noleen that, because she's comped their room as a mark of condolence and she'll uncomp it stat if she hears it wasn't the ambience and delicious free breakfast that brought them our way.'

'And they need our help because . . .?' I said. 'What are their names, by the way?'

'Double duh,' Kathi said. 'Because if we don't help them they're going to be relying on the Cuento PD to solve their parents' murder. I just told you their names.'

'I assumed you were kidding,' I said.

'Seriously?' said Todd. 'Bill and Billie called their kids Phil and Jilly?'

'They've brought their little dog, Tilly,' Kathi said.

'Really?' I said.

'Of course not,' Kathi said. 'You know there are no pets allowed at the Ditch.'

It was a hard and fast rule, often strained by the fact that the spoiled and unscrupulous can buy 'service dog' harnesses off Amazon and strap them on to any yapping little mutt in the world. Kathi cancels the booking of anyone whose harness looks new unless, as she puts it, there are still stitches or crutches or a story in the news. It doesn't help that Diego owns two cats and a rabbit, all of which go outside on little harnesses of their own. And the disgruntled tourists don't even know that inside Casa Salinas-Muelenbelt there's also a well-stocked tropical-fish tank.

We were at the gate now with no more time to discuss the Miller family, because what was left of them was sitting at the worst table by the pool – the one with no umbrella at all and the *Nickelback Rules!* graffiti scratched in – and suddenly it didn't matter what they were actually called because their names were Oliver Twist and Annie. Their parents were dead, murdered, and even in my menstrual fug with the side of disappointment and the Todd-annoyance chaser, I only wanted to hug them.

'Ms Miller?' I said. 'Mr Miller?' Then I stalled. I had no

idea what to say next. *Welcome to the Last Ditch* was a bit heartless if their parents had in fact spent the last night of life here.

'We're so sorry for your loss,' said Taylor, damn him. It was the only thing to say and he had nabbed it.

'Lexy here is our resident therapist,' Todd said. 'And I can offer massage treatments, which sound entirely irrelevant in your current plight, but might help you sleep.'

The two kids, looking very like each other with their straight hair and slight build and huge dark circles under all four eyes, turned to Taylor.

'Ornithology,' he said. They looked even more similar when they frowned in bewilderment. 'If you think spending time in nature might help you in any way, I can take you to the wetlands.'

Damn him twice. Damn the lot of them. I, the therapist, was the only one not helping here.

'And we know Kathi,' the girl said. 'Thank you again for the room. It's one less thing.'

I had thought of something. 'Do you have anyone to come with you when you go to—'

'*Lexy*,' said Kathi, making me jump, 'isn't aware of the distressing particulars of what happened to your parents.' She glared at me. I mean, it was true, but one or both of them was going to have to identify two corpses. Unless they did one each.

I was wrong, as it turned out.

'Can we tell you the details?' the girl said again. 'We told Kathi already but I think the more times we say it the more it might actually go in. Right, Phil?'

'It sounds crazy,' said the boy. 'But Jilly's right. The more times we say it, the more of it I think I'm going to be able to get out of me before I implode.'

Pretty much the opposite of what his sister had said, but both things were probably true.

It took about twenty minutes of bustle and fuss to get ready for the recounting. We went round to the porch of the house-boat, for a start. 'So tranquil,' Jilly said. 'Thank you.' And then Todd sent Taylor on a drinks run, vetoing coffee and letting the orphans choose between chamomile tea, lavender tea and chocolate milk. They both chose chocolate milk and Todd added cookies to the order. Then the three of us from Trinity arranged ourselves with the sombre eyes and not quite smiling mouths of the condoler and waited to be filled in.

'We're twins,' Jilly said, kicking things off. 'And Mom and Dad were childhood sweethearts, so it's always been, I mean the four of us have always been, so . . .'

'Smug?' said Phil.

'I was going to say tight, but, yeah, smug,' said his sister, with a small smile. She reached out and took his hand and they laced their fingers together, driving both points home. I enjoyed the view. It's unusual for me to come across uncomplicated family members showing one another normal amounts of simple affection. In my job, I get mostly the vengeful and the broken. In my personal life, I've got Todd and Kathi. There's Della, it's true, and Roger. But he's usually working. Taylor . . . I'm too close to.

'And we were all really looking forward to the next chapter,' Jilly said.

'Mom and Dad retired,' said Phil. 'They're only fifty but they worked hard and they had big plans.'

My smile might have dimmed a bit. 'Worked hard' is a very rough translation for started lucky and got luckier, nine times out of ten.

'Like this trip,' Jilly said. 'The Redwoods National Forest, Yosemite, Death Valley, the Mojave Desert, the Grand Canyon and the Hoover Dam.'

'Mom wanted to see Vegas too.'

'Where did they start?' I asked.

'Home,' said Jilly. 'Tacoma.'

It wasn't really important in the grand scheme of things but Tacoma was north of here, in Washington State, so they had only seen the redwoods when a stop in Cuento ended their lives. That struck me as indescribably sad. I mean, I like a big tree as much as the next person but, compared with the Grand Canyon, we're talking about a tree, only bigger.

'And they weren't doing it in a van, like our trips when we

were kids,' Phil said. 'Remember, Jilly? Mom saying that her vacations were the same housework in a smaller kitchen with more bugs?'

'They leased a vintage purple Mustang and booked themselves into nice hotels all the way.'

It didn't particularly go with the sensible haircuts and kayaking but each to their own.

'So what were they doing in Cuento?' Todd said, earning a glare from Kathi. Not that he had referred directly to the Ditch. He didn't have to. Cuento's other lodgings ranged from the Hyatt at the top end to the Super 8 at the bottom, with the Last Ditch occupying a spot we weren't going to discuss in front of one of its owners.

'Dad got a migraine,' Jilly said. 'They had to pull off and find the nearest room with decent blackout. If he does that they can usually get ahead of it. That was Friday afternoon. They realised they weren't going to make it to the Fairmont in San Francisco. They decided to stop in the next town they came to and get Dad horizontal in the dark. That was the last time we spoke to them. And it was only Mom. Driving. Distracted. Dad was already—' She gasped.

'Eyes closed, seat tipped, trying to hold it together until they could check in,' her brother supplied.

'So you never knew where in town they stopped?' said Kathi. 'It's not likely to have been here, you know. We're right on the southern edge. They would have passed a lot of places before they got this far.'

'That's . . . That's . . . what I can't stop thinking about,' Jilly said. 'The start of spring break in a town like this, smack between the city and the lake? Smack between the capital and the wine? I can't bear to think about how many places they tried before they found an empty room. Oh, poor Dad. Oh my God, Phil – how can our hearts not just stop with the ache of it?'

Phil said nothing. But not in a cold way, more in a nothing to say because she was right way. The rest of us, ditto.

'And what makes us think they *were* here,' said Jilly once she had honked up a monster sniff and cleared her tubes again, 'is that we can't find a trace of them anywhere else and the cops said that this place was kind of unattended last weekend. Right?'

Kathi glared at Todd, in lieu of glaring at Roger who had paid for the substandard stand-in managers in the first place. Todd glared at Kathi because that was quite a stretch and she knew it. I glared at Taylor, because I was feeling like shit on toast and there was no one else to glare at. Taylor glared at me because he's sweet but he's not a push-over and none of what was happening was his fault. Phil and Jilly stared at the floor and missed it all, thankfully.

'And then we heard nothing until Thursday,' Jilly said, at last. 'Which was good news. The plan had been for them to take a proper break, not be texting and posting and checking-in all the time. We both thought the silence meant they were back on track, didn't we?'

'We did,' said Phil. 'It seems like an unbelievably stupid idea now, doesn't it? Not to call or text or even send a thumbs-up emoji. Six days went by. Six days!'

This was a very modern American take on matters, it seemed to me. First of all, when Brits go on holiday they go for a fortnight. If we go for a week we say it's a week, usually with a wrinkled nose and a rueful grin. Anything shorter than that, we call a trip. This is such a hard-and-fast rule that a Brit claiming they'd been on holiday to Paris, leaving Friday and back Sunday night, would be lying. Not so over here, as I've come to learn. How anyone makes money running a hotel when the average tourist on 'vacation' from home is more like a member of special ops on a night raid . . .

But that's not the only difference between us and them. On those fourteen-night holidays from home? One postcard, if you were lucky. And you usually beat it back because the gift shop at the beach only had second-class stamps.

But these thoughts, even inside my own head, were edging into Grandma territory, which is unaccountable because I'm still in my thirties, as I keep reminding myself. And after Taylor's birthday he'll be in his thirties too.

'When did your parents d—' I began, thinking it was well

past time to get to the heart of the matter. Kathi, Todd and Taylor all shouted me down like hecklers at a roasting.

'In your own time,' Kathi bellowed.

'In your own words,' Todd shrieked.

'If you're comfortable telling us,' Taylor chipped in.

'When did they die?' said Phil, unperturbed. Perhaps he was unperturbable beyond where he'd already got to in the way of perturbation.

Ha! I thought but managed not to say. *Die!*

It's a perfectly respectful, serviceable, unobjectionable word. To the sane amongst us. And I'm not trying to tie this to any particular nationality, you understand, because the avoidance of *die* has started trickling into *Coronation Street*, *EastEnders* and *The Archers*, probably off a cruise ship. So I might actually be admitting there's a national element after all. Here, nobody dies. We pass, pass over, cross over, slip away and pass away. We go over the rainbow bridge, or on ahead, or home, or to a better place. We leave this life and find ourselves at rest. We're a Monty Python sketch, basically.

So I was greatly looking forward to rubbing it in to all my friends that Phil Miller said *die* about his own parents, days after they'd been reborn into heavenly glory. Oh yes, I've heard that one too.

'The police aren't completely sure,' Jilly said. 'They'll be able to be more accurate when they find the . . .'

Murderer? Weapon? County coroner who's gone fishing? I had no idea.

'Say it,' said Phil.

'Right,' said his sister. 'When they find them. When the police find our parents . . . When the police or whoever – a dog walker, or a jogger – finds them.'

'Hang on,' I said.

'Yeah, but, Lexy,' said Kathi. 'Maybe just listen?'

I nodded because it was hard to argue but my thoughts were like a jar of bees. Molly had said 'murder', Phil had said 'die'; I had put them in 'orphan' category in my head and Noleen had comped them a room. Now, it turned out they probably weren't even dead? Because there were no bodies? *Habeas corpus*, I thought to myself, even though I knew that was nothing to do with bodies really. It was more a case of a fair trial, but not the speedy bit and not the getting a lawyer bit and I seemed to be plunging down a rabbit hole and maybe Todd was right about over-studying. I blinked my way back.

'Spit it out, sis,' Phil was saying. He was still holding Jilly's hand in his, and now he rubbed her knuckles with his other palm. 'It'll help. Say it.'

'OK,' said Jilly, with a big breath that looked to me like it had a burp at its back. I was all for her digging deep and saying something hard, in order to get somewhere good, but I hoped that if it got gastric she'd remember she was on a boat, with a railing. 'When the cops, or whoever, find . . . the rest of them.'

Oh.

I eyed the distance from *my* seat to the railing. I had had no idea we were in for this kind of tale.

'I mean, that's maybe a weird way to put it,' Jilly said. 'But if I say "find their bodies" my brain goes like this: missing bodies, so they might not be dead and they might come back. So, you know.'

I didn't. I was completely lost. 'What *did* the cops find?' I said, curiosity winning through over squeamishness.

'Blood, mostly,' said Phil. 'They found the Mustang abandoned and, in it, they found blood. Two people's blood. Mom's blood and Dad's blood.'

'They got the DNA results back already?' said Kathi.

'No way,' said Phil. 'I asked when they swabbed my cheek and the guy said, "This ain't the movies".'

'But it's their car and they're missing and they do know there's two people's blood,' said Jilly.

'But they might only be injured . . .' I began.

'Pints of it,' Jilly said. 'Pints and pints and pints of it.'

I found myself wishing that 'pint' – a general unit of measurement here in the ironically imperial US of A – wasn't also the name of a delicious refreshing drink where I came from.

'They need to get a specialist to do the calculation,' said Phil, 'but best guess is that both of them lost over two thirds of their blood. So that would be like seven pints of Mom's and eight pints of Dad's. At least.'

None of us spoke. Kathi had heard this once already and even she didn't make a sound.

'They bled out,' Phil added, unnecessarily in my view. 'In the car.' We already knew that too. 'Probably around Tuesday or Wednesday.' This was new information, so it was technically worth saying. But it left me with the thought that a locked car, with fifteen pints of blood inside it, had been sitting somewhere in the warm spring sunshine for five days, so I wished he hadn't told me.

'Who found it?' I said.

'Vultures,' said Jilly. 'They were sitting on the roof pecking at the windows. And then a team of guys on their way to plant out tomato seedlings saw the vultures and called it in.'

'One of them walked right up to look inside,' said Phil. 'In case it was a dog or a . . . picnic or something.'

I really wished he hadn't said 'picnic'.

'We should try to meet him and say thank you,' said Jilly. 'And sorry, kind of, somehow.'

Phil nodded. 'Yup. Poor guy.'

'And then,' said Jilly with a big breath, 'they called us as next of kin and we came down here. That was yesterday.' She let Phil's hand go and shook out her fingers. They must have been holding on to one another for dear life.

'Can I ask a question?' Kathi said. 'When you said it was "blood *mostly*" in the car, what did you mean? Did the cops find something else? Like DNA from the killer? Or some other kind of clue?'

'Well, it's a rental, so there's going to be a lot of DNA, you know,' said Phil. 'Did they mention any other clues to you, Jilly?'

'Nothing,' his sister said. 'No real details about anything at all. Just a lot of reassurance. I'm not complaining.'

She could moan her head off, as far as I was concerned.

'The other thing the cops found . . .' said Phil. 'Are you sure you want to hear this, Lucy?'

I looked around for a Lucy. I wasn't thinking all that straight.

'Lexy,' said his sister.

'I'm so sorry.' Phil looked genuinely mortified. His parents might not have worked hard at their lucrative jobs but they had certainly put in a shift on their children's manners.

'Please go ahead,' I said, mortified to discover that I, of the three of us, was the one looking most like she couldn't cope with this.

'They found a chunk of my mom's scalp, with the hair attached.'

Only the fact that Noleen had right at that moment arrived on the bank, about to climb the steps and come aboard, stopped me from dashing to the railing and releasing my coffee into the wild. Not that Noleen's squeamish or anything, but if I threw up in front of her in the morning when she knew I was trying to get pregnant, I'd have to beat her about the head with a soaked tampon before she'd believe that she wasn't nine months from being an honorary grandma for the third time. And, after Phil and Jilly's little tale, I'd be changing my sanpro with my eyes shut for the rest of the week to try and keep from fainting.

FIVE

At first, I couldn't work out what looked strange about Noleen today. Some of it might have been the fact that she didn't have a jug of Margaritas in one hand, as is usual when she comes aboard, but it wasn't only that. I puzzled over it until I noticed her top tucked into her jorts, then it struck me: she was wearing a sloganless T-shirt. On Easter morning, I would have looked for an offensive religious theme, an off-colour swipe at chocoholics, or maybe a mild wish for the return of winter. I'd definitely seen her in one of those last springtime – 'Fuck sunshine: you all look better in more clothes' – and, being married to a professional laundress, her T-shirts last for years. (Her jeans will outlive the sun.)

Today, presumably for the Millers, she was wearing a plain navy-blue cotton top. Funnily enough, the lack of verbal punch from her chest only allowed more scope for her body language and facial expression to come across as threatening.

Of course, Phil and Jilly already believed she had a heart of gold so they didn't edge away, as strangers might, when she stamped aboard.

'That fu— That frigging detective will solve this thing for sure,' she said, as she dropped down into the last remaining free seat. 'I know nothing's going to bring them back, kids, but no way you'll have to live without closure. She's a machine.'

'What happened?' said Kathi.

'Nothing relevant to . . .' Noleen said, not looking at the Millers, but not looking at them so vehemently that her meaning was clear.

'We might go and take a shower and a nap,' said Phil. 'Let you all talk freely.'

How could someone in raw grief be so reasonable? Once this was all over, I fully meant to ask the Miller kids to collaborate on an article for my website. Or maybe a self-help book.

That impulse would pass, mind you: if anyone ever wrote a self-help book that worked, I wouldn't be the only one looking for a new career.

'I put some soothing products in a couple of baskets on your beds,' said Todd. 'And some nibbles in your refrigerator.'

'You're so kind,' said Jilly, her voice shaking.

They went down the steps, hand-in-hand, then Phil ushered his sister ahead of him into the bushes on their weary way back to the front of the motel.

'What shirt did you take off to put that one on?' said Todd. So it wasn't just me discombobulated by the lack of text on Noleen's chest.

'Huh?' she said. 'The red one that says "Maybe later this evening, Satan". Biblical, for the holiday.'

'And what's up with Molly?' I added.

'Some crap about fire regulations and insurance and God alone knows what else that's none of her business,' said Noleen. 'Displacement activity, *you'd* call it, Lexy. I'm not so much with the psychobabble, so I'm calling it being a pain in my fat ass.'

'Displacement activities are for when you wish you could do something but you can't,' I said. Noleen started making her hands go yak-yak like two naked sock puppets. 'If she's hounding you about city stuff instead of investigating the murder, that's procrastination and dereliction of duty. And it's not like her.'

'Eh, hounding's a stretch,' said Noleen. 'She only said, in passing, that she hoped us getting off-book managers in to run the place hadn't jeopardised our licences. So I asked her when she moved in because how was it any of her beeswax otherwise.'

'That's right,' I said. '*She* doesn't live here. She's practically breaking a commandment!'

'Wut?' said Kathi.

'I mean amendment.'

They all looked at each other. 'Which one's that?' said Taylor. 'I've been helping her study for the citizenship test and I thought I had got them all pretty squared away.'

'Never mind,' I said. 'I was stretching too. Go on, Noleen.'

'Psychobabble or constitutional scholarship,' she said. 'When I snap and kill you, Lexy, it could be for either. And I might kill Roger too, by the way, Todd, for setting us up with that pair of bozos.'

'Fine by me,' Todd said.

I parked that to look into later and said, 'If she's taking side-swipes at you, Noleen, it's probably frustration about something. That's not displacement activity either.'

'Oh my God, Lexy! No one cares,' Noleen said. 'Do I come and tell you the nail-biting steps involved in changing the booking calendar over at the end of the month? Jeez.' She looked around herself, probably for the Margarita that would normally be at her elbow. Finding nothing but a bare coaster, she unwrapped a stick of gum and folded it into her mouth before continuing. 'No shit she's frustrated. She can't find the managers. They're not answering their emails and the agency says she needs a warrant unless it comes through me.'

We all waited to hear why on earth it *wasn't* coming through Noleen, even if only to get Molly off her back. Or at least, I had assumed so. Turns out Kathi was thinking something else entirely. 'Molly's investigating a murder,' she said. 'Can't she demand that the agency cough up whatever she's asking for, except health records?'

'You'd think,' said Noleen. 'But the agency knows neither the victims nor the murderer stayed here, so they reckon Molly's harassing them.'

'How does the agency know that?' said Todd. 'I didn't think anyone knew that. I thought Molly was still trying to find out where the Millers stayed. And as for the murderer, how on ear—'

'Because I told them!' Noleen said. 'Happy now?'

'How did *you* know?'

'I didn't,' said Noleen. 'I don't. But they were pissing me off. I called the agency to tell them that it seemed I had left the door on the latch and asked the guests to help themselves last weekend, rather than having the place run by competent professionals, on account of how the records are sketchy and the books are hinky, and you know what the . . . What's that word, Lexy?'

'Jobsworth?'

'You know what the jobsworth had the gall to say to me?'

'Have a nice day?' said Taylor. This wasn't sarcasm and was actually a pretty good guess because nothing refries Noleen's beans quite as much that particular little platitude. She and I are in lockstep on that score.

'Oh, she would have,' said Noleen. She was working herself into a rage at the memory. If a successful holiday calms you down for twice its length, then I supposed that a three-day break that had run out after seven wasn't exactly a failure, but the holiday itself had been camping and it all seemed pretty sad to me. 'She was exactly the type who would have,' Noleen was telling Taylor now. She heaved a sigh. 'If I hadn't of told her to go fuck herself before she got the chance to.'

'We might need to use a different agency another time, huh?' Kathi said.

'She said,' Noleen went on, ignoring both Kathi and the suppressed chortles she had wrung out of the rest of us. Kathi's very deadpan and nothing cracks me up like deadpan, while nothing cracks Todd up like me cracking up when I'm trying not to. Taylor just likes to join in with stuff. 'She said,' Noleen repeated, taking a run at it. 'Why are you telling me?'

'Why are you telling *me*?' said Todd. 'Who else would you—?'

'Exactly. I call up to say very politely that my motel went to rack and ruin over the course of a single weekend and she says, "Why are you telling me?" And also, "After what you did".'

'After what you *did*?' said Kathi. 'You didn't do anyth—'

'I know! But that's what she said. "Why are you telling me?" And, "After what you did." *And* "What did you expect?"'

'What did she mean by that?' I said. 'What did you *expect*?' Or I tried to say it like that, like an echo, like I was agreeing with the incoming outrageousness, but I think what I actually asked Noleen was, 'What *did* you expect?'

'What are you saying?' said Noleen, glaring at me. 'Whatever it is, how about you say it straight.'

'Nope,' I said. 'I'm not an idiot.'

'Because I know what you're thinking. Because I'm not an idiot either.'

'But how did you get from there to telling them we've got nothing to do with the murder, though?' said Taylor, my hero. He had completely distracted Noleen from my accidental and unsuccessfully aborted allusion to the fact that 'What did you expect?' was a sentence she employs regularly when guests who've just paid $140 dollars for a room come back to Reception to whine about the lack of rainforest showers, goose-down mattress toppers and Netflix. Thing is, it had occurred to me that people who start working in the hospitality industry tend to stay put, God knows why, so I was wondering if whoever was on the phone at Rent-a-Pulse had once done a summer under Noleen's iron wing.

'Because,' Noleen said to Taylor, 'I started in telling her that two hotel guests had been brutally murdered and she got all hysterical and goes, "In your motel?" so I say, "No of course not" – which is true – but that the murderers also had to stay somewhere too and she goes, "In your motel?" exactly the same like she's a broken bot, and she's annoying me by now so I say no of course not, exactly the same too, to see if she notices, and then she borrows a brain cell from a friend and comes back with, "Why did you say something so upsetting for no reason?" and I've had enough of her by now, because I'm only human, and so that's when I told her to go fuck herself and there it is.'

'You could call back and—' I suggested.

'Blocked.'

'So you could tell Molly what happened and she—' I tried next.

'Do *you* wanna get blocked?' said Noleen. 'I'm not handing dynamite like that to a woman like Molly Rankinson. She would roast me till the stars winked out.'

This was true.

'So I'm looking for the bright side and I think I found it,' said Noleen. Maybe three nights of sleeping on the ground slapping at mosquitoes had done more good than I thought. 'There's no evidence that the Millers stayed here. There's abso-lutely no reason to think the murderer stayed here, so I don't actually have to deal with either those agency bozos or the PD banana brothers and I can just forget the whole damn rigma-role. Nuttin to do with me.'

Unfortunately, we had all been looking at Noleen as she spoke and none of us had noticed the return of the Millers Next Gen to the bank opposite the porch, where they now stood, aghast and frozen, staring at Noleen as if they hoped she never had another good day in her life.

'Shit!' she said as she spotted them. 'Aw, Christ. I didn't mean it like that. Jesus.'

'What agency?' said Jilly Miller.

'Huh?'

'Is the FBI here?' She sounded bleak and drained, as if even the news that the big boys were on the case wasn't enough to hoist her spirits out of the mud of the slough.

'Shit,' said Noleen again. 'Listen, I was going to say: does it help to be together, time like this and all? Would a connecting door be enough? So you could each have your own room?'

'But *is* the FBI coming?' said Phil. He sounded hardly more hopeful than his sister, but more strained, less defeated.

'Sorry, no. Hotel agency that . . . Doesn't matter. Nothing to do with law enforcement, no.'

They stood on the bank, blinking, saying nothing.

'I'm sorry,' said Noleen. 'My knees are bad today.' Her knees were fine. 'And I can't take any more painkillers because of my blood pressure.' Her blood pressure was 120/80 even when she was bowling. 'And I can't use gummies after I ate too many one time and now they give me flashbacks.' Noleen had never consumed cannabis in any form as long as I'd known her.

'Honey,' said Kathi. She never uses endearments in front of strangers. 'Don't tell lies to protect me.' She turned to the Millers. 'We had a fight.' Kathi and Noleen never fight. It's a miracle. 'She's angry with me, and lashing out. She's prone to what she calls displacement activity.' God, how I love this woman. There was the sacrifice made and the penalty extracted all in the same sentence.

Jilly smiled uncertainly and then glanced at her brother.

'Two rooms would be great, actually,' Phil said. 'With a connecting door.'

'And I really hope that doesn't go for everyone,' Jilly added. 'Wanting nothing to do with all of this, I mean.'

Noleen made a low moan in the back of her throat.

'My offer stands,' said Taylor. The chances of either of the Millers remembering his offer were surely close to nil. Hardly anyone finds birds and their habitats as noteworthy as Taylor.

'And mine and Lexy's,' said Todd. 'Naturally.'

'And mine too,' Kathi said. 'Although I didn't get around to laying it out for you yet.' The Millers looked at her expectantly and then, apparently communicating like the Midwich Cuckoos they were beginning to remind me of, they each put out a foot and stepped aboard. Same foot too, the left one. I had to work not to find it creepy.

'I'm a private detective,' Kathi said.

The Millers nodded.

'And I agree with my wife that Sergeant Rankinson of the Cuento PD will work her butt off for you and your parents and will get you and them justice, but I also want to say I'm here to help in any way I can.'

Jilly Miller put a hand up to her mouth as if she was trying not to cry out with emotion.

'We thought you meant free laundry,' said Phil. 'Like maybe you would wash the stuff they found in the car.'

Maybe Jilly pressing her hand over her mouth wasn't about emotion after all; when she took it away and spoke, her voice was guttural. 'I think if they ever give us anything back from out of the car, we'll just pay to have it incinerated. The cops picked some pretty OK stuff for us to identify but it still wasn't great.'

'They think,' said Phil, 'the murderer was looking for something. Or at least, he tossed the car, you know? So pretty much everything in there got blood on it. And then sat there all that time.'

'Right, right, right, right,' said Kathi. 'Well, no, that wouldn't be something the Skweeky Kleen could offer to deal with. That would be a very specialised service and, as you say, it's probably better to assume you won't be able to salvage anything.' She was doing a fantastic job of looking and sounding normal, for the two Millers. It was the rest of us who knew that the idea of days' old blood soaked into dead people's clothes getting within ten miles of the machines in her precious laundromat was making her want to scream and run and possibly sell her business and move to another state.

'But you're a private detective too?' Jilly said. 'So you know your way around all of this? We've never had any dealings with police or courts or crime or anything.'

'Oh, I think I can say I know my way around a crime and the solving of it,' Kathi said. 'So like I said, anything I can do for you.'

'This is wonderful,' Jilly said. 'We actually came to ask if anyone would be willing to do this one thing for us – we thought maybe Lexy – but this is even better.'

'What about me?' said Todd. 'Although, what was it?'

He wasn't doing such a great job of sounding normal, and that was because the spectre of his cleptoparasitosis trigger was now as close as Kathi's germaphobia one had just been. The Millers needed help with something. They had spontaneously raised the topic of the blood-soaked contents of their parents' car. Everything in that car would have started incubating maggots already. Those maggots soon would turn into bluebottles. Todd was out.

'We would like to view the crime scene,' Phil said.

Todd scraped his chair backwards, putting two deep scores in the surface of my porch floor.

'I can see why you might want some emotional support for that,' I said. I wasn't blinded by panic and I knew the crime scene – wherever the long-removed death car had been parked when the tomato guys saw vultures on it – was separate from the death car itself.

Kathi knew that too, I reckoned. At least, she nodded along and said, 'Absolutely. Is the tape still up or can I have a look around and see if there's anything to learn?'

'The tape's down,' said Phil. 'It was very . . . contained, they told us. They already took all the soil samples and photographs and whatnot. As well as the car, obviously.'

'I have no idea where the car is,' said Jilly. 'And I like it that way.'

Todd jumped his seat forward again in a couple of bunny-hops. 'So when would you like to go?' he said. 'I'll drive.'

'How far is it?' said Kathi. 'We've got a big dinner planned. Oh.'

'Yeah, we've got a lot of friends coming for an Easter thing,' Noleen said. 'Which we can cancel, by all means. It would be pretty much right under your window.' She was still grovelling.

'Please don't cancel your plans,' Jilly said. 'The car was parked in the lot at a museum just south of the college campus. It can't be far.'

'I thought it was out in the fields,' said Taylor.

'Arts funding is precarious in this economy,' Todd said.

The utterance made sense when we arrived, thirty minutes later, at the farthest reaches of the so-called car park of the brand-new Patsy Denoni Museum of Art on the UCC campus.

The museum itself was gorgeous; small in overall size, it's true, but packing an undeniable architectural punch. It looked like a Tiffany lamp that had been dropped and then hastily glued back together in the dark by drunks. The only right angles to be found anywhere were the corners of the posters advertising the inaugural season's exhibitions. The big one was something to do with basket-weaving and the climate crisis and our throw-away culture. There was another, student-led, exhibition too, but I didn't get any of what it was, even after I'd read the explanation twice over and had a close look at the example installation. It might have been a bacterium or an asteroid. Maybe a mung bean.

'What a marvellous enrichment to the culture of such a small town,' said Jilly.

'Are you . . .' said Kathi. I thought she was going to say *kidding*, but it turned out to be, '. . . involved in the Arts?' Mind you, that might be pretty much the only other option, from Kathi's point of view.

'Healthcare,' said Jilly.

'You?' she asked Phil.

'No way,' said Phil. 'Healthcare *or* "the Arts".'

'But you see what I mean,' said Todd. 'About funding?' He turned away from the shards and gestured in the other direction.

I did. The Patsy Denoni Museum car park should have had sweeping curves, urging people to park on swathes of smooth new tarmac between raised beds of . . . Well, I'm no gardener but swanky places generally go in for clumps of grass any colour but green, so they look either like they're dying of some terrible virus that turns all their fronds black or like they're literally dead and gone brown in the sun. Either that or tiny-leaved bushes clipped into balls and cones.

What actually lay before our eyes was *some* tarmac, right enough, for *some* cars to park on, near the doors, and then orange warning signs to mind the bump before the rest of the place was given over to dry dirt. The dirt, in turn, was separated from the fields beyond by a straggling line of trees and some bits of leftover builders' chain-link, except where an area of darker dirt and some wisps of yellow tape showed where the Millers' car had been abandoned and the cops had subsequently been tramping around.

We headed that way, flanking the Millers, and stood in solemn silence when we got there, gazing at nothing.

SIX

A single, half-choked sob from Jilly Miller broke into the stillness.

'I know,' said Phil, putting an arm round her. He was biting his lip.

The rest of us, Todd, Kathi and me, stood there as awkward as we were useless while the pair of them took a series of hefty breaths, then eventually let go of each other and turned to face us with brave, watery smiles on their faces.

'Well, at least we can tell Sergeant Rankinson that they died last Friday night,' Jilly said. 'Or before Saturday morning anyway.'

'You can?' said Kathi. 'How come?'

'They couldn't find a room,' Jilly said. 'We're even farther south than your motel now, aren't we?' Kathi nodded. 'So I think what happened is that my mom couldn't find a room at any of the places in town and – this happened once before, Phil. Remember? – Dad couldn't take driving on and off the lighted entranceways while she tried, so they looked for somewhere really dark to park and ride it out.'

We all looked up at the sheltering hackberry tree above us and then across the dirt and tarmac at how few lights there were in this barely finished car park and I think we all must have agreed that this was probably the darkest spot to leave a car for miles around. But that realisation brought a deluge of questions in its wake.

'How could a car be left parked up here from Friday to Thursday without anyone doing anything about it until the . . .?' Vultures started pecking, I didn't finish.

'I don't know,' said Jilly. 'Phil, that's a really good point. How could it?'

'Is it even open?' said Phil, looking over his shoulder. 'The parking lot's not finished.'

'There's definitely lights on,' Kathi said. 'Easter Sunday or not.'

'But would they tell us anything?' said Phil, reluctant for some reason. 'They probably want to put ten miles between themselves and . . . this.' He half raised his hand and half gestured to the scuffled earth inside the bits of crime tape. I had seen it before: grief making someone's very limbs feel weighted.

'It would be a clear stance if they refused to help you,' Todd said. 'Judging by their opening exhibitions, that's not how they roll.'

I gave him a sharp look as we trudged over to the entrance and then gave the two advertising posters an even sharper one, but I still had no idea what he was on about as the automatic doors swished open and we stepped inside, finding ourselves in a soaring white space with the sun beating down on us from a prismatic arrangement of skylights high above.

'Welcome to the Patsy Denoni Cultural Centre,' said a young woman stepping our way with a big laminated QR code held out in front of her like a shield. 'I'm Fern.' She had an impeccable rainbow dye-job and was dressed in the timeless UCC student uniform Type A: a shapeless faded T-shirt, a pair of unflattering sweatshirt-cotton shorts and grubby trainers with odd socks. (Type B changes every season, but was currently a micro-bustier, low-slung skinny jeans and ironic Birkenstocks (not to be confused with sincere Birkenstocks. Type A students often wear sincere brown Birkenstocks with their odd socks. Ironic Birkenstocks are jewel-coloured and worn with bare feet, pedicures and toe rings).)

Fern had arrived at our side. 'To reduce our carbon footprint,' she said, 'we ask that you scan this code and download the museum map and exhibit discussions. These resources are free and there is no entry charge.'

Right, I thought. But I still didn't see how Todd worked it out from the posters alone.

'But,' Fern went on, 'we encourage you to make a small donation to support our work in celebrating, promoting and protecting the diverse practices of artistic expression by the families of peoples who comprise our communities.'

Wow, I thought, but before any of us could answer or down-load anything, another woman came our way, stalking across the polished marble in spike heels. It took some kind of confi-dence to walk that fast in those shoes on this surface, but she was being powered by irritation.

'Diverse expressions of artistic practice, Fern,' she said. 'The communities of peoples who comprise our family.'

Fern hung her head and let the laminated card drop to her side.

'And that,' boss lady said, 'is the blow-up of the QR code to demonstrate to our more tech-emergent seekers what they're looking for. Not an actual QR code.'

'Oh yeah,' Fern said.

'To be fair, we didn't notice the difference,' I said, instantly on Fern's side. If I'd been handed that script I'd have mangled it too, possibly not even on purpose.

'The suggested small donation level starts at fifty dollars,' Stiletto Sadie said. She spun on one of those heels in a way that surely couldn't be good for even marble floors and stalked off again.

'You're Fern Doyle, aren't you?' Todd said.

Fern raised her head again like one of her namesakes in the spring rain and for the second time that day I got to see the effect of Todd on someone twenty years too young for him, the wrong gender, and not his husband. She filled with pink light as we watched and gave Todd a smile so full of youthful sunshine that it made me want to weep and crawl into a cave to live out my few years left as the wizened crone I was in comparison. Or maybe my acetaminophen was wearing off. Certainly, I could tell from the heavy feeling in my lower middle that I needed, sometime soon, to find a loo.

'Fern's a yarn artist,' said Todd. 'She made the handgun condoms that caused such a stir.'

I vaguely remembered one of the UCC students being fêted, ridiculed, and questioned under caution over the donation of gun cosies to the police department a while back. She knitted them in overly realistic flesh tones, complete with veins, and finished them off with dangling scrotums stuffed with wadded-up news stories of police brutality that she had chewed on and spat back out. The Arts correspondent of the *San Francisco Chronicle* had gushed about the skill with which she switched from chenille to mohair to simulate the growth of hair towards the fat end and Fern had explained that she teased apart the balls of wool with a moustache comb and re-spun them into a continuous thread that she wore around her body under her clothes, working the free end as she revolved, like a human bobbin. The reviewer praised her creative dehiscence. I remembered that detail because I looked it up at the time and marvelled at how much I didn't know.

She was, on the other hand, bloody hopeless at customer service. It's not often I'm tempted to advise a creative knitter to give up the day job and stick to the mohair willies. Today was the first time ever.

'We're not actually visiting the museum,' said Todd, in a pretty Magritte-like way in my opinion. Fern frowned.

'I'm Jilly Miller and this is my brother, Phil.'

Another frown.

'And I'm Kathi Muntz.' Kathi flashed her PI licence.

'Our parents were found in the car that was parked over . . .' said Phil.

'Oh my God.' Her boss's heels had suggested as much but Fern's voice now confirmed that, as well as looking like a million dollars and leaving nothing in the bank to finish the car park, the Patsy Denoni had killer acoustics too.

'I am so sorry,' Fern said. 'And I don't mean for your loss. Although of course I'm sorry for your loss. When my mom died . . . Shit! That's exactly what you're not supposed to say, isn't it? But I really am sorry. I feel so responsible. I want you to know that you can say anything to me or even slap me if you need to. But don't punch me in the middle because I use a stoma.'

We all heard the spike heels come our way again even faster, then falter, stop for a second or two and retreat.

Fern flashed a wicked grin. 'She hates me talking about my stoma, but she can't do anything about it because of her stated commitment to yadda-yadda-yadda.'

I had been ready to like whoever had made those cosies, sight unseen, but Fern was a refreshing surprise. I *really* liked this girl, pink-lit youthfulness or no.

'But why would you feel responsible?' Jilly said.

'Because I asked if my friend could park his car in our lot sometime over spring break because it kept getting broken into where he lives and he was scared to leave it while he went out of town. So when the car turned up away over there, I thought it was Stewie's. I still don't know where *his* car got to! I'm worried that he did leave it here and it was stolen before I even saw it. Although . . .'

'Although the Millers' car was here for almost a week, so probably not,' said Kathi.

'Right,' Fern agreed. 'He most likely left it at his place after all – he's pretty disorganised.'

'And it was OK with your boss for you to offer free parking to a pal?' I asked her.

'I was going to broach it when she spotted the car, once it was too late, you know?'

'But *then* she was OK with it?' I asked.

'She didn't say anything,' said Fern.

'Really,' said Kathi, looking up from her notebook. 'Interesting. Did, uh . . . did Sergeant Rankinson follow up on that, do you know?'

She was feeling her way, I thought. Trying not to undermine the cops in the Millers' eyes, but clearly smelling something fishy. I smelled it too. Why would the boss lady not wonder about an abandoned car?

'Can I change the subject a skosh?' said Todd. 'It's just . . . where is this place in town that's having car thefts?' He's got a beloved Jeep as well as a run-around nicer than my one and only, and Roger's car is like something from the movies.

'Hm, well, I can't really go into *that*,' Fern said, in a low voice. She cocked her head towards the corridor where the footsteps had originated. 'But I can tell you that I was there all the time the cops were here and Yuzula didn't say a word about it.'

'Interesting,' said Kathi again.

'Yuzula?' said Todd.

'Let's talk to her first,' said Kathi. 'And then when's your next break, Fern? We could grab coffee and talk more privately.'

'I'm done at three,' Fern said. 'Meet you out there?'

'Actually, guys,' said Phil. He had put his arm round his sister without any of us noticing that she had started to look wan. 'Can *we* meet you outside at three too? Or maybe just back at the motel? This is . . .'

'Of course,' Kathi said. 'I'll report faithfully but sensitively everything we find out. This is what we do. Leave it in our hands.'

Which they did, disappearing out into the sunshine together.

Kathi's voice snapped into a different mode altogether once they were gone. 'Yuzula!' she said, rolling her eyes and starting along the corridor with her trainer soles squeaking on the shining floor. 'I'll give you both a hundred bucks if that's what it says on her birth certificate.'

She rapped on the half-open door at the end of the passageway and said, 'Can we come in thank you,' all in one sentence, as she stepped inside. I walked into her back and Todd piled into mine. It was the only thing that stopped Kathi from turning tail and fleeing.

Because we had moved from the front to the back of the Patsy Denoni and no mistake. There was no marble and prism action here. What there was was a brown carpet, still new enough to be pocked all over with the imprint of those spike heels, a desk overflowing with printer paper, screwed-up tissues, empty coffee cups and abandoned vapes, and a tower of stained pizza boxes resting on the only unoccupied chair and looking quite like the Cat in the Hat's hat.

'This area is private,' snapped Yuzula, from behind the desk, letting out a cloud of scented vapour as she spoke.

'Perfect,' said Kathi. 'I'm a *private* detective. It's about the Millers' car, Ms . . .'

'Mo.'

'Ms Mo?'

'And you are?'

'We are Trinity,' said Todd, sounding like something from

cheap sci-fi. 'How long has this place even been open? Because that is a lot of pizza. Aren't you concerned about . . .?' He still couldn't say it, but he had recovered enough in recent months to be able to make a series of clicks on the door frame with his fingernails, that could have been either mice or roaches.

'I've already spoken to law enforcement,' said Yuzula Mo. 'I complied to the letter.'

I thought I saw an in, somewhere amongst that pretty strange formulation. 'We, as Kathi here indicated, are concerned with restorative justice for our clients, the Miller children,' I said, almost completely lying. 'Not with the machines of state.' I might have meant engines of state, but she got the drift. She took another suck on her vape and sat back a little.

'Sit down,' she said. 'How can I help you?'

'You could start by showing us where we can sit,' said Kathi.

Yuzula sighed and rose. 'Standing meeting then,' she said. 'How *else* can I help you?'

'It's about the car,' Kathi said. 'The Millers' car? I was just wondering why you didn't wonder what it was doing there for all that time?'

'All that time,' said Yuzula, looking green. 'Yes, well, obviously *now*—'

'But then?' said Kathi.

'I assumed it belonged to one of our neighbours.'

Kathi frowned and I was also trying to think what Yuzula could be on about. There wasn't a building for miles in that direction, due south of Cuento. Muelleverde's northern suburbs were half a day's trudge away.

'Neighbours?' said Todd.

'Work neighbours,' said Yuzula. 'We curate art and our nearest neighbours produce food.'

'Ohhhhh,' Kathi said. 'You mean the tomato guys?'

Yuzula pursed her lips.

'The guys who finally called it in? When the vultures got involved?'

'I'm not sure our neighbours would relish being known as "tomato guys",' Yuzula said. She was pretty prissy for someone with eleven dead pizza boxes in her office. 'We at Patsy Denoni are committed to bedding into our community in a spirit of mutual respect and a recognition of the dignity of all labour.'

'OK,' said Kathi. 'So . . . could you give us the names of the neighbours we should be talking to, perhaps? Maybe you wouldn't be happy passing on their phone numbers but could you call them and pass on ours? Tell them we'd be happy to hear from them.'

Yuzula's pinched glare had become more of a blank stare, fixed and glassy. I would have put money on her having no clue what any of the field workers were called (with a side bet on Kathi knowing that). I would have put more money on her not even knowing that it wasn't the same guys turning up next door to the museum throughout the lifecycle of the tomato plants in that field, but rather a scratch team of whoever was free that day. I would have put the last of my money on her not being able to describe a single one of these neighbours beyond 'small, brown, wears a hat' and I'd have borrowed some extra to bet that she wouldn't admit any of this to us if she was in a snake pit and we were holding a ladder.

'We'll find them,' Kathi said eventually. 'They're probably Sunrise Ag Solutions guys. Right? This time of year?'

Yuzula nodded. I thought Kathi had probably made up Sunrise Ag Solutions on the spot. But I wouldn't put money on it; she's hard to read.

'OK then.' Kathi turned and shooed Todd and me out with her notebook, leaving Yuzula to sink into her chair and scrabble for another vape.

'Total güero,' said Kathi to Todd, once the door was closed.

'Do I want to know what that means?' I asked her.

'Pretend I said "gringo".'

'Güera,' said Todd. 'Gringa.'

'Asshole. Pedant,' said Kathi in exactly the same tone of patient explanation. 'You believe that chick? She thinks one of the tomato guys might have left a vintage Mustang parked at the side of a field for six days? How's he getting to work in the meantime? How's he making payments on the thing? How's he explaining to his family that he won't be sending any money home until *next* Easter because he just couldn't resist the leather seats?'

'Did it *have* leather seats?' I asked, because there's no point I can't miss.

Back in the foyer, Fern was busy with legitimate art fans, getting their app sorted out for a tour of the museum, so we stepped outside. The day was still warming up, a precursor of the summer to come when the mornings would trick you and then by five the heat would make you wish you were dead as you panted and sweated and waited for sunset and that first blessed waft of the cool bay breeze blowing through.

'I wish we had said we'd come back another day,' Todd griped. 'Instead of hanging around for . . .' He whipped out his phone. 'Kill me now. Another hour!'

'Would you rather be back at the Ditch peeling spuds?' I said.

'Aren't Meera and Maria doing it all?' said Kathi. Those two and their husbands, Arif and José, were old friends of ours, from lockdown, and loved nothing more than cooking in industrial quantities, as a succession of Thanksgivings, Christmases, Seders, Eids, and barbecues had shown.

'Not in the mood for Happy Families,' said Todd, reminding me I still hadn't asked why he'd given permission for Roger's murder. In jest, but even that had to come from somewhere.

'Tomato guy!' Kathi said. I thought she was still fuming about Yuzula's phony wokeness until I saw that she was pointing beyond the line of straggly trees into the field beyond, where someone was crouched in the rows of tiny plants fiddling with an irrigation pipe. She set off, hailing him at the top of her voice. 'Señor! Perdón! Para hablar contigo! Señor?'

The crouching figure stood up, shaded his eyes and looked over.

'You sound like an idiot,' said Todd, following Kathi. He raised his voice. 'Ese? Un poco contigo? Huh, güey?'

The guy started walking towards us.

'Felices Pascuas,' I shouted. 'Happy Easter' was about the only relevant contribution I could hope to make. I knew I needed to learn more Spanish. Taylor and I had promised we would dig into Babbel when the baby was born. I still found it strange to think that my kid would be an automatic American but, given that, we were determined it would be a proper Californian too, with Tío Todd helping.

That thought made me realise I still hadn't found a loo and I turned back into the museum. I was about as much use to Todd and Kathi's interview of a Spanish-speaking tomato guy as I was to Taylor's dream of fatherhood. I knew that was egregiously self-pitying and I didn't care. I sat there on the toilet in the all-gender restroom of the Patsy Denoni and cried my eyes dry. Then I washed my face with some nasty pink soap, dried it on a nasty blue paper towel, apparently recycled from a woodchip-sandpaper mix and went back to be useless at my side hustle as well as my primal function. Multi-tasking.

SEVEN

It was going pretty well over there in the shade of the hack-berry. Kathi was sitting on a burr near the stump, laughing so hard she literally started, as I watched, holding her sides. Todd was talking thirty-eight to the dozen: nineteen to the guy and nineteen translating for Kathi. The guy himself was enjoying every minute of it, whatever it was.

I found myself thinking, sourly, that I hoped the Miller kids didn't come back early and witness the jollity their parents' murder was affording.

'Lexy,' Kathi said, when she spotted me. 'Listen to this. Tell her, Todd. You won't believe it. Well, you will believe it, but you'll love it.'

'Teto here said he saw the car last Saturday when they brought the . . .' He fired off some rapid Spanish. Teto answered. 'Brought the trays of tomatoes that had been . . . prepared . . . in a way I've never heard of to sit in the shade until they planted them starting Sunday,' Todd said. 'I don't know the English words for whatever farming tasks these are.'

'Hardening off after pricking out,' I said, my father's daughter. Although here where they had kitty-cats and tidbits so they never had to say *tit* or *pussy*, both procedures were no doubt called something else.

'Wow,' said Todd. 'Hostile much? But get this: Teto's crew saw the blood. Saw the hair. They thought it was an art installation.'

Kathi snorted.

'Sí, como una escultura,' Teto said.

'A sculpture, right,' said Todd. 'Because it wouldn't be the first time.'

'The dumpster,' I said. 'I remember.'

'Right. But here's the funny part. They weren't the only ones who got caught. People were parking and walking over. Walking round it, peering in the window. Right, Teto?'

'Sí,' he said. 'Una vampire y unos abuelitos y un insecto palo.'

'Vampire, some grannies and what's the other thing?' I said.

'Crane fly, I think,' said Todd. 'No. Dragonfly. Something like that.'

'So the usual selection of Cuento residents,' said Kathi. 'Out and about being normal.'

'What does he mean by *dragonfly*?' I said. 'Because you know what I'm thinking? If he means colourful hair he might mean Fern. And if he's saying Fern was over here looking into a carful of blood then she hasn't been completely honest with us, has she?'

Todd turned back to Teto and started in on the Spanish again, gesturing at his head. Teto was having none of it. As far as I could tell from Kathi's stuttering translation, it was nothing to do with hair and he didn't even mean a dragonfly. 'Insecto palo,' he said, doing a weird kind of jerky dance. Todd shrugged. Kathi shrugged. I got my phone out and googled it.

'Stick insect,' I said. 'Not Fern then. Stick insects are plain green.'

Kathi slapped her head. 'The joyless green giant,' she said, referring to a hardcore cyclist who powered around town in ill-judged Lycra clothes, bullying drivers and pedestrians alike.

'A lead,' I said. 'Not to downplay all your chuckles, but that *is* what we came for.'

'But we haven't got to the funny part yet,' said Todd. 'Lemme set the scene: vultures don't normally go much for vegetables and small snacks.'

'Como dije, sí, los zopilotes,' said Teto. 'Los buitres.'

'Right,' said Todd. 'Thief birds, like you said. Turkey vultures.'

Teto said some more and I only really caught one word of it for sure.

'Right,' said Todd. 'So they don't turn up when the earth's disturbed, looking for seeds and grubs.'

'Is "gaviotas" seeds or grubs?' I said. That was my one word.

'Gulls,' said Todd.

'Ajá sí,' said Teto, doing a good impersonation of an angry seagull.

'Also,' said Todd, 'Teto knows about the cows in formaldehyde and the Piss Christ—'

'Piss?' I said. 'Christ? I'm not devout but that's kinda—'

Teto interrupted me to agree vehemently and completely unintelligibly, nodding and swearing – I got that bit – and ending up with a spit on the ground at his side.

'—so he thought maybe the vultures were part of the "installation",' Todd said. 'And, sidebar, I think if anyone hears about this it's only a matter of time until some sculptor somewhere asks for a bird grant. But!' he held up his hand. 'And this is a close translation, Lexy. Teto says, "There is a bird guy who lives right here in town who would break the artist's head if any of these poor vultures' beaks got chipped on the glass." So Teto decided to call it in before things turned nasty.'

'God almighty,' I said. 'He would too. What have I done with my life?' But they were right. I was laughing.

It was almost three o'clock now, so we thanked Teto and headed back, converging on the entrance at the same time as Fern emerged and the Miller kids appeared too.

'Your boss is an idiot,' Kathi said.

Fern nodded. 'Yeah, and related to that: the thing I wanted to say but didn't want her to overhear? It's not true about my friend's car. There's no hotspot for auto theft in Cuento.'

'So why didn't you wonder what the Mustang was doing there?' said Todd.

'But it's not completely false either,' Fern said. 'Thing is, my friend – he lives in Oakland; he's part of an amazing art collective down there – wanted to bring some of that . . . energy . . . to stuffy old Cuento. It's like we finally get a new *space*, not just another *gallery*, selling *paintings*, and right away it's the same old same old, so when he said he was going to mix it up I was looking forward to it, you know?'

'And so when a car full of blood turned up at the edge of your parking lot,' Todd said, 'you assumed it was . . . art?'

'I assumed it was the beginning of a work, yes,' Fern said. 'It was gorgeous, for a start. A mesmerising blue-green car. It looked like art all on its own. And then the blood? Not kinetic, exactly, so slow. Not ephemeral, exactly, too solid. But I know he's been working on the art of decay and like a car – years of rot to come, red-orange taking over – and then blood – all so quick to change – I was excited. When the vultures came, I stood and wept. And then, even when the police came, it only added to the magnitude of it all. I filmed everything.'

'You filmed everything?' Jilly had been standing slack-jawed as Fern told her tale, but now she looked electrified. She clutched her brother. 'A film!' she cried out.

'Do you have a film of Friday night?' said Phil, in a strangled voice.

'Well, no,' said Fern. 'I didn't know it was here on Friday night. And when I got here on Saturday and saw it, I assumed my friend had set up a camera somewhere and was filming for himself. But I couldn't find it. So I started. I caught the visitors—'

'Yeah, Teto told us about the visitors,' I said. 'The tomato guy,' I explained to the Millers. 'Vampires, and grandmas and a green one.'

'It sure sounds like performance art,' said Phil. 'A green *what*?'

'I don't suppose you'd be willing to give us a copy of the film?' Kathi said.

Jilly gasped. For once, Phil didn't seem to be focused on her so I reached out and put an arm round her instead. She was trembling.

'I haven't got it,' said Fern.

'Right, right, you gave it to the cops?' Kathi said. 'But any chance—?'

'Gave it to the cops?' said Fern. 'Do I *look* like someone who would give stuff to the cops?'

I tightened my hold on Jilly Miller. She was beginning to feel like a sandbag.

'I got over myself,' Fern said. 'I realised that if the artist hadn't chosen to film the art evolving then me filming it was no better than every screen-dead zombie with their phone out. It freaked me out so badly.'

'The film did?' said Phil. 'When you watched it?'

'I didn't watch it!' said Fern. 'What do you people think I am? I wouldn't *watch* it instead of attending to the *art*. No, I mean I realised I've been contaminated by this place, curating and recording and cataloguing and . . . *accruing*! I'm horrified at myself.'

'Of course you are,' said Todd.

I gave him a bit of side-eye.

'I mean, I gotta ask if even the murderer of those two innocents can feel any worse about himself than you do right now. *Accruing?* Jesus.'

'Are you . . .? Are you . . . laughing at me?' said Fern.

'Absolutely not,' Todd lied.

It looked to me like she believed him. Meantime, Phil had finally noticed his sister's plight and had rushed to her side to hold her up, freeing me.

'So you started filming the car on Saturday?' said Kathi. She had been writing in her notebook and her tone suggested that she didn't care what the rest of us were up to, because she had a job to do. 'And you stopped on . . .?'

'Tuesday.'

'And you didn't watch the film. And you've deleted it.'

'Yes.'

'Can my sister go inside to sit down and have a glass of water, please?' Phil said. 'Can someone help me?'

Which is how I ended up having a cultural experience on Easter Sunday, when I had started the day with nothing further from my mind. Together, Phil and I helped Jilly into the foyer, where there wasn't a single seat to be found. I spied one through an archway in the gallery proper, though, and after a good glug from the water fountain she made it there under her own steam. I sat beside her with Phil at the other end of the bench and together we gazed at the wall in front of us, at the wriggling busyness of some kind of film projected on to an unrelated lumpy red oil painting. I wondered if the painter knew there was a film playing on their thing. I wondered if the video maker knew their bit wasn't deemed worthy of a plain white wall.

'Imagine hanging that up over the fireplace,' Phil said, trying get a laugh out of his sister.

Jilly made a tiny little snuffling noise, a sort of suggestion of a promise of a small laugh later.

'What is it?' I asked.

'Life,' said Fern, who had followed us. It was a singularly unhelpful answer and – gun condoms or no – I decided I'd had about enough of her for the day. I stood up, and that's when it hit me. Those weren't mung beans, asteroids, or bacteria. They were foetuses. They were little clumps of dividing cells, all jostling about on top of a background of red like they would be inside a body.

'Oh God,' I said. 'They're not . . . they're not real, are they?'

'It's a live feed from three different labs, superimposed,' said Fern. 'Isn't it amazing? I'm only still here because of this one piece. This piece makes up for everything.'

'Life,' said Jilly. 'Right. I see why you thought maybe, if the car was art too, that it was kind of—'

'Magical,' said Fern. 'A serendipitous completion really. Life beginning in here and ending out there. It really did feel like . . . magic. I'm still reeling. Once I find a way to enter the experience as an artist instead of a participant, I'm going to make a work about it.'

I made my goodbyes, after a fashion, and left to go and join Kathi and Todd in the car park again.

'You took your time,' said Todd. What was wrong with him?

'I stopped to look at some of the product,' I said.

'Good!' he cried. 'If you've looked at the art and been impressed or at least diplomatic, that should keep things sweet. And anyway, Kathi, Fern's as dumb as a bag of soup, so I got away with it. Stop nagging.'

'Diplomatic,' I echoed. 'Um . . .' Then I reconsidered. 'Got away with what?' I asked instead. Then I got distracted. 'Why do we need to keep on the right side of the Patsy Denoni?' Then I got distracted from my distraction. 'Who the hell *is* Patsy Denoni anyway?'

'We need to because,' Kathi said, then she interrupted herself.

'The Patsy family – big horde of Irish – made their fortune selling shovels in the gold rush. The Denoni family were in shipping or something but they've got a winery in Napa now. One of them married one of the other bunch and set about filling California with art no one asked for.' She took a breath. 'Totally irrelevant. We need to keep on the right side of Fern and her knitting needles because there must be a way to recover that deleted video. Right? Devin could do it. So we need to try to get her phone off her and give him a clear run.'

'Or tell Molly,' I said.

'Quitter,' said Todd. 'You don't want to try to help? Those kids are going through hell. Didn't you see that poor girl nearly passing out?'

'Wouldn't you?' I said. 'If you thought your parents' murder had been filmed?'

'Body dump, not murder,' Kathi said. 'Although, that's a good point. If they were killed in the car, whoever did it must have been pretty well coated in gore from head to toe.'

'Could you please not?' I said. 'Could you just not, maybe?'

'What's up with you?' said Todd.

'Nope,' I said. 'What's up with *you*? Why are you fighting with Roger? Why are you pissing off witnesses? Why are you arguing with Kathi? What did you get away with?'

Before he could answer, all of our phones rang in unison. Devin, I reflected, could definitely recover whatever Fern had deleted and probably would if Noleen asked him to. He had set up a broadcast function that led from her phone to any and all of the rest of us because she asked him to. And he had done it without touching our phones at any point.

Kathi accepted the call for all of us and put Noleen on speaker.

'Where the hell are you? Dinner is going to be ready in seventeen minutes. In twenty-one minutes, I'm giving yours away to the homeless. Get your lazy asses back here now.'

'For your information,' said Todd, when we were underway, racing through the empty Sunday streets, 'not that my marriage is your business in any way, shape, or form.'

'And he's not even kidding,' Kathi murmured.

'What?' said Todd. 'Anyway, I'm annoyed with Roger because he tried to woke-shame me in front of Molly.'

'I have no idea what that means,' I said. 'Because you just made it up on the spot. And no he didn't. Roger doesn't play games.'

'Gaslighting is illegal in the state of California,' Todd said.

'Roger gaslighted you?' I said. 'No way.'

'You gaslighted me!' said Roger. 'Twice now.'

'What? No, I didn't.'

'Three times.'

'What?'

I waited for him to say four, but instead he went with, 'You told me I didn't experience what I experienced, Then you repeated that. Then you said you didn't. One, two, three.'

'Todd,' I said, 'gaslighting – a serious type of psychological abuse – is illegal inside domestic partnerships, between couples. And rightly so. Sometimes I think you forget I know about this stuff. Telling your friend he's talking shit, when he's talking shit, is not illegal. And if it ever gets illegal, I'm going home to Scotland.'

'Between couples or amongst intimate groups,' said Kathi.

'I can't tell if you're showing off your knowledge of domestic violence law or just *woke-shaming me*,' I said.

Kathi laughed but Todd pounced. 'So you *do* know what it means!'

'Tell me what happened,' I said. 'Roger, the saint, the dreamboat, the catch, the hero, the fantasy come true said . . .?'

'Not that you're biased or anything.' Kathi was murmuring again.

'We were telling Molly about the guests we saw on Friday and then on Saturday morning before we left. There was Leo. He was late leaving on Friday.'

'The construction guy?' I said.

Todd nodded.

'I wish he would tell some more of his friends about our excellent linens and delicious coffee,' Kathi said. 'When we agreed to weekly rates, I thought it would take off and be worth all the rubble in the rugs.'

'So there was him,' Todd said. 'And then Sue and Tony arrived shortly before we set off on Saturday.'

'Who the hell are Sue and Tony?' I said.

'Aaron's parents. He's majoring in psychology, Lexy. You should know him.'

I knew 'UCC parents' and thought I was doing well. Of *course* Todd had all the names and a basic bio.

'And Lara and Kent were pulling in as we pulled out, so we saw them too. Just to wave to.'

'How's their kid's GPA?' said Kathi.

Todd was silent.

'Don't you care?'

'But the one that caused the trouble was late on Friday night,' Todd said, ignoring her. 'That's the first point. It was dark. And this person was dressed in black. I described him to Molly not just in detail, but with such specificity and flair that if he walked down the street she could arrest him on the spot.'

'For what?' I said.

'Well, I mean if he was the murderer. But listen. He was a Goth, but he was Nu Goth, you know? Hipster Goth. Slight shading in to Cyber Goth. But by no means a standard "Goth".'

'I'm lost,' Kathi said.

'By which people usually mean Trad Goth. And certainly not a Romantic or Victorian Goth. No lace mittens here, no boned bustiers, no pineapple explosion hairdo. He was a sleek, modern, *Nu* Goth.'

'Are you sure he wasn't just a guy in dark clothes?' said Kathi.

'Oh yes,' said Todd. "John Lennon sunglasses in the pitch dark of night, a Nehru jacket with an inverted inset vinyl crucifix on the back. He had on velvet Chelsea boots.'

'My God, did you pin him to a corkboard?' said Kathi. 'How the hell do you know what his boots were made of? They might have been leather in need of a shine.'

'How the hell do you know what a Chelsea boot is?' I said. 'Aren't they from Chelsea?"

'How meticulously you wound me,' said Todd. 'You finally use the fashion singular, but do it while accusing me of not knowing shoes.'

'And how exactly did he cause trouble between you and Roger?'

'Roger said he was a woman.'

Kathi and I waited. It took a moment to realise that was all we were going to get and it was supposed to make sense all on its own.

'So . . . you thought the person was a man and Roger thought the person was a woman,' said Kathi. 'That seems like a really low-stakes difference of opinion and like it would only help Molly, in the long run.'

Todd said nothing, but he made his feelings known: we had arrived back at the Ditch and he pulled on the handbrake so hard it screeched. It sounded like the rending of a stiff piece of cloth, such as you might use to make a Nehru jacket with a vinyl crucifix right down the back.

'I agree with Kathi,' I said. 'I think if you said "guy", a basic type like Molly might get it into her head she was looking for . . . who's the most masculine man you can think of?'

'Kenny Rogers,' said Kathi. She's such a deep pool, in some ways.

'But Roger saying he thinks it was a woman,' I went on, 'means that Molly will keep her eyes peeled for likes of . . .'

'Brittney Griner.'

'It was a man!'

'OK, jeez. Then . . . Cillian Murphy. I'm just saying.'

'But Roger's *not* saying he thinks it was a woman that I stupidly mis-saw as a man,' said Todd. 'He's saying it was someone presenting as a woman that I shamefully mis-gendered.'

'Ah,' I said. 'Roger reckoned he saw a transwoman and recognised her identity and thinks you saw the same woman and acted like a grunter in a red pickup truck?'

'I explained to him about the Chelsea boots and the Nehru jacket and do you know what he said?'

'Did he say, "What's a Chelsea boot?"' said Kathi.

'He said,' Todd stopped and climbed out of the Jeep, to give himself time for a big build-up, 'that she was wearing pixie boots and a shift dress.' He slammed the door, leaving Kathi and me to crack up in privacy, and stalked over to where Noleen, Meera, Arif, José, and Maria were trying to set the Easter table, with kids running around high on chocolate.

'He's not pissed about "woke-shaming" at all,' Kathi said, when we had recovered and got out of the Jeep to follow him. 'He's pissed that Roger questioned his garment-identification skills. God Almighty! For that he almost derailed our in at the Patsy Denoni but "got away with it". Thank God you fixed it, Lexy.'

'Got away with what?'

'Mocking her for freaking out about accruing instead of murder,' Kathi said. 'But like I said, you fixed it.'

'Yeah.'

'Right? You fixed it?'

'Well, about that. I, um, when I was saying goodbye to Fern and the Millers? Thing is, I did say goodbye to the Millers, see? But that museum has some sick shit on its walls – subtype, foetuses – and I didn't deal with it very well. So I might have said more than goodbye to Fern.'

'Oh?' said Kathi. She stopped walking. 'What might you have said?'

'I might have said she was an idiot to think that her skanky Oakland art collective buddies could afford to wreck a classic Mustang and if the Millers never got justice it would be partly her fault. That's why they didn't come home with us. They stayed on to comfort her and also, I think, they didn't really want to hang out with me. I might have come off a bit angry.'

'I'm sorry, Lex,' Kathi said.

I ground to a halt and stared at her.

'It's not something I ever wanted for myself,' she said. 'But I get that it's a big deal to you.'

'Have I got a sign on my back?'

'Pretty much,' said Kathi. 'And like I say: I don't get it but I do care.'

'Cos you're American,' I said.

Kathi frowned.

'And the enumeration of certain rights doesn't disparage others.'

'Christ on the cross,' Kathi said. When she's pissed off but trying to be kind, she goes right back to Sister Mary Carmelita from middle school, a nun with a salty tongue if ever there was one. Kindness won as she went on, 'You wanna go to the boat and I'll bring a plate to you?'

I opened my mouth to say of course not, that I wanted to sit on a hard wooden bench and hang out with other people's kids, then I imagined putting on a pair of grey, sweatshirt-material shorts and a vest top with no bra and eating Meera's food with my feet up and something completely without artistic or cultural merit on my telly. 'Oh yeah,' I said. 'Double potatoes. No salad. Outside crispy bits of meat, please.'

'All three desserts?' said Kathi. 'All three desserts,' she replied to herself. Then she hugged me and let me slink away.

EIGHT

I will never get used to the Monday after Easter not being a holiday. It's even got a name – Easter Monday. Granted, it's not a name you'll find in any creed. It's not like Palm Sunday, Maundy Thursday and Good Friday, being more garden-centre-related than church-based, but it's printed in my DNA and so it felt profoundly wrong for the alarm to go off at quarter to seven in the morning to get me up and ready to face a full day of whinging clients.

I saved a bit of time on breakfast at least, because I was still full from the three puddings the night before and also quite hungover. That was one benefit of finding out I yet again wasn't pregnant, or at least it should have been.

When Todd sprang on board and rapped on the closed door of my shower room, it seemed he was there purely to bug me. Taylor was long gone down to the wetlands, or I'm pretty sure he would have offered protection.

'I've got a bottle of this amazing stuff I just found for you,' Todd shouted through the door. 'It's a fertility-support bundle but don't assume it's just vitamins.'

'I wasn't,' I muttered to myself, getting shampoo in my mouth and making myself feel worse than ever.

'Because it's going to replace all the boost you're missing from giving up caffeine and it's got all the natural relaxants you're missing from no longer drinking alcohol, and it's packed with minerals that you might start to need since you've prob-ably given up all dairy instead of just soft cheese. So really it's four bottles of absolutely unparalleled self-care that—'

'It was one bottle a minute ago,' I shouted. 'Did it have triplets?'

'I can't hear you,' Todd said, opening the door and leaning in. He had his eyes shut but he was still letting steam out to wreck my hallway panels and the size of the shower room meant that water trickling along the floor wasn't unlikely either. 'Taylor told us you weren't feeling good. So don't tell me you don't need this. Just for once let people help you.'

'I wasn't feeling good,' I said, 'because I really thought this time I was up the duff and I'm not and also I'm sore and I'm bleeding and, if there's a barista in this town who knows how to make a soft blue cheese and brandy latte I'll tip them forty per cent.'

'Let it all out. Let the rage flow like your—'

'Do NOT finish that sentence,' I said. 'Is that all you came to tell me?'

'Also, Phil and Jilly want to retain our services on a formal footing and it's a bit of an ethical dilemma. So there's thaa-at . . .'

'And . . .?' I was annoyed with myself for letting it happen but the truth is he had me. I was straight-up showering with the door open and having a conversation now.

'And . . . don't get all uppity and start telling me I'm over-stepping,' he said, 'but I don't think you should assume it's you. I've seen Taylor's underwear. I mean, I tried to block it out for crimes against style but also it's not healthy. So I've put some super-drapey satin boxers in his top drawer and removed the offending items. But still, you should send him to have a sperm test.'

'He's twenty-nine,' I said. 'I'm thirty-seven. And what on earth made you think I'd see this as over-stepping?'

'Oh,' said Todd. 'Well, good. I just never know with you. But to your main point. Investigating your fertility is invasive and expensive. Given that your cycle is regular and you're tuned into it, and given that Taylor can find out how his guys are after ten fun minutes with a magazine, it makes sense to dot that i first.'

'And you're basing the notion that my cycle is regular on . . .'

'The fact that I gave you a link to an ovulation app months ago and you would have told me if it wasn't.'

'Right,' I said, turning off the shower. 'Can you hand me a towel, please?'

Eyes still shut, Todd faffed about until his hands lit on the bath sheet hanging on the half-open door. He held it out to me. 'Say when.'

'When,' I said, still standing stark naked and dripping, with my tampon string plastered to one wet thigh.

Todd shrieked and ran.

'It's part of my fertility bundling,' I shouted after him. 'Everyone knows you have to park your modesty to give birth. I'm starting early.'

'I'm going to have to watch Bruno Mars dance videos until Fall to rebuild my retinas!' he shouted back, but at least he was laughing.

'So why the ethical dilemma?' I said, joining him on the porch with my enormous bath sheet securely wound right round me and tucked in tight under my armpit.

'Because Jilly's decided she doesn't believe her parents are dead,' Todd said. 'And she wants us to find them. Kathi's playing it straight. She told them to go to the police and lay out the theory for Molly.'

'But Molly's not going to shred a murder enquiry and start a missing persons instead because a grieving daughter can't face the facts.'

'Exactly,' said Todd. 'So we need to decide what to say to the Miller kids if – more like when – they come back to us again.'

'What's Kathi think?'

'She's all for it,' said Todd.

That was surprising. Kathi, with her PI licence, had most to lose from stepping on the toes of the PD and she was usually the voice of reason, while Todd went careening off on his usual helter-skelter of unquestioning enthusiasm.

'Let me get dressed and come to the laundromat,' I said. 'We need a plan.'

'What are you wearing?' said Todd. He can't help himself.

'White jeans of course,' I said. 'The better to slide down the back of my white couch.'

He frowned. Maybe he didn't pay as much attention to tampon adverts as I do. 'White jeans before Memorial Day are

fine in California, of course,' he said. 'Fine anywhere really
except Black Church, as I found out to my cost once when we
went to visit Roger's family, but you don't own a white couch,
Lexy. And until Hiro stops juggling raisins and then sitting on
the missed ones, I can't recommend it.'

I started to loosen my towel and Todd scrambled down the
steps and leapt on to the bank to get away from me.

'Glad you rethought it,' he said, when I arrived in the Skweek
fifteen minutes later, in a pair of drawstring linen trousers and
a cotton jumper in shades of grey to suit my mood. 'Kathi,
you were saying?'

'I like our chances,' Kathi said. 'And I need the work.' As
she looked around the sparkling, gleaming laundromat, all set
up for another week, I'd never seen such a lack of avidity in
her eyes. It was almost as though she'd rather be grubbing
about in pools of blood and webs of lies than polishing quarters and folding shirts into such sharp rectangles that two stuck
together and twisted could be used as jumbo throwing stars.

'So . . . Jilly's new notion?' I said. 'Based on what?'

'You missed this, of course,' Todd said. 'Last night at dinner
when the Millers got back from the museum. What the hell
did you say to Fern, by the way? Never mind.'

'Yeah,' Kathi said. 'Jilly's got an idea into her noggin, planted
by Fern with some help from the Oakland dude Fern thought
had put the car there? It goes something like this: if you can
fill a car with blood and call it a sculpture of decay then you
can fill a car with blood and call it a crime scene. She wants
us to start by asking butchers about any special orders recently.'

'But . . .' I began.

Kathi was rearranging her shirt pins into a double helix
pattern, subconsciously I'm sure, but it made me feel better to
know I wasn't the only one that all this blood, blood, blood
talk was getting to. I felt like an extra in a remake of *Carrie*
and I could have done without it.

'Of course "but"!' Kathi said. 'Even if they haven't got the
DNA back yet, they decided already that it was human blood
and that it was from two different people. How long can typing

it take?" Enh, she was upset. But, even after we talked her down from that, she still thinks there was no reason for the killer not to leave the bodies there in the car and since he didn't – no bodies.'

'How can she know there was no reason to—?' I said.

'She can't!' said Kathi. 'I'm not agreeing, I'm just reporting. She's feeling hurt and helpless and she'd rather feel hurt and like she's doing something. If she's willing to pay us to find her mom and pop, who are we to turn down work?'

'What am I missing?' I said.

'Highlighter, contouring, a really good blow-out, a well-fitting bra . . .' said Todd. 'Just kidding. Not. Yeah, Kathi, what are we missing? Because everything you've said so far sounds like we'd be taking money under false pretences from vulnerable people and probably getting arrested for interfering with a police investigation too.'

'Not false pretences,' said Kathi. Then she ruined it. 'Not exactly. What I think we should do is defer the retainer until the case is closed to the Millers' satisfaction. *They're* going to think that means finding their mom and pop alive and well and rebuilding their iron levels on a tropical island. *We* know it means giving them proof that their parents are dead, even if it's the cops who take over and work out whodunnit. I can live with that.'

'But what makes you think we can do either?' I said. 'Quicker and better than Molly, I mean?'

'For one thing, we'll be trying,' Kathi said. She held up a hand as I started to interrupt her. 'I'm not saying Molly won't be trying to solve the case; I'm sure she will, but she'll be working for the deceased, the state, and her own promotion prospects. Not the kids. They're orphaned in more ways than one.'

'Like DC,' I said. 'Gotcha.'

'What?' said Kathi. 'DC . . . Universe, you mean?'

'If only she did,' said Todd.

'The District of Columbia,' I explained. 'Phil and Jilly are like DC before the . . . Shit! Which one is it?'

'*What?*' said Kathi.

'No one *cares*,' said Todd. 'Oh, don't look at me like that! Of course I care about the Miller kids having someone in their corner and I'm even willing to let it be us. But literally no one cares which amendment gave DC . . . No one even knows!' He started clapping. 'It. Will. Not. Come. Up.'

I filed that claim away, all set to cast it up to him if he was wrong, like he'd been wrong about no one knowing or caring what the stopping distances were at different speeds. I'd had to sit my written test twice because of Todd's excessive breeziness. I'd made him pay the extra thirty-eight dollars, rounded up to fifty for the emotional damage. 'What did you mean "for one thing"?' I asked Kathi.

'Thanks for noticing,' she said. 'The other factor is – are you ready? – I have a clue that Molly's missed,' said Kathi. She is a serious woman. Even when she laughs it's usually down her nose with her lips pressed together, but right now she gave an impish grin I had only seen on her face a handful of times before in all the years I had known her. The last time was when she saw the weals and dents my wedding underwear had put on my flesh and she had opened her tuxedo shirt and showed me her own plump and unmarked skin under her softly fitting sports bra.

I grinned back, partly at her and partly at the happy memory of burning my bra, knickers, suspender belt and garter in a trash barrel in the slough, against all the fire regulations of Beteo County, and making my first post-wedding vow to Taylor as the flames died down. I'd wear a thong again any day he wore a thong, I'd promised him. It had yet to arise.

'Go on, then,' I said. 'Clue?'

'They were seen.'

'Who was seen?' I said.

'Have you given up coffee like an idiot?' said Kathi. 'Switch your brain on, Lexy. The Millers were seen. "Who was seen?"!'

'I know they were seen,' I said. 'All over town, trying to check into hotels and failing. If you hadn't been off camping – speaking of whether brains are switched off or on – you would have seen them too.'

'Yeahhhh, about that,' said Kathi. 'And still on the subject of whether brains are on, off, or decommissioned and broken up for parts. I cannot believe you people really think I went camping. Sleeping on the ground? In dust? Or mud? In a tent that sits out all night then gets rolled up and reused next time?'

'But you always go camping,' Todd said.

'I have never been camping,' said Kathi.

'I should know,' Todd went on, as if she hadn't spoken, 'because oftentimes if you were going to stay in a nice hotel like human beings do, I would come with you to escape my loneliness, what with Roger working all the damn time, but ohhhh no. Camping it is and so I've never had the chance . . . Wait.'

'There it is!' Kathi said.

'Well, I must say that is incredibly hurtful,' said Todd. 'You left me here and went off just the two of you? Every single time?'

'We did,' Kathi said. She was polishing the legs of her folding table now, crouched down and craning up to get her duster right in where they joined the underside of the surface. How *did* we ever believe this woman had gone camping, actually?

'But you took a tent,' I said, trying to stop myself from feeling too foolish.

'Yup, a tent, a groundsheet, an awning, a bear bag, a cooler, a camp stove, pots and pans, big bag of marshmallows. You wouldn't believe the crap people leave behind in their motel rooms when they've over-shopped on a trip. None of it cost us a penny and, because we never use any of it, none of it will ever wear out.'

'So you pack your car with camping gear and then you go off to a nice hotel?' I said. 'As a therapist I can't applaud the deception but as a friend I say good for you.'

'Call yourself a friend?' said Kathi. 'And yet you know nothing about either of us. Yeah, sure, Lexy, Noleen and I go to another lodging somewhere and compare the business with ours. We also run into people we know from the CHLA chapter and spend our evenings talking about the board members. It's so relaxing.'

'OK, I see that,' I said. 'So where do you go? You can't sleep in your car if it's full of bear bags and marshmallows. Do you sneak back in here and lie low with the curtains shut?'

'No, they don't,' said Todd, 'or I would find them when I go to do wardrobe triage while the coast's clear. And there's even less room in the car than you thought, Lexy, because they take all their clothes.'

'Why . . . Oh, so Todd can't do wardrobe triage?' I said.

Kathi pointed her finger at me, clicked her tongue and winked.

'So where do you go? Actually, you know what? That's not what we should be talking about, is it? What we should be talking about is who saw the Millers and what makes that sighting different from everyone else who saw them?'

'It does matter,' Kathi said. 'Because *we* saw them, Noleen and me. At least, we saw the Mustang.'

'You mean you saw *a* Mustang,' I said. 'But even if it was the right colour . . . What colour was the Millers' one again?'

'Well,' said Kathi, 'if you remember, Jilly said they rented a beautiful purple vintage Mustang.' Neither Todd nor I are petrol heads but we were both willing to believe her. 'And then Fern said it was a magical arty-farty blue-green colour, right?'

Todd gasped. 'Oh my Gordon Highlander plaid swatch collection!' he said. 'It's not their car! The car full of blood isn't the Millers' car! The two bloodless dead folks, one bald as well, aren't the Millers! They've disappeared and we can find them?'

'Almost completely wrong,' said Kathi. 'It *is* the same car.'

'Someone's colour blind?' I said.

'No, it's a Mustang Cobra Mystichrome is all. Jilly called it a *vintage* car presumably because her folks told her they were renting a classic car and she's really dumb about cars. And you know what? It's a stretch even to call it a classic. It was made in 2004. Assuming it wasn't a convertible and everyone forgot to say. A convertible would put it back in the nineties.'

'But how is it one car when it's two different colours?' Todd said.

But I was on it. 'Mystichrome?' I said. 'Does that mean what I think it means?'

'It looks purple when you look at it one way and green when you move your head and look at it another way. Yep.'

'OK, so the Millers are dead again,' said Todd. 'But I still say you and Noleen wherever you were – so cruel – saw *a* Mustang.'

'Yes,' said Kathi. 'We saw *a* Mustang Cobra Mystichrome coupé. Ask me how many Ford made of the things.'

'Say, Kathi,' I said, very generously, 'how many did Ford make of the things?'

'Five hundred,' Kathi said.

'In the whole country?' said Todd.

'In the whole world. Twenty years ago. I think it's safe to say that the one I saw on the street, in Cuento, Friday night, is the same one that was abandoned, in a field, in Cuento, Friday night. Don't you?'

'I do,' Todd said.

'I do,' I said.

'And now you're married,' said Kathi. 'God help you both. Anyway, I *could* tell Molly. You might even say I *should* tell Molly, but honestly? It wasn't until Fern said green after Jilly said purple that I realised what car we were dealing with. And the fact that Molly didn't hammer that bit hard, in interviews and press conferences and flyers? That is so dumb. It's like . . .'

'Not mentioning that a guy's wearing stilts?' I said.

'Random,' said Kathi. 'But essentially, yes. That dumb. So I'm going to do a little digging around on my own and rub her face in it when I hand over what I got. Wanna help?'

'Potentially,' said Todd. I think he still hadn't completely accepted that Kathi and Noleen didn't go camping and he didn't want to sign up for anything until he was sure.

'So,' I said, 'if we promise not to tell anyone and we promise – no, we vow – not to muscle in, right, Todd? Will you reveal where it is you and Nolly go when we all thought you were under nets in the forest?'

'I will,' said Kathi. 'An Airbnb.'

Talk about a let-down.

'We go to a little cottage owned and rented out by a friend of mine. We met at an intensive graded-exposure weekend course for germaphobes, ten years back now, and she is the only person whose cleaning I trust enough to go and live there, sleep there, wash there and eat there.'

'Pretty hopeless course then,' I said.

'First afternoon, the instructor licked a toilet and told us we'd all be doing it by the Sunday.'

'Ewwww,' I said. 'Did anyone stay on for the rest of the weekend?'

'It wasn't a real toilet,' Kathi said. 'Well, it was a real toilet, but new from the home improvement store, still with labels, and it wasn't plumbed in. But ewwww is right. Belle and I got out of there before the instructor had stood back up again. We bought a twelve pack of beer, a box of Clorox wipes to clean the tops of the cans and went for a ride in her car. She's the one who showed me how to clean inside the ignition keyhole with hot chewing gum.'

'Have we ever met her?' Todd said, his nose still badly out of joint.

'She doesn't go into other people's houses much,' Kathi said. She spoke in awed tones, not in the least offended that her forensically disinfected and scrubbed-silly home was deemed too grubby for Belle to enter. Instead, she seemed to be bowing at the feet of a recognised master. I should have said something. None of it was remotely healthy. But there were bigger fish to fry.

'And where is it that this "Belle" runs the Airbnb equivalent of an operating theatre?' said Todd, still pretty waspish.

'The dream streets,' Kathi said. '*That's* where we go.'

Todd pursed his mouth so hard that his lips disappeared. And he has to work at that, being blessed with the kind of lips that make you remember Nastassja Kinsky eating a strawberry.

The dream streets – 9th to 12th between B and F – were broad and shady. And *quiet*. They led nowhere that better streets didn't lead quicker and there were no businesses to tempt passing trade. They were simply quarter-acre lot after quarter-acre lot of smooth lawns, or crazy paving or raised beds or gnome villages, with snug little 1940s ranch houses set back behind deep porches, red-brick chimneys puffing up scented smoke on chilly afternoons and elderly neighbours toddling back and forth with covered casseroles on holidays. I had no idea what any of them looked like inside because I'd never been in one, but judging from the beige Volvos in the driveways and the original window frames, I was guessing there would be a lot of carefully tended porcelain in the bathrooms, hardwood in the living rooms, painted cabinetry in the kitchens and not a granite island in sight.

'You were right *there*?' said Todd. Because the dream streets were a fifteen-minute walk away from the Ditch. Ten minutes for someone running on outrage like Todd was right now. And besides that, 'dream streets' wasn't a Cuento word; it was a Last Ditch word because all we Ditchers loved those four blocks of northern Cuento, and would live there in a heartbeat, only no one ever moved out to let newcomers in. Oh, there were suburbs with winding roads, further out, and there were McMansions with glittering pools and Sopranos kitchens, but you can't buy taste and we all judged the residents who settled there. No, the dream streets were it. Della and Devin walked them with Hiro asleep in her buggy after they'd dropped Diego at library story time, Taylor and I laughingly agreed that we'd more likely win the lottery and raise a deposit on one if we ever bought a lottery ticket. Todd had been heard to say that if he moved into one of the houses on the dream streets, he wouldn't have to do any remodelling. And now it turned out that all these 'camping' years, Noleen and Kathi had been bunking off there to live out everyone's daydream on the sly.

'So what were the Millers *doing* on the dream streets?' Todd said, with admirable focus on the point, given that he was still stewing.

'Finally!' said Kathi. 'What indeed. The only sensible possibility is that they were trying to find somewhere to stay. Now, they might have googled Airbnbs, in desperation, once they realised they'd had it with hotels, but they wouldn't have found one.'

'How can you be sure?' said Todd.

'Because Belle's books up weeks out and she's fussy. Any others in those four blocks would be even more choked on Spring Break weekend. So . . .?'

'So . . .?' I said.

'So someone in those streets knows the Millers. The Millers knew someone who lives on those streets. It's the only explanation. They were trying to lean on a friend and get a place to spend the night.'

'Some friend,' said Todd. 'Turning them away to sleep in their car.'

'That's one possibility, yes,' Kathi said. 'But don't you think these mean excuses for friends would have come forward? To the press? To the cops?'

'How do you know they *haven't* been to the cops?' I asked her. 'Not going to the press, I understand. They must feel absolutely wretched with themselves.'

'Didn't you watch the press conference Molly did?' said Kathi. 'It was a masterpiece. The strangers in our midst, the values of this town, the unspeakable tragedy of two innocent people seeking refuge in their hour of need and finding only violence.'

'You think that would make the friends come forward?' I said. 'It might make *me* crawl under a rock.'

'Also, she put their route up on the screen, right along the hotel corridor either side of the freeway, finishing at the Patsy Denoni, no mention of them being downtown or up in the dream streets. Nobody else knows about their detour except for me, and now you, and these pals of theirs.'

'Even though it's such a distinctive car?' I said.

Todd made a noise with his tongue obviously meant to make us ask him for a contribution. When neither of us obliged, he rolled on anyway. 'This is exactly why we had to get to the city! Friday night in downtown Cuento and no one's out and about to see a vintage mystical Congo car cruising around.'

'Barely classic Mystichrome Cobra,' Kathi said. 'And it was nearly midnight, to be fair.'

'And their friends *still* turned them away?' said Todd. 'May they never have another night's undisturbed rest in their lives.'

'I'll say it again.' Kathi gave us both a patient look. 'That's one of the possibilities.'

'List the others,' said Todd.

'Just one other that I can think of,' Kathi said. 'The Millers were on a street in Cuento where they knew someone. The Millers got murdered. The someone hasn't told the cops a damn thing . . .'

'No way,' I said.

'*Someone* did it,' Kathi said. 'We don't have a long list of other suspects. And think about it: if you had killed two people and their very distinctive car was parked outside your house, wouldn't you want to take it to the edge of a dusty field miles away and leave it there?'

'Without the bodies?' I added. 'I don't know. If I was going to drive a car full of blood through the town I might make sure I was one and done. Dump the bodies too.'

'Those dream streets houses have basements,' Todd said.

'So?' I said. 'We're getting ahead of ourselves like we've been catapulted!'

'Same as "Someone did it",' Kathi said, 'Bodies gotta be somewhere.'

'Ew but true,' I said. 'Right then. Not how I imagined this day if it ever came. I was hoping for an open house one Sunday afternoon, but OK. To the dream streets!'

NINE

B ut first, at Kathi's persuasion, we had to go on a whistle-stop tour of 'the competition', as she was still calling it, despite the fact that there were no winners in this particular bout: the Millers had been turned away from everywhere in town. We were all losers.

'Why?' I asked. 'What can we find out that'll make a difference?'

'A lot of empathy,' said Kathi, 'from a professional empath.'

'Counselling isn't . . .' I said, but she wasn't listening so I agreed to go. So did Todd, of course. No show without Punch.

Besides, it didn't take long, that evening after work, to drive from one to the other to the next Cuento lodging spot, parking in the fifteen-minute spaces and following Kathi inside to quiz the desk staff about that fateful Friday night.

'So . . . these folks who got killed,' she opened. 'Oh, I'm Kathi Muntz, by the way. You're new, right? Oh you've heard of me? Good. Yeah, I'm just going round checking and double-checking. I can see a world of shit coming our way, all of us in the local hospitality trade. But you really were full, weren't you? Not a broom closet to be had? Us too.'

It worked just as well on the junior-type new arrivals as on the old-timers and the manager sorts. Although there weren't many of the lowly probationer kind of staff on duty on this quiet Monday evening (which should have been the end of a raucous three-day Easter weekend, but nobody knew that except me); they get stuck with Friday and Saturday nights, and the check-out tsunami on Sunday morning.

Still, whether Kathi had to introduce herself and wave a hand in the direction of the Ditch or had to trade salty stories about regional conference weekends of yore, every single one of the desk staff we dropped in on confirmed that the Millers had been there, that they turned them away, and that they only did so because the hotel was truly, to the rafters, full.

The sole interesting moment was when a career-hospitality woman at the Best Western said that she would have sworn it was Mrs Miller who had the migraine.

'She might well have had a bit of a headache too, before they got this far,' Todd said, the Best Western being only two hotels up the freeway from the Last Ditch, after all.

'No, it's not that,' the woman said. She was straightening leaflets in the Perspex stand on the desk as she spoke, one of the band of customer-service true believers who are never not straightening something. Once the leaflets were square she came out from her station and went to bang cushions in the foyer. 'What I meant was that I would have sworn it was the husband who came in and said his wife had a migraine and was in the car. But then I saw their pic in the *Voyager* and they were practically twins, weren't they? *She* made no effort what-soever to look pretty and *he* was kind of a weed.'

So much for not speaking ill of the dead.

Too late, she seemed to take her first proper look at Kathi, who didn't so much not make an effort to look pretty as make active efforts to look plain bordering invisible. The woman coloured, turned to Todd and said, 'I like a man to look like a man.' Then she blinked, coloured a deeper shade of pink and latched on to me. 'It had been a very busy night and I was . . .'

'Tired?' said Kathi.

'There had been a reception with complimentary wine and it turned out everyone was driving. It was all poured in the glasses already.'

'So you were hammered?' said Todd.

'Ignore him,' I told the woman. 'He's upset about something else and lashing out very unpatriotically at you.'

'Huh?'

'It's your right to drink alcohol if you want to and it has been for over ninety years.'

'What the hell?' the woman said. 'I'm fifty-eight!'

'Ignore both of them,' Kathi said. 'And thank you.'

*   *   *

'What am I supposedly upset about?' asked Todd, as we left. 'That's made me lash out at Mel Gibson back there?'

Kathi frowned.

'Drank so much she couldn't see gender,' he added.

'That's nothing like Mel Gibson,' I said. 'And there's no supposedly about it. Pixiebootgate is bugging the shit out of you.'

'Chelseabootgate,' said Todd. 'How many more, Kathi?'

'Two,' Kathi said. 'Las Palmas and the Ditch.'

'And we're not counting the Ditch,' said Todd. 'Yay. Last one.'

'But we most certainly are counting the Ditch,' Kathi said. 'We need to work out if those – what did you call them, Lexy? Sounded like a tropical disease? – actually had a reason for bouncing the Millers. Because I don't believe the Ditch was full last Friday night. Unless those . . .'

'Locums.'

'Right, locums, were giving rooms away to their pals. The takings don't say "full house" at all.' She sighed. 'It's pretty sketchy the way the agency won't give up their names. Even if Noleen did . . .' She stopped talking like the good wife she is.

'Put their backs up like an airbag,' I supplied.

'I'm not saying it was empty,' Kathi said, giving me a quick nod of thanks. 'There's Leo's late check-out, assuming the locums were too lazy to go in and turn the room round in time to re-let it. Plus my room, Todd's room, the emergency room, the Ds' rooms. That's six rooms accounted for. But we have twelve, as you know.'

'But doesn't Molly know that too?' Todd said. He had pulled over to the kerb. Actually, he had slowed to a standstill in the middle of the road, then pulled to the kerb when honked at. Thank God we'd left the freeway by now. 'Kathi,' he went on in the soberest voice I'd ever heard him use, 'this fact-finding mission around the hotels that you've got us doing here? Are you trying to spread the blame?'

'What blame?' Kathi said. 'I didn't exsanguinate the Millers. I wasn't even there.'

'Oh yeah,' said Todd. 'You were off seeing the death Mustang.'

'What the hell is this?' Kathi said.

'Because it really *would* be pretty sketchy if the agency refused to tell Noleen the relief managers' names.'

'*Would be?*' said Kathi. 'I can't believe I'm hearing this. You're sitting there telling me Noleen knows the names and so do I and I'm *lying* to you? We weren't even at the Ditch that night.'

'No,' said Todd, 'you were camping.'

'This is some bullshit right here,' Kathi said. 'Lexy, what do you think?'

'I genuinely think that whoever answered the phone at the agency worked at the Ditch for at least a summer and harbours a grudge against Noleen. Can't imagine why.' Neither one of them so much as raised a smile. 'But anyway, they are refusing to cooperate with her, after the . . . somewhat unprofessional exchange of views when she called them. However, I also think there is no reason to suspect that anyone with a working braincell would turn away business, so we can assume that either the Millers didn't even stop at the Ditch for some reason, or the motel was genuinely full. Look, we know there was the man in black that Todd saw . . .'

'Thank you! Tell Roger,' Todd said.

'Seven rooms gone if we count him. And there was the barbershop guy that I saw on Saturday. If he was there the whole weekend then that's us up to eight. And you forgot that the managers themselves had to sleep somewhere, and presumably they didn't share a room – I wouldn't – so that makes ten.'

'And leaves two,' Kathi said. 'I mean, we needed the break – Todd, I swear to God, if you say "camping" again, I will hurt you – but we come back and the Ditch computer is in chaos and the managers are nowhere to be found and there's been a murder and we're the only innkeepers in the whole of Cuento that can't put our hands on our hearts and say we couldn't have done any more than we did to give the Millers a safe place to stay.'

'Hang on, what?' I said. 'The managers were nowhere to be found? Seriously? They left before you got back? Noleen shouldn't just be asking for names then. She should be banging heads. She should be reporting the whole shebang to the . . . somebody. Chamber of Commerce? Better Business Bureau?'

'Except we told them when we booked them that we would be back by happy hour Sunday and we didn't get back till almost midnight.'

'But they can't just walk out!' I said. 'What if you were trapped up a tree, with rabid wolves circling.'

'Oh, Lexy's allowed to refer to you "camping"?' said Todd.

'Yeah, but we didn't want to pay them overtime,' Kathi said. 'We called Devin and asked if he would take the desk a few hours until we got there.'

'Which of course he did,' I said. 'Sunday night? When Della and her sisters group chat to her mum? And it's big bathtime before school in the morning?'

'Yeah,' said Kathi. 'I felt kind of guilty about that, but the thing is Belle's got this hot tub on the patio at her rental unit and, as you know, I can't ever use hot tubs – Legionnaire's Disease, feet . . .'

'Genitals,' said Todd. 'Ass cracks.'

'OK!' said Kathi.

'And has anyone spoken to Devin?' I said. 'Maybe the locums gave him a report when they handed over.'

'Molly asked him,' Kathi said. 'But he can't remember what they talked about.'

'Sounds like he's been taking tips from Taylor,' I said.

'I don't understand how people can be uninterested in people,' said Todd. 'We see faces in clouds, in toast. People should see people!'

'All right, Barbra,' said Kathi.

And whether he had finally done enough moaning about perfect Roger disagreeing with him or he was just thrilled to be compared to such an icon, that was the end of the great camping/gender huff. If we had carried on the conversation even a little bit longer, we might have made some headway with the case.

Instead, we drove up through the rapidly emptying downtown and on to the start of the residential neighbourhood, meaning to take a crack at finding the Millers' dream-streets destination.

Kathi parked outside her friend Belle's cottage. It was on

the small side for this neck of the woods, but cute as a button, painted a soft moss green with smoky blue trim and steps the same weathered red brick as the chimney. There were swing seats at either end of the porch and tubs of tulips.

Kathi got out of the car and strode up the path.

'Stop,' I hissed at her. 'You can't disturb someone else's minibreak! We need to do this from the road.'

Kathi gave me a screwball look. 'Duh,' she said. 'We just rented it last weekend, Lexy. Belle won't even be halfway through the cleaning yet. Breathe in.'

I did and felt my nostrils prickle as they were assaulted by a hit of pure chlorine bleach. No wonder the bricks were weathered. The porch furniture too was scrubbed until it squeaked when Kathi ran her finger along one of the wooden slats.

'Good,' said Todd, who usually has a big problem with porches. It's one area of anxiety where I get it, mind you. There are black widow spiders in California, and they like to hang out in peaceful corners: under wicker chair legs; in the gaps between the slats of picnic tables; in amongst the agave spikes and cactus bumps and yucca fronds where they won't get bugged by watering cans or inquisitive fingers.

'So where did you see the car?' I asked.

'We were in there,' said Kathi, pointing. 'The bed is opposite the window and we were sitting up, sipping tea.'

'You crazy kids,' said Todd. 'Tucked up in bed by midnight, sitting up, sipping tea.'

'We had actually just finished a marathon,' said Kathi. 'Of *Extraordinary Attorney Woo*.'

'Nice pause,' I said.

'And I saw it go by, under the streetlight. I knew what it was straight away. Leapt out of bed and went to catch another glimpse before it passed out of sight.'

'Lexy, if I ever notice the make and model of a car going past the window when I'm in bed with ma honey on a weekend break, will you support me through the divorce and the dating afterwards?'

'But it had parked,' Kathi said. 'Almost right opposite. So I went to put a robe on—'

'Oo-oooo,' said Todd. 'Nekkid. That's more like it.'

'Over my PJs,' said Kathi. 'What is wrong with you today? By the time I got back, the car was still there but whoever had been driving was gone. I think – only *think*, this is – that she either went in to that house, that house or that house, or she walked along the street thataway.'

'And you know it was a woman how?' I asked.

'Because Mr Miller was flat out on the back seat having his migraine.' Kathi heaved a hearty sigh. 'So it must have been Mrs Miller who got out of the car and walked to wherever her friends live.' She sighed again.

'Are you having breathing trouble?' said Todd.

'I'm just thinking,' Kathi said. 'If I'd had a sturdier robe, I'd have probably gone out for a closer look at the Mustang, and I'd have seen the guy in the back seat and . . .'

'Invited a visibly ill stranger to come and join you in your AirBnB?' I said. I was trying to stop her beating herself up, but I only succeeded in rattling her.

'Belle would kill me, and I'd deserve it, if I turned her cottage into a party house. But I could have done *something*. Surely. I could have told them that there's no college in Muelleverde and so no spring-break hotel room overload. And they might have driven on another five miles and be on their way to the Hoover Dam as we speak.'

'OK, but to get back to detecting instead of flaying yourself over absolutely nothing,' I said, 'if you didn't actually see her, how do you know which way she went?'

'Exactly why I wanted to come here and scope it out.'

'Did you see her return to the car and drive away?' Todd said. 'But then how come you don't know which direction for sure?'

'Fell asleep,' said Kathi. 'All's I know is the Mustang was gone by morning.'

'But then she could have gone anywhere,' I said. 'She could have walked for miles. We might need to do a proper house-to-house of all four blocks.'

'You're just being nosy,' said Todd.

'Well, that too and I won't deny it, but you see what I mean?'

'I don't,' Kathi said. 'Why wouldn't Mrs Miller just park as near the right house as she could?'

'OK,' I said. 'As we were. Back to how come you know which direction she went from the car?'

'Look,' said Kathi, backing up to the window and pulling me in close to stand beside her on one side, with Todd on the other.

I pressed myself up against the glass to get as close to the right spot as possible. She was right. The sightline was unimpeded for quite a way coming towards us, so Mrs Miller would have been visible much longer than it could have taken Kathi to jump out of bed and shrug into her dressing gown.

'Might she have crossed the road?' I asked. 'Let's ask the houses on this side too, eh?'

'You really do just want to look inside these beautiful homes,' said Todd. 'You don't fool me. And neither do you, Kathi. What's the real reason you didn't go outside for a closer look, because I've seen your robe. It's a triumph of sturdiness. What aren't you saying?"

'You've never seen my weekend-away robe,' Kathi said. While Todd was gasping like a goldfish on the hearthrug, she added, 'We can't pound on doors in this neighbourhood when Rachel Maddow's on. So we better get going if we're going.'

'It won't take long,' I said, as we trooped down the path again. 'I mean, surely we'll know as soon as whoever opens the door, right? Wait, what are we going to say?'

'You're not going to say anything,' Kathi told me. She stopped with one foot on the pavement and one still on the path. 'And Todd? You're not going to say anything either. Got it? The only reason you're here at all is to watch their faces while *I* say what *I'm* planning to say, seasoned and licensed professional like I am.'

'Sounds like a fish,' said Todd.

'It's a good plan,' I said. 'Something's going to show on their faces. Whether they're rightly guilty that they turned their friends away, wrongly guilty because they weren't here that night, and now you steam in like Nemesis—'

'Fish again,' said Todd.

'That's Nemo or Neptune.'

'Will you both for the love of God get your heads in the game?' said Kathi. 'You forgot option C, Lexy: they did it and they think they got away with it. We might be about going to confront a murderer, people!'

When she put it that way . . .

In fact, we were lucky to get away without eating dinner at the first place. Kathi rapped on the door and arranged Todd and me flanking her like nightclub bouncers while she waited for an answer. After a minute, a woman appeared, with an apron on and a ladle in her hand

'Hello!' she said. 'You work at the laundromat that does the crisp shirts, don't you? My husband retired years ago now but oh he looked smart every day once we found you, dear. What can I do for you?'

'I'm not just a starch specialist,' Kathi said. 'I'm also a private detective.'

'Now there's a combination you don't come across every day,' the woman said. 'Are you detecting right now?'

'I am,' said Kathi. 'It's about Bill and Billie.'

I was watching the woman's face as if she was a roulette wheel with my life savings riding on her, and there wasn't a flicker. She raised her eyebrows a fraction and leaned in, waiting for more, hoping understanding was on its way.

'The Millers,' Kathi said.

'Millers? Millers?' the woman said. 'Now, why does that ring a bell?'

'They were murd—' Kathi began.

'Oh! Oh! The people in the canoe? Oh yes, of course. How silly of me. I must have read their names in the *Voyager* article but it didn't stick. Wasn't that terrible? Terrible.'

'Awful,' I agreed. I had promised to keep silent but I reckoned I'd fulfilled my obligation now.

'And so how can I help you?' the woman said. 'Would you like to come in? Dinner's almost ready. Have you been out canvassing residents of Cuento all day? Are you deputised?'

'That won't be necessary,' said Kathi.

'It's meatloaf,' the woman said. 'And there's plenty. I can't cook for one.' She wiped her hand under her eye, ignoring the ladle she was holding. 'I still make meatloaf every Monday like I always did.' She scooped fragrant air out from behind her and wafted it out the front door to where we stood on her step. 'Bircher potatoes. You know what they are? Same guy who invented muesli? Total whack job but he knew his way round a spud. And asparagus.'

As we were walking back down the path, Todd said, 'You have a heart of stone and a will of iron, Kathi. That poor old lady.'

'She was waving that big spoon about in the open air and practically wiping her nose on it,' Kathi said. 'No way was I eating from her kitchen.'

'Savage,' said Todd. 'It was a ladle and you know what that means? Gravy. But we can stop for tacos once we're done, I guess.'

'Onward,' Kathi said.

I was concentrating on not letting my stomach rumble, which is not actually possible and anyway, that's a lie. I was concentrating on controlling the trapped wind that was the result of too much booze, three puddings, period squits, and a long day of grazing on Hiro and Diego's chocolate overstock.

'Are you OK?' said Todd. I hadn't realised I was doing the rear premises equivalent of a pee-dance.

'If I walk away,' I said, 'don't follow me. Apart from that, I'm fine. Can we go to the Red Racoon for food afterwards, though? You can't let me smell meatloaf and then make me eat tacos, not on top of everything else. You must see that, surely.'

'Well, step it up then,' Kathi said. 'It shuts at nine.'

We zipped round the rest of the possible Miller destinations. There were no more meatloaf offers. What there were was: a retired UCC professor, with round spectacles on his wrinkled dome of a forehead and actual leather patches on the elbows of his cardigan, who answered the door carrying a scholarly looking book and a pen for making clever notes in the margin; a retired UCC administrator with a book club gearing up in the living room behind her – we heard the first cork pop while she was claiming with her words and proving with her face that the Millers were just a news story to her; the very smug middle-aged daughter of one of the original dream-streets residents who had moved in after her divorce and had the place to herself because her parents were on the road most of the year, reliving the summer of love in a VW campervan (she was rattled about the Millers, but only because she didn't want her mum and dad to find out that a pair of retired adventurers had been murdered on their jolly, in case they took fright and moved home); and then they started to merge – a succession of comfortably off, trim and healthy, ageing gently, white people backed by glimpses of original art, imported rugs, overflowing bookcases and more than one Latina carer. All with a waft of spices, or herbs, or soup, or gravy as they opened their front doors.

'Has anyone else gone off this neighbourhood?' Todd said as we trailed back to Belle's and the car. 'I can't put my finger on it, but . . .'

'Boomers,' said Kathi, with her usual in-depth analysis.

'It's still Cuento, though,' I said. 'It's professors and campervans, not oilmen and cruises.'

'I suppose there's *that*,' said Todd, pointing out that under the nearest street lamp was a Free Stuff corner. They tend towards baby clothes on some blocks, garden produce on others, textbooks down near the campus. Just a block along here on the dream streets, though, I had once found a black, sequined, evening clutch bag, with a matching folding fan inside. I took it and was still waiting for the occasion when I'd need it. And Diego had once come back from the library with a tattered copy of *Cheech y su Autobus Escolar* from the children's section and a pristine fold-out and pop-up copy of *Señorita Mariposa* from the dream streets' Free Stuff corner.

'Yeah, this isn't such a bad place to live, I suppose,' Kathi said. 'No HOAs. No ordnances against growing tomatoes in the front yard or painting your house purple.'

'There's a mosque,' Todd pointed out. 'And there's a PRIDE flag at the mosque every June. Cuento's OK.'

Someone had to say it. The silence was threatening to deafen me. 'Apart from all the murders,' I obliged. The other two breathed in relief and agreed with me.

TEN

B ack at the Ditch, the curtains were closed on the Miller kids' rooms and lamplight showed behind both windows.

'Phew,' Kathi said, nodding in that direction. 'I know they're our clients but it's hard to stay focussed on solving a murder and keep listening to how no one's dead at the same time.'

Todd and I exchanged a look. But I had said the hard thing no one wanted to say last time so I left this one to him.

'So . . . you still think you can try?' he said, at last. 'Even though your advantage didn't pan out?'

'Yup,' Kathi said.

'So . . . you don't think you should just tell Molly about the car being up on that street now?' I said.

'Nope,' Kathi said. 'Hey, cool!'

This last bit was because the door of Della and Devin's room had opened very slowly and completely silently and the two of them had slipped out. This was their nightly routine: once Hiro and Diego were safely asleep, the parents sat out in the evening air with the door ajar, close enough to hear any calls, but far enough to have a laugh together. It's always struck me as a pretty perfect marriage, and it helps me believe in Taylor and me to see such a mismatched pair so content together.

'Can we join you?' Kathi said. 'Just a few questions.'

'You don't have to ask,' said Della. 'What about?' It was a speech of two halves, definitely.

'Well, last weekend,' Kathi said.

Devin, still close enough to his teenage years to be able to do that thing where they slide bonelessly down in their chair but manage not to topple right out of it into a heap on the ground, did it now. He added a groan for good measure.

'I told Molly,' he said. 'And I took the sh-ugar for it. I'll only go over it all again if you promise not to laugh at me.'

'Can't,' Kathi said.

'OK, not to openly mock me.'

'Dicey,' said Todd.

'Well, don't mimic me,' said Devin. 'I don't even sound like that.'

'Deal,' I said. I couldn't do Devin's voice anyway, although I did laugh along when the rest of them got going on it.

'Right,' he said. 'What do you want to know?'

'Anything the locums said about guests while they were handing over the desk on Sunday,' said Kathi. 'Any details on any guests you saw over the weekend and any indication you can give me that the Ditch was full.'

So she was still smarting about the possibility of the Millers being turned away from the motel that might have saved their lives then.

'They didn't say anything much,' Devin began. 'Noleen texted me she was going to be late back and would I step in on the desk to let the managers go before their overtime kicked in. I said sure. I went to the office and told them they could go and it was like they couldn't get out of there fast enough.'

'Not surprised if it's true about the mess they left the place in,' Kathi said.

'Did they?' said Devin. 'It looked OK to me.'

Della said nothing but her tongue poked into her cheek so hard it looked like she was eating a whole candy cane, sideways. Devin is not the tidiest man ever born.

'The booking system,' Kathi said. 'Not the paperclips. The finances. Noleen can't even find basic contact information for all the guests that were booked in last weekend. It's a mess.'

'I heard,' said Della. '*What do you expect?*'

'So that's why they panic-skedaddled when I let them off the clock?' Devin said. 'I thought it was because they had given discount rates to the Walnuts.'

'The who?'

'Walgreens?'

'Devin, what are you talking about?' Kathi said.

'The family who left early Monday. They had four rooms and only got charged for three.'

'Do you mean the grandparents, parents and seven children in two vans? How do you know their name when no one else does?'

'Hang on, did someone call them the Waltons?' I suggested, making the connection. 'Devin, have you really never heard of *The Waltons*?'

'I've never heard of the Waltons,' said Della. 'Who are they?'

'Doesn't matter,' Kathi said.

'OK, good,' said Devin. 'Yeah, they were in four rooms and their bill was for three.'

'If only that was the worst of it,' Kathi said. 'But there's also the fact that two *more* people stayed here – a person of indeterminate gender who might have been some sort of Goth and a lonely barbershop singer who'd lost his three pals – and, if we believe the record-keeping of these goddam locums, they got their rooms for free too.'

'Shit,' said Devin.

'What?' said Kathi.

'I just realised something.' He paused. 'OK, before I tell you though, promise you won't get upset. Because it's actually good news.'

'Good news doesn't usually upset me,' Kathi said.

'I mean, potentially good news,' said Devin. 'Is Noleen in the office? I just need to check something. Be right back.'

He slid out of his chair and stoner-shuffled along the fore-court to Reception. He was sober and responsible these days and he didn't even dress in baggy shorts and pool slides most days, but that walk wasn't going anywhere.

'What's this all about, Kathi?' Della said.

Kathi let her head fall back against the warm plastic of her Adirondack chair and puffed out a big breath. 'I don't know what to tell you, Dell. I just really wish we hadn't left town – shut up, Todd – last weekend of all weekends. But who can resist a freebie? We had racked up so many loyalty points over the years – seriously, Todd; I can hear you thinking – and there wasn't another weekend to use them.'

'It's not your fault,' Della said. 'I don't think the Millers could have stayed here even if you had had the best managers in the world on the desk.'

'Except that if the best managers in the world hadn't been here they wouldn't have been staying in rooms and those rooms would have been empty.'

Before Della could answer, the door to Reception banged open, rebounded off the wall and then got a vicious kick from a Timberland boot to encourage it back open again. The boot belonged to Noleen, who stamped along towards us. The ground shook. Truly not even a brand-new Dr Marten ten-holer is as inflexible and perfect for stamping as an unbroken-in Timby. Devin mooched along in her wake, looking even more abject than usual.

'What the hell?' I said. Then I noticed that Noleen was waving what looked like two murky green pom-poms.

'No wonder the guests last weekend were such a bunch of freaks and weirdos,' she said. 'Those idiot . . . what did you call them, Lexy?'

'Locums?'

'Exactly. Those total locums were giving deep discounts for *cash*.'

'They told me,' Devin said. 'They said they'd locked it up nice and safe in that weird little closet thing but then they left and I got hooked into a monster FPS and . . . I forgot.'

Noleen wheeled on him. 'That weird little closet thing?' she said. 'It's called a safe!'

'Perfect name for it,' said Devin.

Noleen ran through a few possible responses, looked over to see if Della could help, then gave up, visibly deflating.

'I get that the discounts are annoying,' I said. 'But what's wrong with cash?'

'Cash?' said Noleen, re-inflating and turning my way. I shrank back a bit. 'Are you kidding?'

'Is it because it's dirty?' I said, guessing. But if the grubbiness of banknotes and her wife's germaphobia were what was bothering her, then she wouldn't be waving fistfuls of it practically in Kathi's face.

'The problem with cash is that the IRS don't believe in it. Especially not cash discounts. We're gonna get audited or my name's not Noleen Shirley Muntz.'

It wasn't the moment to react to 'Shirley' and we all dug deep and managed not to.

'So, how many discounted rooms' worth of cash is that?' asked Kathi.

'Three,' said Noleen and Devin, in chorus. Devin carried on with an, 'I told you that part. Three charges for four rooms. For the big family who couldn't drive any more on Sunday.'

'Sunday?' Noleen said. '*Sunday?*'

'We don't care about Sunday,' said Kathi. 'We care about Friday. We care about Friday night. How full was the motel on Friday night? Why did the locums turn the Millers away?'

'The motel wasn't full?' Della said. Her eyes were enormous; that's where Diego got his from.

'You were here, Della,' Kathi said, pleading. 'Did you sit outside Friday night? *Was* it full? Who'd we miss? I can't stop thinking about those brain-dead locusts saying we were full because they didn't understand how a booking system works, or they were holding rooms for pals, or they couldn't be bothered with the work. Two people *died*.'

So did all conversation, for a while.

Funnily enough, it was Devin who sprang back to life. 'OK, first,' he said. 'The Ditch is always way busy. Way *way* busy. Think about it, Kathi. Della and I have two rooms. You have a room. Todd has a room. Then there's your shared emergency evacuation room. There's five right there. And Leo makes six. And the UCC parents.'

'They checked in on Saturday,' Todd said. 'As we were leaving.'

'But there were the two – did you say locusts? – so how many does that make?'

'Eight,' I said.

'Unless the two . . . what is that word? . . . were a couple.'

'They weren't,' Della said.

'And I saw the man Roger insists is a woman,' said Todd. 'Nine.'

Della leapt on him. 'Are you still *at* that?' she said, narky for her; she's usually pretty mild. 'Did you all get together and decide to start wearing sticks up—' She caught herself before the crudeness, and clicked her fingers.

'What?' said Todd.

'You saw a woman and Roger saw a man. Were you together when that happened, Roger and you?'

'What diff— Ohhhhhhhh,' said Todd. 'Ten!'

'How come?' said Noleen. 'How are we suddenly at ten?'

'Because I know fashion *and* I know my husband,' Todd said. 'He would no more pick a fight with me than I would mistake a shift for a Nehru, a pixie for a Chelsea. It was two different people. But hang on. Two black-clad Goths staying at a motel on the same night? They were probably a couple. Back to nine. Sorry.'

Della was giving him a look that could curdle milk. 'You didn't see the woman, Todd. What part of shift dress and pixie boots says "Goth"? It's ten.'

'Speaking of couples though, babe,' said Devin, 'Remember? *If* the locusts were one, we might be back down to nine rooms anyway.'

Now Della turned her death stare on her husband. He loves her so much that all he noticed at first was his honey looking at him and he beamed back at her. Eventually, though, he noticed the drop in temperature, swallowed hard and started babbling. 'But I'm only saying that because you didn't know what you were looking at, right?'

Della narrowed her eyes.

'Or you did! So it would totally be ten! Ten rooms gone on Friday night.'

'And if the barbershop guy I saw had been here since Friday, that's eleven,' I put in.

'Why doesn't Della know what she's looking at?' said Todd. 'Just out of interest.'

'Because she said the locusts – is that an industry term, Noleen? – were just a regular middle-aged coup— pair of people, with no distinguishing features.'

'I always thought that was a guy thing,' I said. 'Like how Taylor can look at a barbershop singer and not even see the stilts.'

'Sometimes,' said Noleen, giving me a thoughtful look, 'I don't reckon I drink enough. *What?*'

'It's not gender,' Devin said. 'It's zones of interest. I dunno if they were a couple because I don't care. But when I do care? I see everything. Della saw a middle-aged coup— two middle-aged people dressed in clothes she'd never wear and that's all. I saw a middle-aged coup— two middle-aged people, I mean, dressed in a Venger hoodie and a Tiamat hoodie with a roll-the-dice backpack for one and a Mimic-the-tongue-lashing fanny pack on the other. And . . . polyhedral die ball caps. And freaking roll-to-win pool slides. I told Molly. She laughed.'

'She's ahead of me,' said Noleen. 'If she laughed that means she understood what you were banging on about.'

'D&D,' Devin said, to blank stares all round. 'Dungeons?' he added. 'Dragons?'

'Drugs?' said Noleen. 'Brain damage?'

'The lady locust was wearing a classic Venger hoodie with roll-to-win pool slides, a Mimic fanny-pack and, like I said, a ballcap with a . . . polyhedral die on it,' said Devin. 'The fanny pack was slung over her shoulder on account of the baby carrier, but I'd recognise it anywhere. And the guy locust had the same slides and a . . . similar ballcap, but he was all Tiamat in the hoodie department, you know. But he hadn't updated his backpack, or maybe he didn't care. Although, that was a lot of merch for someone who didn't care.'

'Dungeons and dragons the board game?' said Todd.

'It's not a board game,' said Devin.

'What baby carrier?' said Kathi.

'I don't say this lightly,' said Noleen, 'but I think you're right. Sorry about the room tally, Kathi, but it's undeniable. Two people the same age, coming to fill in as managers at the same motel on the same weekend, decked out in leisurewear devoted to the same niche cultural activity, and I use the terms "cultural" and "activity" *very* loosely, sure sound like a couple to me.'

'Um,' said Devin. 'It's not that niche, you know. It's—'

'You are a good father and a sweet husband,' said Della, 'but Oh. My. God.'

'What baby carrier?' said Kathi again.

'Exactly!' Della said almost loud enough to wake her own

babies asleep on the other side of the open door behind her. 'They weren't the locums, Devin. Lo*cums*, by the way. Not lo*custs*. For this, we'll be paying off your tuition loan until our kids are retired? You saw an old lady dressed like all she was missing was her skateboard? You saw an old man dressed like he still lived in his mother's basement? *And* you saw their baby carrier? But you still think they were the locums?'

'Uhhhh.'

'Adults don't dress that way to go to work,' Della declaimed. Like she was trying to manifest her husband out of his Osgemenos T-shirt and board shorts and into a blue shirt and a pair of chinos with the pure force of her conviction.

'So who were they?' Devin said.

'The other grandparents,' said Della. 'From the big family that checked out early Monday from their free room? Dios mío!'

'So . . . they weren't here on Friday night?' said Kathi.

'I could have sworn they were,' said Devin. 'But you're right, babe! The locussums on Sunday were wearing totally nother clothes. Like a sweater and maybe a sweater, but not merch. I thought they had tried to look a little more professional for the gig, you know.'

'You didn't notice that they were "totally nother" people?' I said.

'I only saw the D&D merch, if I'm honest. I shared it on my subreddit. Kind of a timeline cleanse.'

'Is any of that relevant?' I asked him, wondering how much it mattered that I didn't understand a word of it.

'Not so's you'd . . . No,' said Devin. 'Anyway, when I saw them again, I assumed they were the locussums because—'

'I swear to God,' said Della. 'Locusts. *Rayos!* Locums.'

'—because . . . Yeah, why was that, actually?' said Devin.

'Hang on,' said Kathi. 'Hang the hell on. This is getting away from me. Devin? You saw the big family on *Friday*? I thought you said you checked them in on Sunday? And you didn't notice that they'd paid in advance and got a free room.'

'No, I just saw the one pair on Friday,' Devin said. 'With the Tiamat hoodie and the—'

'Let's just call them the D&Ds, eh?' I said. My head, fogged with period and hangover and general upset, was going to start fizzing if he ran through all that again. 'Are you sure you saw them on Friday? Not Sunday, with the rest?'

'I don't recall,' said Devin, very formal suddenly, 'if it was Friday or Saturday I saw them. But it wasn't Sunday. Because it was across the forecourt, kind of guest to guest, you know? Not when I was behind the desk with a job to do.'

'If it *was* Friday,' Noleen said, 'and assuming the locums aren't a couple, then we're getting there.' This was met with silence. 'OK, listen: if Devin saw slacker grandma and stoner grandpa on Friday, *and* the locums aren't a couple, *and* the lady in the pixie boots isn't a Goth so why would she be with the guy who *is* a Goth, *and* the guy Lexy thinks is a minstrel on a unicycle or whatever the good god damn you said—'

'Barbershop singer on stilts,' I said.

'—got a *late* check-out on Saturday – and why wouldn't he? Since it was anarchy all over – meaning that he could have been leaving when you saw him, Lex, rather than arriving, then Leo's late check-out on Friday gets us to twelve. And there was no room at the inn, Kathi. You can stop beating yourself up. Yay.'

'If,' Kathi said. 'If. If a circus freak stayed for three nights and only Lexy saw him, and if two of the Waltons came two days before the rest, even though they were all on a road trip together. Nah, that's too many ifs. I think the locust zombies turned away business like they let people pay cash and like they comped a room for no reason. The Millers should definitely have been here at the Ditch on Friday night. Noleen, I know this is bad publicity, but we need to tell Molly to get on to the agency and start taking names and kicking ass.'

'But what makes anyone think the D&Ds were connected to the rest of the . . . Waltons?' I said. 'I don't want to start everyone off counting rooms and describing clothes again, but I don't get that bit.'

'Because they were all set up to take some of the kids,' Della said. 'There were seven kids and four adults rolled up on Sunday, squished into two vans. Legal but not comfy. And the other grandparents came equipped with booster seats and whatnot, to take some of the seven and let the other two vans spread out a little.'

'Does that actually change anything?' Kathi said.

'Makes it more likely to have been Saturday,' I said. 'If they were all heading off together on Sunday, why come two nights early? Sorry.'

Noleen nodded glumly. 'You're right. There *was* room at the inn. We need to tell Molly. Someone needs to speak to those agency bozos. They might have been the last ones to talk to the Millers. Except for . . . well, you know.'

'I'll do it,' Kathi said, sounding about as keen as a veterinary nurse about to squeeze some canine anal glands.

'Can I come with you?' I said. 'You need moral support.'

'The whole of Trinity should go,' said Todd.

'Two-thirds of the whole number is a necessary quorum,' I said.

'Not *now*, Lexy,' he said. 'This isn't Congress. And I disagree. You can give one hundred per cent of the moral support, if you insist, but the whole of Trinity needs to take joint and several responsibility for checking out the dream streets for ourselves before we spoke up.'

'Oh yeah,' Kathi said, sounding as if she'd just found out the glands belonged to an Irish wolfhound. 'That too.'

ELEVEN

Once the three of us had been kept waiting by the part-timer on dispatch, getting inspected like a sub-standard produce delivery by every cop who passed through the front door, we were finally ushered into one of the windowless, airless and soulless interview rooms. Almost immediately, Molly burst in looking exactly as chummy and serene as you'd expect, four days into a double murder with no suspect (so far as we knew) in view.

However, she was so incensed by the news about the relief management agency's unhelpfulness that she barely registered what Kathi said about – to quote the good sergeant herself – 'What you *think* you saw, twenty *feet* away, in the *dark*, through a window and the overhanging branches of those trip-hazard *street*-trees, when you were probably hammered anyway.'

'A very clean window,' was all Kathi said in reply.

'What's the name of the agency?' Molly barked. Quite a hard sentence to bark.

Kathi told her and added, taking her phone from her pocket, 'I can give you the numb—'

'We can get numbers,' Molly said, holding up her hand. She stood up and swept out.

'So . . . we just sit here?' said Todd. He had his legs crossed twice and his arms knotted like a stick of barley sugar too. I think he was trying to levitate so no bit of his body was touching the plastic chair. And he had a point. I always wondered whether the cells at the police station could be any worse than the interview rooms. At least they would have blankets and pillows – or so I assumed – and maybe a window with a view of tomato fields. This little bunker had nothing except bolted-down furniture, a strongly ingrained stench of sour mop and, for entertainment, the graffiti.

Where's the lettuce and tomato? was one of the wittier

entries. *Bitch be dead* had less to recommend it, I felt. *Carbon neutral by 2030* seemed a bit out of place, but perhaps Cuento PD had once unglued some activists from the freeway and brought them in for questioning.

'What would you write if you had a penknife handy?' I said.

'Todd Kroger is a God,' said Todd.

'Dumb ass,' said Kathi. 'They'd know it was you and arrest you for criminal damage.'

'Why would they think it was me?' said Todd. 'They'd assume it was someone sick with love for me. Who would write that about himself?'

Kathi shook her head. 'I'd write "Richard Nixon's ewe's milk cheese". Just to give people something to ponder.'

I couldn't argue. I could feel my eyes narrowing right now as I looked at her, pondering like mad. I was so engrossed that I jumped out of my skin when the door handle was assaulted on the corridor side and Molly leapt back into the room.

'I really and truly thought that I had heard everything about you people,' she said. 'All the incompetence and unprofession-alism and general . . . fuckery.' She stopped and licked her lips. It wasn't clear whether she was relishing the taste of that word or trying to work out why her mouth had formed it. 'But here we are,' she finished off.

I'm sure it wasn't only me thinking: *where?*

'So, I got on to the hotel relief management agency,' Molly said, sitting down opposite us and placing her hands flat on the desk in front of her as if she was trying to balance herself or start a séance, 'and they told me what you didn't.' She paused. 'You wanna tell me now before I get annoyed?'

'I have no idea what you're getting at,' Kathi said. 'Unless the woman who answers the phone there really did work at the Ditch one time. Is that what you mean?'

'Quite the reverse,' said Molly, a mystifying statement. 'Not only did the gal on the phone never work for your motel, neither did the relief managers.'

'That's what I've been saying,' said Kathi. 'The place is a mess. Thank God I closed the Skweek and didn't ask them to take care of it too.'

'Wait,' said Molly. '*Wasn't* it you? You *really* don't know?' She took her phone out of her back pocket and dialled someone. 'Mrs Muntz?' she said, when someone – presumably Noleen – answered. 'I've spoken to the hotel cover agency. Do you have something you want to tell me? Last chance to say it with no comeback?' She listened a while, and then added, 'That is a very full rundown of your thoughts and feelings, ma'am. You have a nice day now, you hear.'

I said, 'I take it Noleen just exercised the hell out of her right to free speech.'

'Name the other four freedoms,' said Molly. 'Pop quiz.'

'Press, religion, assembly and petition,' I said. 'Ask me another. And not one of the biggies.'

'One of the biggies,' said Molly, shaking her head. 'Anyway, to get back to the matter in hand. Both owners of the motel are currently denying that they told the relief managers their services were not required last weekend and I have no idea why that would be.'

'What?' said Kathi. 'Someone cancelled the locums? It wasn't me. And it wasn't Noleen. Why would we? We were going away on the first busy weekend of the year.'

'Camping,' said Molly. 'On Twelfth Street.'

'OK, yes, camping wasn't true, but it was a lie for Todd that you got swept up in. I'm not lying about this new thing.'

'How could I doubt you after that?' Molly said. Sarky cow. 'But to be clear: you're telling me you didn't try to get by with your friends covering the desk and then try to blame the agency when that particular penny-pinching back-up plan didn't work, like anyone could have told you it wouldn't?'

'No!' Kathi said. 'Like I just asked you: why would we?'

'And how could they?' said Todd. 'We were gone. The permanent residents were coming and going all weekend. No one agreed to fold in covering Reception and delivering towels to their plans. I didn't. Lexy?'

I shook my head. 'Devin only stepped in late on Sunday, when Noleen called him.'

'So who was it?' Molly said. 'With the towels and the welcome?'

'What exactly did the agency tell you?' Kathi said. 'Because
I'm lost.'

'They said their employees arrived to begin work as arranged,
around eleven a.m. on Friday morning, and were told by the
motel owners that their services were not required after all.'

'That's not right,' Kathi said. 'They didn't arrive till noon,
a little late but no harm done, and we did *not* send them away.
We handed over and everything seemed completely normal.
This isn't making any sense to me.'

'Apparently they didn't even get into the office,' said Molly,
as if Kathi hadn't spoken. 'They were met out in the parking
lot and turned away pretty decisively. The agency is not happy.
If I were you, I'd look somewhere else for your next stand-in.
And *I'm* not very happy either. I don't much care if Mrs Muntz
made the decision and didn't tell you or if you decided and
didn't tell her. I do care – I care very much – that one of you
is lying to me. This should have been an easy box to check in
a very complex investigation, Mrs Muntz: one last full hotel
that the Millers tried to stay at. It's borderline criminal that
you're wasting so much police time for your own screwed-up
entertainment.'

'Wait a minute . . .' said Todd.

'Molly, I swear on Dolly Parton I didn't turn them away,'
said Kathi.

'I swear on Beyoncé she's telling you the truth,' said Todd.

'I swear too,' I said. 'On . . . It's really hard now the Queen's
gone . . . I swear on David Attenborough. Something weird is
going on.'

Molly gave us all a long, hard look. 'Likes of what?' she
said, at last.

'Someone met the stand-in managers in the parking lot at
eleven in the morning and sent them packing,' Kathi said. 'And
then that same someone – two someones – came in to the office
and pretended they *were* the stand-in managers. That's the
only thing that makes any sense and it also makes sense of
why everything was such a mess. But what doesn't make sense
is . . . why would anyone do that?'

'You're asking why would someone want control of a motel

for a weekend?' Molly said. 'It's pretty elaborate and usually, when things are that elaborate, it's organised crime of some kind. Drugs, guns, sex traffickers . . .'

I might have let out a gasp. I hated to think of the Ditch being used for anything so ugly. I could picture a ring of desperate men . . . Actually, I couldn't. I couldn't picture a ring of desperate men pretending to be the relief mangers for a roadside motel at all.

'Or the handover in an illegal adoption, or an organ harvesting, or an—'

'OK!' Kathi said.

'But if all you've found since you got back is poor paperwork . . .'

'And a comped room,' said Kathi.

'And a comped room,' said Molly, nodding graciously, 'then I'm going to ask you to be very patient, for a very good reason.' She didn't exactly smile; that would have been unsettling, but she definitely gave Kathi a softer, less granite sort of look than her usual. 'I will – we will – look into this for you and get you answers if we can. It's fraud, even if it's hard to see what the fraudsters hoped to gain. But right now we have a double murder on our hands.'

'And it won't impede your investigation, if you're prevented from establishing what time it was the Millers tried to get a room at the Ditch?' I said. 'You know, by interacting with the amazing disappearing fake locums? Wouldn't it help to pin that down?'

Molly shook her head.

'I mean, shouldn't you ask the fake locums to come forward?' I said. 'In exchange for clemency?'

'Clemency?' said Molly. Maybe that's not what it's called here.

'About the prank,' I said. 'The switcheroo.'

Molly shook her head again but there was a faraway look in her eyes.

'There's something else that's just occurred to me,' said Todd. 'Talk me down, please. But I have to say it. Kathi, when you thought the Millers had friends on the dream streets and

CATRIONA McPHERSON

you were wondering why they hadn't come forward, and we were saying they must feel terrible about turning them away. And you said that was one possibility. Remember that?'

'Uh huh,' Kathi said.

The faraway look in Molly's eyes got a bit closer, like a cowboy galloping towards us over the farthest hill, a long way off, but definitely approaching.

'And now here we are again,' Todd said. 'We're saying we don't understand why the fake locums bothered doing what they did. And we're saying the fake locums were amongst the last people to see the Millers alive. And we're saying that the mysterious motive for the takeover of the motel – drugs, guns, trafficking, organ harvest for God's sake – might be why they wouldn't come forward without a proffered deal. Well, I'm thinking that, to quote you, "that's one possibility".'

We all sat in silence, staring at one another, wondering who was going to voice the other possibility: that the fake locums faked being locums to kill the Millers.

'Or, alternatively,' Todd said, after no one had spoken for a really long time, 'the fake locums were murdering maniacs and they reckoned strangers checking in to a roadside motel would make ideal random victims and the Millers happened to be in the wrong place at the wrong time.'

'It must be that, if it's anything,' Kathi said. 'Because the Millers didn't plan to be at the Ditch. But for a migraine and spring break combined . . .'

'True,' Molly said.

'But it can't be that, even if it's anything,' I said. 'Because how would the murdering maniacs know that locums were coming?'

'Hacking,' Molly said. 'Connections at the agency.'

'Or,' said Kathi, in a tiny voice that sounded nothing like her, 'because one of the innkeepers put it on a public message board that the commission fees the agency charges are daylight robbery and if anyone wanted to work off the books, these were the dates in question.' She put her head in her hands.

'But we don't think it really is anything,' I said, looking at Kathi's parting. 'Molly? Do you?'

'It's a . . . loose end I'd rather have tied,' Molly said. 'Mrs Muntz, how about I come back to the motel right now and have a look around.'

'In case the Millers' bloodless corpses are stashed in a closet in one of the rooms and we didn't notice?' Kathi said.

'Just . . . let's say this box feels a little more worth checking suddenly. You go ahead. I'll follow you with a couple of my guys.'

'What guys?' said Kathi.

'No need to worry,' Molly said. 'An abundance of caution. Crossing Ts and dotting Is, that's all.'

It's always really bugged me how, when the weather forecast says a twenty per cent chance of rain and then it rains, people complain that they got it wrong. Noleen does it all the time. She shakes her fist at the weather and says, 'Twenty per cent, my fat ass!' and no matter how many times I tell her that we're *in* the twenty per cent, she still doesn't get it. Same thing when someone says an abundance of caution. Are they wrong when abundance turns out to be the perfect amount of caution? It fries my brain to think about it, but Molly descending on the Last Ditch with 'her guys' – a black-light technician and a general CSI – was not wasting any of her precious murder-solving time on abundance. She had got the caution level just right.

It was a perfect night for letting police crawl all over the Ditch, looking for evidence of violent crime. Only one room had travellers in it, with one more lot expected if they ever got through the mountains and the never-ending Sacramento rush 'hour'. And Jilly and Phil Miller assured Kathi they were more than happy to do anything that might help, including pitching out of their rooms to let cops in.

Molly started with the empty rooms anyway. The rest of us sat outside Della and Devin's again, watching the show, listening to Hiro snore – she had a little sniffle from allergies and her blocked nose was causing quite a symphony.

I hurt for the Ditch. *That* room there was the one my parents stayed in when they came for my wedding. *That* room over there was where Meera laid her sleeping son down on the bed and took her first steps to leaving a bully of a husband, not even knowing that sweet Arif was waiting for her just around the next bend, aka two doors down. *This* room right here was where José and Maria spent the lockdown and, beside it, Todd's mom Barb had reversed her pick-up truck full of beer right up to the door to start unloading.

All of the rooms were like friends by this time. Even the one where I'd found the dead guy, delivering his early morning coffee the day after Thanksgiving. Even the one where a racoon had decomposed in the bath and filled the air with blowflies.

And it wasn't just the rooms. There had been so many feasts and fiestas here on the forecourt: pool parties and kids' birthdays and impromptu gatherings that turned into classic all-nighters. I had been picked up and dusted down after a brutal divorce here. I had fallen in love here. If the gods could be persuaded to smile on me one last time in my life, I would bring a baby into the world here.

The thought of some twisted individual looking for a setting to play out a sick fantasy and hitting on my beloved Last Ditch was making me feel physically ill. Or maybe it was the poutine versus chips'n'cheese'n'curry-sauce tournament we were running. Della loves poutine – soggy fries and gravy with bouncy little balls of weird cheese – while I know them to be Satan's butt scrapes but will go to the wall for good chip-shop chips with yellow curry sauce and grated cheddar. Todd, probably just to be irritating, says they're much the same thing. Tonight we had decided to settle it once and for all and we were beginning to feel as sick as dogs.

Watching Molly and her guys popping in and out of the upstairs rooms wasn't much distraction from our insides, but there was nothing else doing so, when she came out of Room 203 and didn't immediately open up 204 with the master key and go back inside, we were all following along from our seats and we saw her plod down the metal steps and come our way to stop by the long table.

She gave a twisted look at the congealed chips and glop. 'We found something,' she said.

'I knew it!' said Kathi. 'There was something hinky about that room. It wasn't just clean. It was—'

'Almost Kathi kleen,' I said. 'I remember you telling me you thought someone had gone in there and then switched to down-stairs.' It's one of Kathi's screwed-up superpowers: knowing when someone has been inside a hotel room even if they didn't stay. 'If people want to look at a room before they commit, they should use the website,' she always says.

'I'm sorry I didn't listen,' Noleen said. 'Kathi wanted to re-clean 203 but I said the towels were folded Kathi-style and the toilet paper had a Kathi point on it and told her she was imagining things and she should come and watch *Matlock* with me. Love us some Kathy Bates.'

'Me too,' Molly said. 'But thank God she lured you away, Mrs Muntz. Otherwise, we wouldn't have what we have here. Speaking of which, where are the Miller kids?'

Noleen pointed to the two ground-floor rooms she had comped the grieving orphans.

'Why?' said Kathi. 'What *do* you have there? What did I miss?'

Molly said nothing, just trudged over, knocked and waited. I stood up. 'They're vulnerable,' I said. 'They need support.'

'Lots of support,' Todd said, also rising from his seat.

'And the perspective of the detective they employed,' said Kathi, wiping her lips and joining us as we trotted over that way.

We were too late to be in at the announcement. We heard Jilly wail before we had got to the door and Phil came bursting out and almost knocked Todd over.

'Where?' he said. 'Where? Which room?' He scanned the balcony and, seeing one of the techs emerge from 203, he sprinted up there and barged along the walkway, Todd in hot pursuit. The tech put his armload of bulky equipment down at his feet and gripped Phil by both biceps, stopping him in his tracks without even trying. Todd came up behind and put an arm round the young man, drawing him away.

The wailing hadn't stopped, so I ducked inside the room, where Molly – better at sharing bad news than dealing with the aftermath – was standing uselessly at Jilly's side, almost patting her on the shoulder, but not quite making contact. Reiki comfort looked to be as good as Reiki everything else, because Jilly sounded as if she was going to turn herself inside out sobbing.

'Can you stay with her until I can get victim support?' Molly said.

Try and stop me, I thought. 'Of course,' I said.

I sank down on the bed and put an arm around Jilly's shaking shoulders. Molly gave me a wild look and then headed out, edging round Kathi who was standing in the doorway as if turned to stone.

'Have they . . . Did she . . . Is there . . .' Kathi said, no part of her moving except her lips.

I knew what she was asking: are there really two corpses in my motel that have been there for over a week, because if so I am going to burn it down and still never sleep again in my life?

'What did Molly say, honey?' I asked the girl at my side, translating.

'They found—' Jilly said. 'It happened here. They died here. They were killed here. It happened upstairs in a room. Right here.'

'What did they find?' I said. A bit more plain-speaking than I might have gone for but Kathi was going to either explode or faint if she didn't get answers soon.

'They found glue.'

'Glue?'

'From tape.'

'Tape?'

'From tarps,' Jilly said. 'They found the glue residue from where plastic tarps were spread all over the floor and up the walls and taped down at the edge. And they found dust from the plastic. They dust it in the factory before they roll so it doesn't stick.'

'Well, but that might not be . . .' I said. 'I mean, it might be. But it might also be . . . maybe an artist stayed in the room. Or maybe a wedding party did spray tans.'

'And blood,' Jilly said.

'Oh.'

'Not where the tarps ran out but around the sink drain and the place where the faucets are sealed on to the vanity.'

'But that might have been a guest with a heavy period. Or a bad shaving nick,' I said.

'And my mom's earring,' said Jilly. 'Molly showed me a pic of it just now.'

For the third time, all I could say was, 'Oh.'

After that, the Ditch became a circus. Noleen called the Best Western and the late tourists and introduced them to each other. And she tried to move the one lot of travellers who were already here into a downstairs room, but lost them when they found out why they had to shift. And, of course, she rang round all her contacts in the motels, hotels and inns of Cuento to secure the very best room available for the Miller kids when they could gather themselves enough to leave. All this with cop after cop after cop and tech after tech after tech running up and down the metal steps with shoulder units crackling and phones chirping.

After a while, we went round to the boat, all except Noleen who was still dealing with the desk and Devin who stayed with the kids. As we sat on the porch, we could still hear Hiro snoring through the open back window of her room.

'This might be it,' Kathi said. 'I don't see our business surviving.'

'We've survived everything so far,' Todd pointed out. Sweet of him to say 'we'.

'But this time Noleen told the world we were looking for sketchy folks. She invited them. I mean, she didn't invite them but that's what people will say and I don't think I can argue.'

I looked around the deck. Forty-eight hours ago I had been pregnant – I thought – and settled, surrounded by friends and set fair for the future. My biggest problem was the fact that Easter is annoying in America. Now, the Ditch was probably going to close and so the boat was probably going to have to move and we were all going to scatter and I was a shrivelled old crone with no business trapping a young man like Taylor into a barren marriage.

At least, I told myself, it couldn't get any worse.

Hey, I've never said I'm not an absolute moron.

When Molly appeared round the side of the building and asked if she could come aboard, I thought – we all thought – she was here to say they were done for the night and would be back at some semi-sociable hour in the morning.

What she actually said was, 'OK, no way to dress this up, folks. We're going to dredge the slough.'

TWELVE

S ome of my new clients, over the years, have baulked at being counselled onboard a houseboat at the best of times. But, as well as Free Stuff corners, a tight community of CHLA chapter-mates, far too many coffee shops and the constant threat of wildfires in the hills to the west, one thing Cuento has to offer is a good selection of shared workspaces in the downtown. So, since it wasn't ideal – therapeutically speaking – for any of my clients to explore their issues with police right outside the window who might bring bloated corpses to the surface of the water at any minute, I could have moved them into a blank little rented office with bad art and tweed armchairs. Instead, I cancelled all my appointments and went to the wetlands with Taylor for the day.

I hadn't been for longer than I felt comfortable admitting, and given that I was both failing to provide him with progeny and was about to suggest something he was bound to run a mile from, I was glad to be balancing my books even a little by sitting there in the rain, with the first of the year's mosquitoes, dutifully training his second-best binoculars on egrets, grebes and loons, all of which sound to me like under-species in a science-fantasy world, where the books are eight hundred pages long and each one gets turned into three movies.

'How are you feeling?' Taylor said. He's nothing if not attentive. Sometimes I think he's got an alert set on his smartwatch to tell him to say *I love you* or *How you doing?* at appropriate intervals. Or maybe I'm a complete cow.

'I'm fine,' I said. 'I'm not sore today and I'm not flooding. Day three onwards is when you can forget to change your tampon and end up with toxic shock syndrome.'

'That doesn't sound good,' said Taylor. 'What should I look out for?'

'Me dead, and too many unused tampons in the box on the cistern,' I said. 'If it happens, will you promise me something?'

'I know,' Taylor said. 'You told me: bury you with a photograph of Jason Ralph in your bra.'

'Next to my *heart*, I told you. If you bury me in a bra I will come back and haunt you.'

'Please don't talk about dying,' Taylor said.

'I wonder which one of us will though,' I said. 'We'd be pretty lucky to go together like the Millers, so either you're going to kiss my cold forehead one day or I'm going to kiss yours. And can I remind you of the age difference? Pucker up, baby.' Which wasn't completely 'not talking about dying', I suppose.

'Can *I* remind *you* that I have no idea about my genetic history,' Taylor said. 'And don't be so defeatist, Lexy. We might get divorced.'

'I love you,' I said, cackling with laughter, but quietly so's not to disturb the nesting action. 'Divorce isn't looking too likely as long as you keep cracking me up.'

'I aim to please,' Taylor said. 'Anything else I can do for you?'

'Yes, as it happens,' I said. I needed to say it quickly before I lost my nerve, and yet I was hesitating.

'Go on,' he said, but he was only half-listening. Something out on the water was claiming most of his attention. My guess was: a bird.

'Can you go and get your sperm count judged?' I said. 'I don't mean judged. Sorry. I mean could you go and have your sperm counted?'

He said nothing.

'Not that I'm saying it's you because obviously, it's me. Hello? Rancid eggs you wouldn't throw at Trump here! But would you?'

Still, he said nothing.

'Sorry,' I said. 'Of course, I'll get tested too, only for me it's abdominal surgery under general anaesthetic and for you it's . . . not. And not to throw a dear friend under the bus or anything but it was Todd's idea.'

'I know,' Taylor said. At least he was speaking. So I knew

he wasn't shocked to his core and I also knew that he had heard me. Depending on what kind of bird he had spotted that was far from a given. Although maybe he wasn't listening, because that was a weird thing to say in response.

'You know?'

'Todd told me too. About the intrusiveness and the expense for you and the . . . not, for me. So I did.'

I said nothing.

'I went. And I got checked. And I have the results.'

Still I said nothing.

'I've got two hundred and fifty million sperm per millilitre with eighty per cent motility. Which is high-normal.'

'Well,' I said, finding my voice. 'That's good. Isn't it? That's great. That's good news. That's excellent. That's a relief. That's a worry off our minds. Isn't it? That's half the battle.' At some point in the middle of saying all those jabby little sentences though, tears had started to roll down my face. Because that meant it was me. (Of course it was me.) I was old and stale and useless. (Like I didn't know how old I was. Like I needed evidence.) And that wasn't even the worst of it. The worst of it was that I was disappointed I wasn't going to get to be generous and lovely and show him I didn't mind and it didn't matter. No, I was going to have to be grateful and not bitter. And that's a lie, because that wasn't the worst of it by a long chalk; the absolute worst of it was that I knew that Todd would have given me sperm if I'd asked and he was absolutely gorgeous and even Roger would probably have given me sperm if I'd asked and he made Todd look like Shrek and Taylor was the love of my life but he made Shrek look like Timothée Chalamet.

'I'm a terrible person,' I said.

Taylor nodded. 'Because you hoped it was me, so you'd get to be all magnanimous and not even mind if I got resentful of having to be grateful to you?' he said. 'Tell me about it. I've just been there. It nearly stopped the . . . not.'

'OK,' I said. If he wanted to believe that was the worst of it, who was I to prevent him?

'But at least you wouldn't have had to ask Kathi to be a surrogate,' he said. 'Oh yes, I went there too.'

I laughed so loud the birds all took to the wing and disappeared off to another part of the reserve, so we called it a day and trailed home.

Noleen heard the car and came out to the door of Reception as we arrived, beckoning us her way and looking around like a pantomime villain. Taylor parked, shot round to the passenger side and opened my door for me.

'How long have you had that tampon in?' he said. I was going to regret that wind-up, clearly.

'Is that your idea of sweet talk?' said Noleen. 'Gross. Can I talk to you, Lexy?'

'What's up?' I said, as she shooed us inside and shut the door. 'Oh God, don't tell me they found them.'

'Not the bodies,' Noleen said. 'But they found their luggage and they found bloodstained clothing. At least, they found luggage and bloodstained clothing. They haven't asked the Miller kids to identify anything yet. They were waiting for . . . Well, they're waiting to ask a mental health professional to evaluate Jilly before she tries.'

'What's the hold-up?' I said. 'Oh my God, don't tell me! There's a Mexican stand-off between the Millers' insurance company and the only psychiatrist on call and the . . . what would the third party be?'

'If the PD's legal representation didn't recognise the only psychiatrist the Millers' insurer would cover to indemnify them against a suit for causing excess anxiety,' Noleen said. 'Lexy, you'll never get citizenship if you can't even set up an insurmountable financial obstacle to necessary healthcare.'

'You mean I'm right?'

'No, of course you're not right,' Noleen spat. 'The cops have got their own doc they provide for free as long as the witness signs away all right to legal recourse.'

'I was close then,' I said.

'Nah, what it is is Jilly wants you to be with her,' Noleen said.

'Can't Phil do it?' said Taylor. 'Lexy has had a rough day.'

'Phil is gorked,' Noleen said. 'His cheese slid off the cracker in a big way when he saw the police diver bringing up a duffel bag. He was watching out of a back window and I guess it must have looked like a body. So he's out of his gourd on tranqs and Jilly's up. If you'll help, that is.'

'He was watching out a back window?' I said. 'Why were they still here?'

'Right?' said Noleen.

'I thought you got them into . . . where was it?' Taylor said.

'I did. The Sole Pitch Downtown. In a two-bed suite with a whirlpool bath and a mini-kitchen. The balcony didn't even overlook the trash cans. But they want to stay here.'

This was a diplomatic work-out of a sentence to respond to. The owner of this motel wouldn't think it was insane for someone to want to stay here, instead of there.

I flaked. Taylor stepped up and whiffed it badly. 'Well, I suppose they feel it's where they're closest to the last of their parents.'

But for once, Noleen didn't jump down his throat. 'I know, right? They even said they'd like to move into 203 once the cops are finished with it. That's just weird.'

'As long as we don't all get invited to a séance or anything,' I said, 'I don't think we can judge them. None of us have ever had to deal with our parents being murdered and we have no idea how it would take us.'

Noleen considered my words for a moment and then said, 'Nah. Weird as fuck.'

'So weird,' I agreed. 'When will the cops be done?'

'Tomorrow,' said Noleen. 'And then Kathi needs a day to clean. You heard the latest? She wants a black light of her very own. I told her I was pretty sure she didn't. Can you imagine? Anyhoo, she's written up an hourly schedule to remove latex powder and fingerprint powder and duck tape residue and whatnot. I'm thinking maybe the Miller kids will have changed their minds by the time all that's through. Because how can Phil think he's going to sleep in the death room if he loses his shit over a soggy duffel bag?'

Behind me, the door dinged open, making all three of us jump. Nolen was pouring scorn on Phil but none of us was that relaxed, actually.

'Lexy,' said Molly. 'I got something to ask you.'

'Noleen asked me and of course I'll help,' I said.

'But you've got to go to the bathroom first,' Taylor said. Oh boy, I was going to be very sorry that I mentioned toxic shock syndrome.

'He's got you on a bathroom schedule?' said Molly. 'You know the code to alert us about coercive control?'

'I do,' I said. 'But I'm pretty sure you're not supposed to say "coercive control" in front of my abuser, Molly.'

'Your sense of humour makes a black hole look like a daisy chain,' Taylor said. 'Makes the Sahara Desert look like . . .'

'Bill and Billie Miller's duffel,' said Molly. 'Come on. Let's go.'

There had been quite a sensitivity failing on the part of the Cuento PD, in my opinion. They had laid out the Millers' soggy belongings in an empty hotel room . . . on a tarp.

Jilly gasped when Molly ushered us in.

'Is that . . .? Is that . . .?' she said.

'Uh, that's what we need you to tell us,' Molly said, still not getting it.

'I'm sure the plastic sheeting is police issue,' I said. 'Right, Sarge? Just rolled out to save Kathi's carpets from river weed and tadpoles. I live on that water, Jilly, and I tell you!'

'Oh,' Jilly said. 'Of course. Sorry.'

Molly made a big cartoon grimace behind Jilly's back. 'Do you recognise any of these things, Ms Miller?' she said.

'So I already told you about the earring,' Jilly said, pointing to a little nub of silvery metal that sat on a sheet of paper, so it wouldn't get lost. 'But I don't see . . .'

On the tarp, besides the sheet of paper with the little silver stud earring and the infamous duffel bag, empty and wrinkled, sat a pair of grim-looking water-logged pillows, their pale blue pillowcases streaked with mud. Besides them was a pair of suitcases, that annoying size that's too big to roll aboard but actually not any roomier. Each of those had a kind of fan of soaked clothes arrayed in front of it.

'They bought new is the thing,' Jilly said. 'All new clothes for their trip, so I don't actually recognise any of it but I could – can I touch it? – I could check the sizes.'

'I'll call them out,' Molly said, snapping on a blue glove and crouching. 'Do you know your mom's bra size?'

Jilly gave a tiny laugh. 'She never would buy a right-sized bra. That thing could be any size at all and I'd believe you. But her dress size was an eight.'

Molly pawed in the neck of a linen dress that was lying there like a dishrag. 'Eight,' she said. 'And your dad?' She crab-walked over to the fan of menswear beside the other suitcase.

'I don't know sizes,' Jilly said. 'But my dad loved a brand. His underwear will be Fruit of the Loom. His shirts will have the polo player and his pants were probably made by Indochino.'

Molly nodded. 'Fruit, Ralph, Indochino,' she said, then she tried to tidy the disarranged pile of wet clothes as best she could. I concluded it wasn't her that had fanned them out to start with because she failed, big time.

'That's good enough for me,' she said. 'But if you felt like looking over the rest, that'd be helpful. Just in case any of this stuff was in there already and didn't belong to your parents at all.'

Was it my imagination that she flicked a glance in my direction? Did Molly think I was in the habit of jettisoning unwanted items off the deck and into the water? The slough wasn't deep enough for one thing. After a couple of years it would all have been sticking up like shark fins. Plus, obviously, the environment and everything.

Jilly looked it all over, nodding and not quite weeping. There was a toilet bag, again with contents laid out beside it. 'Jo Malone,' said Jilly. 'Harry. That tracks.' There was a set of straighteners. She frowned. 'My mom wasn't a high mainten-ance kind of a gal,' she said, 'but they were staying at fancy hotels, so maybe she meant to give it a shot.' I personally thought that no one who used Jo Malone toiletries could really be called low maintenance, but then I walk around in a cloud of Target's best. 'The toothpaste is right,' Jilly said. 'Arm and

Hammer, because we used to tease them. Who uses salty tooth-paste? And that's my dad's toothbrush. Hey, it's paired with an app on his phone. Could you find him that way?'

Molly shook her head. 'The toothbrush *sends* data. One way.'

What a world.

Lastly, there was a mini-cooler – essential equipment for Americans on the road, as if there wasn't a Starbucks every ten miles and fifteen fast-food emporia in every town. Laid out beside the cooler was a selection of drowned snacks: bloated grapes, packets of salty crackers turned to mush, little shrink-wraps of cheese that looked OK, actually – maybe fish don't eat cheese and why would they – and some loose, truffle-style chocolates, a bit past their best, in that they looked like brown oysters.

'Yes,' said Jilly. 'Those are Mom and Dad's snacks. Cheese and crackers, grapes and chocolates. I don't recognise the cooler but it's exactly the brand they've always gone for. We used to have a monster of a one, when we went camping. It kept cold for a week on a boat once. Yeah, that's definitely theirs too.'

'Thank you,' said Molly, lumbering up to standing. She's the same age as me and clearly needed to do some stretches. She had uncrouched silently at least – no grandma groans – but you could tell they wouldn't be long in coming.

'And what happens to all this stuff now?' Jilly said. 'There's one thing I would like to—'

Molly was already shaking her head. 'We need to take all the DNA we can find for forensic analysis and then dry it all out and store it in the evidence room until the close of the trial. What is it you wondered about? Because it could take a long time and I'm not sure any of this will be—'

'The earring,' Jilly said. She even stooped as if to pick it up as she was speaking.

Molly was too quick for her. She stepped in front and put one arm out, one arm round. It was half comfort and half barrier. Meanwhile, I took a good look at the apparently precious object. It had no jewel in it and no decorative tooling of any kind. It was just a little cone, like a tooth, of metal.

But maybe Jilly could picture it in her mother's ear like I'd be able to summon so many happy memories from one of my mum's pairs of specs or my dad's array of cufflinks and tiepins. He might be the last man alive who wears cufflinks and tiepins but he's too old to change now.

'It's actually broken anyway,' Molly was telling Jilly now. 'The post is missing. It might be in the slough, but my point is you wouldn't be able to wear it. I'm sorry.'

'A broken earring,' Jilly said. 'That's . . . My God, how pathetic is that?'

'Jilly,' I said. 'If I could step in here for a moment? Is there anyone up there in Washington where your parents lived – a neighbour or somesuch – who could pop into their house and get a little item to send down to you? If you need an object, that is. It's very understandable, and in my opinion, it's healthy too. Like a talisman, or a charm. Anything that would comfort you.'

Jilly's face flooded with an emotion I couldn't pin down. It was probably seven different emotions and no wonder. 'Thank you,' she said. 'I can call Auntie Press. She's lived next door forever and she has a key. She wouldn't mind, I'm sure.'

'She wouldn't,' I said. 'People always ask if there's anything they can do. It's wonderful when they hear "yes, you can". She'll be delighted to help, I assure you.'

'I'll go ask Phil if he would like something of Dad's sent to him,' Jilly said. 'If I'm free to leave?'

Molly held out an arm towards the door. 'And put all of this out of your mind,' she said. 'We'll be taking it all away soon and you don't have to see any of it again.'

When she had left, Molly looked over the pile of stuff, shaking her head. 'Those poor people,' she said. 'New clothes, new cooler, bringing their own pillows for a good night's sleep. They really were going for it on this trip.'

'I'm glad she didn't think too long and hard about how a stud earring gets broken off its post,' I said. 'That must have taken some violence.'

Molly, still in her glove, reached out and picked the little nub of silver up, rolling it between her finger and thumb like a plug of snot. 'Yeah, but it was under the bed,' she said. No blood, no skin. I don't think it broke in the attack. I think it was a cheap pair that fell apart before all the action happened.'

'Probably,' I said. 'Sentimental value only. Must have been, when you think of it, which is why Jilly didn't want to let it go.'

'That true what you said about charms and mascots?' said Molly. 'I thought you psychology freaks were all about cold harsh reality and facing up to it.'

'I really hope you fired the counsellor who made you think that,' I said. 'I'm all for wearing the clothes of loved ones you're missing and having pinches of their ashes welded into lockets. We're creatures, Molly, not brains in jars. Comfort's OK.'

'If we ever get as *far* as Miller ashes,' Molly said. 'Via bodies, a charge, a trial, a conviction and a release of remains. We're at square one. Well, square one point two five, perhaps.'

'Oh?' I said. 'What's the point two five?'

'There's a tiny bit of evidence that the murderer was injured in the process of the attack.' I waited. Molly was in a talking mood and I thought as long as I didn't spook her she might just tell me what it was. 'Possibly. Any other motel it wouldn't have meant a thing.'

'So . . . something . . . left behind in the room that must have come from the murderer because no way would Kathi overlook it, while cleaning in between guests?'

'Bingo,' said Molly.

'What was it?' I said, like an idiot. Unbelievably, though, Molly answered me.

'A part of a wrapper from a bandage,' she said. 'Just one part. Caught under the rim of the trash can. Stuck with static. Like I said, anywhere else . . .'

I nodded. 'I once stayed in a hotel in Edinburgh where there was a pair of black stockings drying over the curtain rail when I checked in. They were kind of hidden by the folds of the curtains but still, right?'

'I once spent two nights in a hotel thinking the lightshade was abstract art and wondering why there were so many flies.

It was pizza crusts the last occupants had been throwing up there for fun.'

'Don't ever tell that to Kathi,' I said. 'Did you hear she wants a black light now you've given her the idea?'

'Waste of money,' Molly said. 'This place is as clean as a whistle. Tell her that from me.'

I did.

'Hey, Kathi,' I said, when I found her in the Skweek, predictably enough cleaning the glass fronts of the washing machines with half a lemon and a shake of salt. It was a waste of two thirds of a Tequila shot, in my opinion.

'Why are you glaring?' Kathi said.

I held up my hands. 'Peace,' I said. 'It's not my lemon and salt, nor do I have the power to legislate its use, therefore your right to waste it is reserved.'

'Is that what you came to tell me?'

'No,' I said. 'Molly wants you to know that this motel is the cleanest she's ever found. No black-light action whatsoever.'

'Must be true,' Kathi said. 'It's not like her to be kind.'

'She was pretty friendly all round today,' I said. 'She told me something she thinks is a clue about the case.'

Kathi reared back in astonishment, as well she might.

'It's a bit of the wrapper from a Band-Aid, stuck with static to the rim of the bin,' I said. I was proud of my translation. When I first moved to America and heard people talking about bandages, I used to think they were slicing themselves to ribbons left, right and centre. Now I knew they meant plasters, and weren't – in this one instance – over-reacting like stressed-out divas.

Kathi squinched up her eyes and considered the news. Then slowly she started to nod. 'I'm with Molly,' she said, 'If it was the whole wrapper that would make sense, because someone might innocently have left it behind, but part of one? Someone tried to leave nothing behind and failed. I reckon it was one of the little strips that you peel off the adhesive sections. They're way staticky. I once had one stuck to my sweater and it wasn't even mine!' She sighed. 'I liked that sweater too.' In other words, she had thrown it out when she discovered the 'problem'. I looked up, thinking about Molly's room with pizza crusts in the lampshade. Here, the box shades on the strip lights were blinding white and completely empty, not so much as the shadow of a single dead fly.

'Of course, it might have been one of the Millers who used the Band-Aid,' I said. 'Even if it was the killer who tried to clear up. Mr or Mrs might have had a bite or a plook.'

'Zit, right?' Kathi said. 'Or a rowing stress injury,' she added. 'In fact, how recent was that picture of them kayaking?'

'No clue. Why?'

Kathi pulled her phone out her back pocket and called up the *Voyager*. 'See?' she said. I took a good close look and was half sure I *had* seen something, when Kathi starfished the picture until all it showed was Bill's hand, every finger wrapped in plasters.

'You should take that to Molly,' I said. 'If she can tell what brand those are and what brand the static scrap was, she might be able to confirm it one way or the other. These guys were extremely brand loyal, Jilly said.'

'That is excellent detective work,' said Kathi. 'You don't want the glory for yourself?'

'I'm in credit with Molly already,' I said. 'Knock yourself out. You could probably still catch her.'

THIRTEEN

Molly and the rest of the PD gang were no doubt busy with all sorts of investigative angles overnight on Tuesday and all of Wednesday too, but we at the Ditch never heard a peep out of them.

Jilly and Phil stayed close to their rooms, strolling along the road as far as Swiss Sisters at one point on Wednesday morning, but the rest of the time presumably resting and gathering themselves and telling relatives the news by text and phone. They certainly weren't on the case in any way.

And Trinity had to let it sit too. I had clients most of the day and a visit to my doctor in what should have been my lunchtime. Todd had a wardrobe 'Afresh, Afresh' at the UCC Faculty Club. Kathi was freaking out about her neglect of the Skweek, actually breaking out in blotchy hives at the thought that if she wasn't there to wash people's clothes, they might re-wear dirty ones. Then stand near her in town somewhere.

'Or wear something that does nothing for their figure and colouring and stand near *me*,' Todd said, as we met briefly over breakfast before going our separate ways.

'How's Afresh, Afresh going?' I asked him. The name had been my idea, or rather my contribution to his portfolio of ideas. He had wardrobe sessions for hen parties, called 'Meet Cute', for stag parties – 'Yass, Queen' (There was nothing a bunch of straight guys liked better than a little of that *Queer Eye* action. California is not like other places, truly), and a monthly standing gig at the Senior Living Centre, called 'Still Got it'. 'Afresh, Afresh' was what he called springtime make-overs for academic types, since it was a quote from a poem and there's nothing professors, straight *and* gay, like better than showing off what they know. His winter offering was called 'Whose Woods'. We hadn't come up with a summer title yet, because I thought 'Shine Kindly' sounded stupid.

'I've got fifteen hairy-legged and grizzle-headed takers,' he said. 'Time to pretend to be more body positive than I am.'

'I hate that expression,' Kathi said. 'Body positive only ever means "You're fat and I'm woke". They never say a skinny chick in a minidress is body positive, do they?'

'I'll be using that line this very day,' said Todd. 'Thank you. Lexy?'

'What?' I asked. Was he telling me I was fat? Warning me never to wear a minidress, or buy better conditioner, or shave my legs more? Asking me my opinion? None of those would be out of character for him, except that he'd ignore my opinion once I'd given it if it wasn't his opinion too.

'What are you doing today?' he said, clarifying. 'The first half of the cycle is the most important period in which to—'

'I'm going to the doctor to tell her I can't get pregnant,' I said. 'If that's OK with you.' I stamped off round to the boat, leaving two mouthfuls of cinnamon roll on my plate and one good swallow of coffee in my mug. My phone pinged while I was sidling past the oleanders. It was Todd.

'Good idea to step down your caffeine and sugar gradually,' he said. 'But before ovulation you should try to be at zero. Case meeting on the boat at six.'

So, possibly, I wasn't in the best frame of mind to listen to my first client work through how she felt about her kid going to college in Iowa instead of Palo Alto, and listen to my second client try to unpick whether she was parenting in response to how she was parented or in freedom from it, and if, in response, was she parenting in spite of it, or still bound by it.

'Can you give me an example?' I said. 'If we work through one concrete example it might shed light on the general problem.'

'Categories emerge from instances,' my client said, nodding sagely. 'Yes, I see.'

All in all, when I set off at noon to go and tell my young, rosy-cheeked, bike-riding GP that I was a dried-up husk of a woman-shaped hole in Taylor's wasted life, I was feeling pretty glum. I got weighed by the nurse, ticked all the boxes to assure them that I wasn't suicidal that day, re-confirmed that they could tell the CIA about my hay fever if national security demanded it (or whatever. I never read the declaration. No one does. I've learned what HIPAA stands for for citizenship reasons, of course, but no way am I ever going to learn what it enforces). Finally, I got shown into the doctor's consulting room to await her arrival.

She waddled in five minutes late. Her belly was three minutes late at most. In fact, as I gaped at her, the thought struck me that she wasn't just pregnant, not normal pregnant like I was trying to get; she was some different kind of pregnant that needed a new word to express it. She was like a warm bottle of Champagne the second before someone untwists the wire, like one of those ripe watermelons you're scared to touch with the tip of a knife unless you're wearing safety goggles and Kevlar, like the corpse of a possum at the side of the road in summer that you keep looking for every day, thinking no way could it still be intact, and then the next day, no way in hell, and you start speeding past it, because you're over your fascination now and when it finally goes, you do not want to be anywhere near.

None of which I told her, obviously. Booze, knife, rotting corpse. I can behave myself when I need to.

'Wow!' I said. 'Better lay off the pies, Doc.'

She laughed. She's Welsh. She gets sarcasm.

'Congratulations,' I said. 'When is it due? After lunch? Should I hurry?'

She laughed again. 'What can I do for you today, Lexy? As long as it doesn't involve bending over.'

'Yeaaaahh, well, don't feel bad,' I said. 'But the thing is I've been trying to get to where you are for well over a year now and there's nothing doing. Taylor's been checked. So it's me. What do I do first? Adoption?'

Give her her due, she wasn't fazed. She didn't grimace or grovel or pretend that her state was anything to do with mine, and she didn't put her head on one side and lift the middle of her eyebrows to say she felt really sorry for me and I was being amazing. Good thing, because how would I have felt if I'd karate-chopped a pregnant woman in the throat, even if she deserved it.

'A year,' she said. 'This last year?'

'Since a year past Christmas.'

'So that's the Christmas where you were on a big trip and there was a skeleton and you were supporting your partner with new grief and then you were planning a wedding and there was a murder and then . . . November happened. That year?'

'Well, yes,' I said. 'Did I really share all that? Sorry.'

'So it's not "you",' she said, ignoring me. 'It's not in any way "you". Are you worried about it?'

'Of course, I'm bloody wo—' Just as well she is Welsh. I'm pretty sure you can't swear at American doctors. It wasn't that that made her interrupt me.

'OK, so *that's* you,' she said. 'Worrying yourself out of conceiving is you. You should stop that, you know.'

'I'm thirty-s—'

'I know how old you are. And I know your periods are regular and you ovulate and you don't have excessive menstrual pain or any pain upon deep penetration.' On the other hand, an American doctor probably wouldn't have just said "deep penetration" either, which would have been nice. 'Relax, Lexy.'

'OK,' I said. 'I'll relax. I'll staaaaart . . . NOW!'

It was loud enough to make her jump and I felt a bit mean but she laughed for a third time after she came down again.

'I will start the ball rolling on a laparoscopic investigation,' she said. 'It will take at least three months to schedule and the co-pay is smaller if you wait six. I would like to make a small bet that you won't need the procedure by the time six months has passed.'

'What's a laparo— What you said?'

'There is a happy medium,' she said, as she often does, 'between coming here with printouts from the dark corners of the internet, and coming here without the smallest under-standing of what is happening to you.'

'I disagree,' I told her, as I always do. 'I think you need to tell me what that word means. I trust you. That's good enough for me.'

'We're going to check that your tubes are clear,' she said. 'Small incision, home the same day.'

'Sign me up,' I said. 'Six months sounds fine.'

'And the bet?'

'A thousand dollars,' I said, trying to activate Sod's Law in my favour. I couldn't afford to lose a thousand dollars. My minimum co-pay for surgery was two-fifty. And double that if anyone gave me an aspirin in the recovery suite.

'I was thinking of a pan of muffins,' the doctor said, looking startled.

'Pan of muffins it is,' I agreed. 'And no flaking just cos you're up all night with a screaming baby in six months, OK?'

'Agreed,' she said and waved me on my way.

I like my doctor so much that I got through the afternoon of clients on a wave of goodwill and – yes possibly because of what she'd said – hope too. There was a depressed teen who was too depressed and too teen to hear that it would only matter that girls were mean and puberty was cruel for a couple more years and then he would be off to college where the weirdos ruled, especially if he chose wisely. The place in Iowa got a mention and my morning client got a moment of gratitude she'd never know about. My middle client was years and years in to the therapy game and didn't need me to say more than 'healthy choice' and 'understandable' and 'keep on with it' as she outlined another week of no problems at all. And then the last customer of the day was a couple who didn't much like each other and couldn't afford to get divorced. My honest advice would have been for them to get divorced anyway and drop their living standards. Or maybe agree to have outstanding professional lives and an adequate marriage, because nobody gets everything. I wasn't stupid enough to suggest either of these two solutions to a pair of Californians, mind you. MFTs get online reviews, just like restaurants, and both 'be poor' and 'you'll do' are cockroaches in the kitchen.

Finally, at six o'clock, I finished writing up notes and dancing with insurance companies, and prepared for a night of Trinity head-scratching, with a side of Taylor which always helps. It's easier for me to keep my happy marriage secret from my warring couples than it was for the doctor to keep her humongous belly from intruding into my infertility, but it's true. A side of Taylor is like a side of fries instead of a side of over-onioned coleslaw. Except calorie-free and with no threat to heart health.

They were all waiting for me, I knew. I had felt Kathi hop

aboard and then Todd shimmer up the porch steps, in new trainers unless I was mistaken. I had heard Taylor drop his boots and, after a pause for him to peel his socks off, had heard him come up the corridor to the bathroom with his sweaty feet slapping down on the floorboards and sucking up off them again. The shower was running as I left my office.

'I'm only peeing,' I said, edging round the door. He was cloudy behind the shower curtain. 'Good day?'

'The best!' Taylor said. 'We've got so many more nesting pairs than we had last year. It was totally worth it.'

'Yay!' I said, standing and flushing. I thrust my hands in to wash them under his hot shower water. He truly believed I knew what kind of birds there were so many pairs of and what 'it' was.

'Can I hole up in your office and share the news with them all?'

He thought I knew who they were.

'Of course!' I dried my hands on a corner of his towel instead of the middle and left him to it. My marriage really is a thing of wonder.

'I've been inside all day,' I said to Todd and Kathi, who were settled on the porch with sharpened pencils. 'I just need to walk twice round the forecourt and I'm all yours.' Literally with sharpened pencils and a big pad of paper. I thought this was a brainstorming session but I knew the signs of a summation and regathering and I had to have a break before pitching in.

'We're outside now,' said Todd. 'I love that you've taken to California life, Lexy, but don't turn into a weirdo.'

'Five minutes,' I said. 'Brain cleanse.' It's the sort of inanity that Todd goes in for.

'I'm setting my timer,' he said.

'I'll help you ease the stick out,' I said back. 'In five minutes' time.'

Kathi said nothing. She was preparing a report in her head, I reckoned.

Round the front, Devin was just arriving home – from where, God knows, since he worked in one of the two rooms where he and his family lived – and he flagged me down as he was parking.

'Is like counselling anything like like ethics?' he said, close to but not up there with his personal record, which had been a 'I like *like* like the early *Simpsons*, but I don't like love them'. None of us will ever forget that day.

'Counselling *has* ethics,' I said, 'but so does friendship. Anything you want to tell me, Devin, I will keep to myself. Unless you're stepping out on Della.'

'I don't know what that means in British,' he said. He popped the boot of his car, which was full of baby equipment (like this day was determined to rub my nose in it). 'Stepping out means cheating in American.'

I smiled. He could so much not imagine cheating on Della he couldn't even hear about it and comprehend.

'Anyways,' he said, 'I meant can you counsel me on ethics.'

'If it takes three minutes or less,' I said. 'Can I help you in with all this . . . Wait. What *is* all this? That's too small for Hir— Oh my God, you are kidding me!'

'Wut?' Devin said.

'I can't counsel you on the ethics of telling me Della's pregnant before she chooses to let me know,' I said. 'If you don't understand what a betrayal that is, I have nothing to say to you.'

'Wut?' said Devin again. 'Della told you—? Della's—? She can't be. I got neutered.'

'OK,' I said. 'Right. She can't be. You're kind of lovely, you know.' He didn't understand what was sweet about not comprehending Della stepping out on him either. 'What's the ethical question?'

'This,' said Devin, but he didn't point to anything or show me anything. I waited.

'Times are hard,' he went on at last. 'And like you do what you can, you know?'

'Even if it's unethical?' I said.

'Exactly. So I've been driving around with this gear in my trunk – well, parked mostly – for days on end because I don't know what to do.'

'Whose is it?' I said.

'Mine?' said Devin. He's not as big an up-talker as he is a

like-er, so I knew he was genuinely asking. I took a closer look
at the equipment he had unloaded. It was two baby seats, a
teddy-bear-design car window-shade, a high-end jogging stroller
and a collapsible playpen-cum-cot-type thingy. They all looked
to be in great condition; I couldn't see a mark on any inch of
upholstery, not so much as a crumb in a single seam.

'Yours?' I said.

'Now it is. If it is.'

'Right,' I said. 'But Della's not pregnant? So you're not
asking if it's wrong of you to get second-hand baby stuff for
Child Three, in hard times?'

'No.'

'Because, if you were, I don't think you should worry about
it. This stuff looks pristine to me. There's still a sticker on the
cage thing – whatever it's called – and there's no dirt in those
tyres. It's all practically brand-new.'

Devin groaned. 'I know, and so it would be a godsend to
someone. It would have been a godsend to us, when Hiro was
coming. So I should pass it on, right? Or give it back? I definitely shouldn't sell it, like I was going to. Right?'

'Give it back?' I said. 'Devin, did you steal it?'

'I don't know!' he howled. 'But if I did, I could still unring
the bell and I need an ethics guru to tell me if I have to.'

'OK,' I said. 'I'll try. Where did you get it?'

'Free Stuff.'

I let a huge breath go. I knew all along I'd been holding it,
mind, but it still surprised me, the size of it. 'Well, what are
you twatting on about?' I said. 'You didn't steal it if it's there
on the street corner literally asking to be taken.'

'Taken and used,' Devin said. 'Taken by someone who needs
it. Not taken and sold.'

'By someone who needs the money? Why not? What's the
difference?'

'It's against the Cuento Code,' Devin said.

'Is that a real thing or did you just make it up?'

'Well, it wouldn't pass the sniff test at Burning Man,' Devin
said.

'Nothing at Burning Man passes a sniff test, D,' I said. 'Not towards the end of the week anyway. Relax. Sell the gear. Buy whatever it is . . . What is it? As long as it's not . . .'

'Like Crypto?'

'As long as it's not like Crypto,' I agreed. 'Or . . .'

'Like foie gras?'

'Or like foie gras. Or . . .'

'Like mink?'

'Or like mink. And if the Cuento Stasi catch up with you, exercise your right to silence.'

'Plead the— So you *do* think it's sketchy?'

'I think it doesn't matter in this world of ours these days. I think the wrong people are worrying about whether they're good enough. And I think if we started a list of sins, we'd die of old age before we had to add "selling Free Stuff" to it.'

'Sins,' said Devin miserably.

'And now your time's up. I need to go.'

I stopped at the corner and shouted back to him. 'But ask Kathi how to clean it all before you list it, eh? It looks spotless, but one of the reasons to offload brand-new stuff would be . . .'

'Like bedbugs?'

'Exactly.'

'I kinda hope so,' he said, staring into his boot and chewing his lip. 'I was thinking like maybe the baby didn't need it after all, because it . . . died. Cos of why wouldn't the mom give it to a mom pal? New moms know a ton of other new moms, you know? Della can't shake them off even now Chihiro's in full-time daycare.'

'Give yourself a break!' I shouted, shaking my head as I rounded the corner, because there was ethics and scruples and morals and values and then there was tying yourself in knots for absolutely nothing. The other thing he'd said was harder to ignore. Packs of new moms roving the streets of Cuento, devouring any woman who dared to have a baby and not immediately spend every minute of every day competing with the rest of the pack on milestones and bloody Cuento ethics. Della had been a pro about freezing them out of her life and carrying on with her real friends. If I ever got pregnant, I would ask her to train me up. And if I never got pregnant, I had just identified the first glimpse of a bright side.

FOURTEEN

'You still paying UK tax?' Todd said, when he spotted me. 'That was no way five minutes, Lexy.'

'I'm here now,' I said. 'Hit me.'

'OK,' Kathi said. 'We wasted a ton of time early on. We can't get that back now so . . . screen wipe and refocus.'

'What?' I said. 'What time did we waste? I didn't.'

'Real team player,' said Todd. 'All the time trying to work out if there was an empty room at the motel last weekend, in case the Millers could have stayed here, safe and sound, instead of sleeping in their car and being hacked to bits by a passing maniac.'

'When, in fact,' said Kathi, 'they'd have been much better off, not to mention – you know, still alive – if they *had* slept in their car instead of coming to the very motel where spree killers had intercepted the locums to get in place and pick off a random victim.'

'Or two,' Todd added, quite unnecessarily.

'Oh yeah,' I said. 'That.' Then I thought a moment. 'But I still don't think we were wasting our time, trying to work out who stayed here. If we could find the big family or Pixie or Chelsea or the stilted singer, they might be able to tell us some detail about the fake locums that leads us straight to them.'

'And we could totally do that except for all the cash and comped rooms and lack of any receipts or records of any kind,' Kathi said. 'Oh my God!' She smacked herself on the front of the head loud enough to disturb all the little birds that were settling in the scrub trees and hard enough to leave a mark. 'I am so dumb. We all are.'

I didn't doubt it. I was so dumb I couldn't work out why I was so dumb. I had to wait for her to explain.

'No one uses cash,' she said. 'It was crazy to swallow that story. Think about it, Todd. If you were checking into a motel and were offered a deep discount for cash, would you have the cash to take them up on it?'

'I would not,' said Todd. 'But I could go and get some. Is that what you mean?'

'What? No,' Kathi said. 'I mean this: obviously all the guests paid with their cards as usual and it was the killers, the locums, who purged all the details of those transactions and put cash in the safe instead. So, you see what that means?' She waited. We let her down. 'A forensic tech head could find everything that's missing, by looking in the dusty corners of the motel booking platform. Don't you think? And then we'd have a slew of witnesses who . . .'

'Might have noticed intriguing tattoos or unusual moles on the perps?' I said.

'Right?' said Kathi.

'Probably,' I said. 'Or possibly no way and we all watch too many movies. What was it *you* were thinking, Todd?'

'Just this. If multiple guests went to get a ton of surprise cash last weekend, they'll all be on the bank cameras. The cops could find them.'

'And *then* we'd have our potential witnesses who might be able to yadda yadda,' I said.

'I'm not saying it's a breakthrough,' Kathi said. 'But it's something. What else have we got? A mysterious stop somewhere in the dream streets and half an adhesive strip from a Band-Aid?'

'Hey,' said Todd, 'did anyone get around to asking the Miller kids if that kayak photo was recent?'

'I did,' said Kathi. 'They didn't know. Their parents went kayaking all the time, and cycling and hiking and climbing and . . . fricking spelunking, for I know. It was hiring a Mustang and taking off to stay in fancy hotels that was unusual for them. Poor bastards.'

'Can you even tell what brand a plaster is from a bit of the waxy bit?' I said.

'We could try,' Todd said. 'Call up all the brands of bandage on Amazon and see if we can tell. If the picture quality in the online *Voyager* is good enough anyway. Lexy, get your laptop: bigger screen.'

'OK, but don't open my email again,' I told him.

Taylor gave me a grin when I scooped my laptop off my desk. 'Lot of crow getting eaten, babe. They all doubted me.'

'Fools,' I said and left again.

'It's not bad,' said Todd, when he'd been working on the kayak picture with all the filters in the editing tool and it was as clear as he could make it. 'But they're not novelty strips. Barbie or Bluey would have been nice.'

I went to look over his shoulder and Kathi joined me, Todd being one of the few people besides Noleen that Kathi was happy to be that close to. I was *always* happy to be close to Todd; he wore a perfect faint whisper of a scent he had once told me was 'moss'. I didn't know moss had a scent, unless a dog had peed on it, so hugs and huddles with Todd were the only place I ever smelled it.

'Call up the biggies on your phones,' Todd said. 'Band-Aid, Target, Amazon Basics, anything else?'

We found another couple of brands I'd never heard of and got close-ups of each, ready to compare with the rings of wrinkled pink on Bill Miller's fingers in the photo. We learned . . . nothing. Except how much fun it is to talk yourself into ridiculous hopefulness about a shot so long it made *War and Peace* look like a haiku. How much? None.

And yet I still couldn't take my eyes off the picture. It was a great shot. The water of the lake or river they were kayaking on was sparkling in little wavelets all around them and the drops of water scattering from their oars looked like diamonds. Bill leaned one way to let the camera see Billie, seated behind him, and she was leaning the other way and laughing. They looked lean and strong and fit and happy. That was why their kids and their pals would gaze at the image. Presumably that was why their kids had chosen this image. But that was not why I couldn't peel my eyes away from it. Just like last time, something was bugging me.

'Something's bugging me,' I said. My job, navigating and interpreting all the mixed messages that can screw up a life, has turned me into an open book.

'That drunk at the Best Western?' said Kathi. 'She's bugging me. Is that it?'

I didn't answer. Todd said, 'Because she can't tell the difference between a man and a woman? Tell Roger how annoying it is. I'm already convinced.'

'Do you think the locums comped a room for that big exhausted family because they'd run out of cash?' Kathi said. Her thoughts were in slot-machine mode. It's annoying to listen to, but I'd never stop it because every so often it comes up three cherries in a row.

'Why did they bother with the cash at all?' said Todd.

I was trying to concentrate on the picture. Band-Aid, Band-Aid . . . Would it help if I translated into the language of home? Elastoplast, Elastoplast . . .

'Because if we'd come back to no money, we'd have called the cops on Sunday and they'd have had a lot less days to get away,' Kathi said.

'But, they can't have thought they were going to get as many days as they did,' said Todd. 'They couldn't have relied on mad Fern and that weirdo Yuzula and even Teto being such a fan of conceptual art. They must have expected the car to be discovered days before it was.'

'Maybe they're sitting holed up somewhere with their sphincters in spasms because no one's found the bodies,' Kathi said. 'Is there anywhere up in the dream streets that would be any kind of a dumping ground?'

'Dunno,' said Todd. 'Lexy?'

I didn't answer. I was staring so hard at the picture of the two Millers in the kayak that my eyes were starting to water. What *was* it?

'Ho! Lexy,' said Kathi. 'You with us?'

'I'm this close to getting a hold of something,' I said, holding up my finger and thumb almost touching. I flashed on a vision of blue fingers and blinked.

'The adhesive strip?' said Todd. 'It was the only mistake they made, Lex, but I don't think it's going anywhere.'

'That and the earring,' said Kathi.

'Bingo!' I said. 'That's it!' Those blue fingers were Molly's glove holding up the little silver cone. And that's what was sticking in my throat like a fish bone. I pointed to the photograph of Billie Miller's tanned neck and sweaty hair and crash helmet strap mark and earlobe, making a big, grand, full-arm gesture. 'She hasn't got pierced ears,' I declaimed, and waited for their stunned response.

'It could have been a clip-on,' Todd said.

'Or she only just got them pierced recently, 'said Kathi. 'We don't know how old the pic is, like we said.'

'A clip-on earring wouldn't break,' I said, pretty evenly given that they had both just practically said 'Duh' to me. 'It would just come unclipped. We'd have found the whole thing. And, Kathi, how many women that age suddenly up and get their ears pierced for the first time? You're not taking this away from me. I'm telling Molly.'

For once, the switchboard put me straight through. Maybe that was how badly the case was going.

'Ms Campbell?' Molly said.

'That earring,' I replied, going straight for it, 'it's not.'

'What makes you say so?'

'Have you got the kayak pic handy?' I said. 'And any other pics of the Millers? You must have. Look at her – at Billie – and tell me what you notice.'

The line went quiet except for some clicks and buzzes, the sound of Molly breathing with her phone tucked in at her neck.

'Well, butter my butt,' she said. 'She doesn't have pierced ears.'

'And neither does he.'

'Not that I needed any more evidence,' Molly said. 'We already knew: it's not an earring.'

'What is it?' I said. 'It's not a bit of a bullet, is it?'

'You feeling good about citizenship?' Molly said. 'Bit of a bullet! No.'

'So what is it?'

'What's she saying?' hissed Todd, very happy to get in on it after he'd just tried to tell me there was nothing to get in on.

'Oh, it's jewellery,' said Molly. 'But not for ears.'

'Stone the crows,' I said. 'Right then.' I hung up the phone.

'Stone the crows?' said Todd. 'As in the "stone the crows" that comes right between "Blimey" and "Fuckaduck"?'

'That's the one,' I said. Their facility with British reactions was unnerving sometimes.

'So?' said Kathi. 'What did she say?'

'It's body jewellery,' I said. 'Wherever it's supposed to go, it's not an earlobe. No wonder Jilly was so keen to get it out of Molly's hands and away.'

'Over to you, Todd,' Kathi said. 'I don't even have holes in my ears, never mind points south.'

'What did it look like?' Todd said. 'I didn't see it, remember.'

'Sort of a . . . well, like a little cone shape but presumably it had some kind of an attachment apparatus in the hollow side.'

'Hmmmm,' said Todd. He ran his hands over his body in a pensive way. I tried to look uninterested. I knew about the eyebrow, cartilagey ear bits, belly button and nipples. When he dropped his hand into his lap, I focussed on the wall behind him.

Kathi wasn't so discreet. She was watching and commenting. 'Ew, ew, ouch, why, ewwww, yikes, no way!' She shuddered. 'What is wrong with you? Leave yourself alone! How do you . . . Don't tell me!'

'I can't bring to mind anything where the fastening is tucked inside the— Wait. I need to google body adornment for women. How thin are labia?'

'Todd!'

'Maybe it's a clitoris topper.'

'Todd, for God's sake!'

'I can't believe I'm saying this,' I told him, 'but I think I'd rather ask Jilly what it is than listen to you any longer.'

'Good, because I don't much want to look at women's genitals, pierced or unpierced,' said Todd. 'Kathi?'

'Unpierced, I could cope,' Kathi said. 'But wearing knuckle-dusters? Nope.'

'Right then,' I said. 'I'll go and ask a grieving daughter who wanted to shield her dead mother's privacy to tell me what her mum had a bolt through. Or her dad.'

'What did I just tell you?' Todd said.

'You know what I only just realised though,' Kathi said. 'It can't be body jewellery. These guys cycled!'

'Ow,' I said. 'Cycling is bad enough just with anatomy.'

'You don't have anatomy,' said Todd. 'You have an absence of anatomy. You have no idea what we men go through.' He stopped speaking, but not because he had belatedly realised how outrageous he was being. Something had occurred to him.

'What?' said Kathi.

'Cycling,' he said. 'The joyless green giant. Someone should really ask when exactly he was there near the Mustang, in case he saw something.'

'Cool,' Kathi said. 'Two tasks. One more and I'll call it multiple fruitful avenues of enquiry.'

The gal in the Best Western?' said Todd.

'Thank you,' Kathi said. 'She'll do. Three lines of enquiry.'

'Four including the bank cams,' said Todd.

'We can't watch bank videos,' said Kathi. 'Even I can't watch a bank video. A PI licence isn't a magic wand, you know.'

'I bet I can get us in to watch at least the Credit Union,' Todd said. 'It's closest. That's where I'd go for a sudden cash-flow emergency. And you know what else? I bet Devin could poke around in our booking system and uncover deleted records.'

'Could we pay him for his time?' I said. 'He's feeling the pinch, you know. He's getting entrepreneurial to make a few extra dollars and it doesn't suit him.'

'We could do,' Kathi said. 'The Miller kids paid their deposit and retainer. Cash again, wouldn't you know? Did I miss a memo? Is cash *back*? Was it like this before Covid and we've forgotten?'

'Right, I'm going to talk to Jilly,' I said. I didn't have answers for any of her questions anyway. 'Just me? Do either of you want to chum along?'

Todd raised an eyebrow and Kathi snorted.

Just me then.

I knocked on the door of one of the two rooms Noleen had given the Miller kids. I had no idea which was which. When

Phil answered I apologised for disturbing him and said I needed a quick word with his sister.

'She's . . .' said Phil. He looked haunted. His face was pale and his breath was sour as he let a big shaky breath go. He came out on to the balcony, pulling the door to behind him. 'You're the counsellor, right? She's . . . I'm worried about her. She's . . .'

'Grieving,' I said. 'She's had a terrible shock. You both have. However she is right now is probably perfect for the circumstances. As long as she's not physically harming herself.' He shook his head. 'So. Angry, sad, energetic, exhausted, fasting, bingeing, you name it. Except for one thing. Not for ever, but just for now, I would kind of "prohibit intoxicating liquors".'

'Huh?'

'Don't drink too much. Or take hard drugs. But what you do need to do, Phil, is take care of yourself. As well as looking out for Jilly. Ask for what you need. We're all here to help.'

He looked like he was going to say more but, in the end, he opened the door at his back and showed me into the room. Jilly Miller was at the little breakfast table, a closed laptop in front of her to one side and a squared-up pile of paperwork in front of her to the other. She sat with hands clasped on the table-top between the two. Was Phil going to say 'frozen' when he couldn't work out how to describe what she was. 'In a fugue state'? She looked powered-down, less stricken than her brother but less present too.

'Jilly,' I said. 'Did you get a hold of Auntie Press?'

She flashed a look at her brother. 'How do you know about Auntie Press?' she said.

'You mentioned her name when we talked about getting some memorabilia,' I said. 'When Sergeant Rankinson couldn't let you take the "earring".' I hoped my heavy scare quotes would cause some kind of reaction and they did. She looked back at her brother for a second time and swallowed hard. I heard the gulp of it and saw her neck move.

'Phil,' I said, turning. 'Would you be willing to go and ask Kathi and Todd to come and meet me here? They're on the boat.'

'Of course,' Phil said. 'But what's going on?'

'Oh, just the investigation,' I told him. 'We work well together but it's hard to explain.' I gave him a warm smile and kept it on my face, waiting for him to leave. It's a good tactic. It takes a lot of ignoring social cues to keep standing there when you've been dismissed. He managed about forty seconds before he left the room.

'Jilly,' I said, 'do you need some support separate from your brother?'

'What? No. I see what you mean. No. We had a small . . . Well, we didn't agree about something. And then you mentioning Auntie Press when I hadn't told Phil that I'd mentioned her. I thought he might get angry again. We're just hurting. It's fine.'

'Of course it is,' I said. After a pause and just to keep her talking I added, 'It's an unusual name. Is that her last name?'

'What? Oh. No, Priscilla. She's my father's . . . cousin, maybe?'

'And she lives next door to your parents' house?'

Jilly looked boggled. 'Is that what I said? When? No, the neighbour is called . . . I can't remember and anyway I think she died.'

'The neighbour?'

'Auntie Press. I'm not one hundred per cent sure, but I think so.'

I nodded. Grief and trauma do strange things. Jilly had only just found out her parents were dead. It wasn't too odd for a name from her childhood to pop out of her mouth, the name of another who might be gone too. 'So,' I said, 'you could still get a small token sent down. Since the "earring" is in evidence.'

She nodded in recognition of the quote marks but volunteered nothing.

'I wouldn't worry about Molly,' I said, 'Sergeant Rankinson. She's seen it all. And for God's sake don't worry about me. I've heard it all. It was a natural impulse to want to keep your mum's private life private.'

'What do you mean?' Jilly said.

'That little stud wasn't an earring,' I said.

'I know. Do the police know?'

'They do. They don't care, really. And, when you think about it, your mum will never know that they know so if you decided not to be embarrassed then that's it dealt with.'

Jilly Miller looked up at me for the first time. 'Embarrassed?' she said.

I paused. Had I picked up the wrong end of the stick here?

'Do you know what it is?' I said. She had to, I told myself. If she wasn't sentimentally attached to it as a bit of her mum's jewellery, then what else would make her want it except knowing what it was and fearing the cops cackling and judging.

'I thought I did,' she said. 'Why, what is it?'

'What did you think it was?' I said.

At that tantalising moment, Phil came back. 'They're not there,' he said. 'Did you straighten out whatever it was?'

'We did,' I said. We hadn't, of course, but I wasn't entirely buying what Jilly was selling about the harmless little disagreement with her brother and I saw no need to set him against her again. This pair might not after all be the close and loving set of siblings they appeared to be a day or two ago. Cracks were definitely forming. And, despite what I said about all grief being good grief, I was having a hard time interpreting the vibe in this little pressure-cooker of a motel room.

All in all, I wished I had made someone else ask Jilly about the 'earring' and volunteered to go and accuse the Best Western hostess of being a drunk.

As I left, the only thing I could think of to do was google Priscilla 'Press' Miller, Tacoma, expecting to find an obituary if I was right about her lineage and therefore her name. I was more lucky than that. Auntie Press wasn't, in fact, dead after all. The second result after White Pages was Facebook and there she was! Priscilla 'Press' Carmichael (Miller) in Tacoma. She posted basic cats, dogs, Far Side cartoons, and changed her profile picture for Pride and vaccination boosters. She hadn't posted anything yet about the death of the Millers. So I sent her a message asking if she was the cousin of the Bill Miller who had just died in California, along with a link to the *Voyager* article. If she said yes, I was going to suggest that her young relatives needed her. Why else would Jilly have blurted out her name when she meant someone else entirely?

I stood awhile on the balcony surveying the landscape. The sky was turning from pink to navy blue and the stars were beginning to wink into existence. Spring time in California is not as wondrous as autumn, when the ground is letting go of the summer heat and the air is gentle against you as it gives in. In spring, there can be a chilly breeze or even a cold snap, same as anywhere. But it's still pretty lovely to be outside in April in a T-shirt not getting soaked to the skin. The tomato fields to the south were brown corduroy with tiny green stitches. I thought of Teto and his fellow workers, probably sitting over a beer in their camp right now. The town to the north was rumbling with a little Tuesday evening traffic coming and going, the buildings studded with lamplight, the pavements empty except for dog walkers and a few students mooching along for a slice of pizza somewhere. The only thing moving in a deter-mined way – and it really was moving in a very determined way – was a bobbing light heading south out of town towards the underpass and the Last Ditch. As it drew closer, I could see a virulent green backing to the light, shiny and fizzing with movement. And I knew what it was!

I threw myself down the metal steps and sprinted across the forecourt to the road, stepping out and waving my arms. It was! It was the joyless green giant, his Lycra legs pumping and his Lycra arms gripping his handlebars for grim death as he powered along. I shifted to the middle, straddling the yellow line and wheeling my arms like someone about to lose her job at the airport.

'Stop!' I shouted as he got close to me. 'Stop!'

I thought he was going to blow right past. In fact, he *did* blow right past, but only because he was going along at such a lick that he was fifty yards beyond me before he could wheel round and come back. It couldn't be safe to pelt along at that speed, surely.

'Have you ever had a speeding ticket?' I asked him. 'What were you doing as you came past the cop shop there?'

'Thank you,' he said. He was as thin as a peeled rake, with a face so used to creasing up against the oncoming headwind that his default expression was now a kind of desperate grimace, the crow's feet at his eyes meeting the deep lines bracketing his mouth, which themselves merged into the stringy tendons all up and down his neck. He looked flayed. And, as for the Lycra, all I can say is that one quick glance allowed me to conclude that he didn't have any piercings.

'Can I ask you a quick question?' I said.

'Five hundred miles,' he replied. I must have blinked. 'That's my weekly count.'

'That wasn't what I was going for,' I said. 'But holy Proclaimers anthem, Batman. Every week?'

'Thank you,' he said again. He seemed to be able to translate any incredulity about his hobby into a compliment, missing out quite a few steps. Maybe it was a good idea, but it did make him come across as somewhat bonkers.

'What I wanted was to ask you about the Mustang,' I said.

In reply, he put a finger to one side of his nose and blew out the other side on to the road beside him. 'Mustang?'

'The car down by the Patsy Denoni. The Millers' car. The murder car?'

He cleared his other nostril.

'I don't drive,' he said.

'OK,' I replied. 'But remember a week and a bit ago when you were in the car park – parking lot – at the new gallery – museum – at the edge of campus and you went to have a look at the . . . Oh God, what's it called? At the misericord . . . That's not right. Mesmerchrome . . . Nope. The bluey-green-purple Mustang that was abandoned there?'

'Me?' said Joyless. 'Not me. You can't get out of the campus there.'

'Across the fields?'

'I can't cycle on fields.'

'But you could have walked, right?'

'Why would I walk?'

I bit back my first response – because you've got legs – and went instead with, 'One of the field workers thinks he saw you there.'

'Without my bike?' said Joyless.

Which was a very good point. If Teto had seen a guy with a bike, he'd likely have called him a cyclist, not a stick insect. Unless Todd's Spanish had seriously let him down.

'Does this guy know me?' Joyless said. 'Did he give you my name?'

'What is your name?' I said, thinking maybe if it *sounded* like the Spanish for . . . God, I was really clutching at straws here.

'Bob Chubb,' said Joyless. It took all my years of experience not cracking up at clients' deepest secrets to keep my face straight; it had to hurt the tallest, skinniest, stick-insectiest guy in Cuento to have a name that sounded like a dumpling.

'Well, don't let me keep you any longer, Mr . . . Chubb,' I said. 'You wouldn't want to slip to four hundred and ninety-nine this week. Although it's only Tuesday.'

'That,' said Joyless, fitting one of his clompy shoes on to the spiky bit of his pedal and preparing to push back, 'could never happen. I have discipline. Do you cycle? I could send you a starter's plan. I could hook you up with a beginners' group. I could introduce you to the local chapter of the . . .' He started pedalling and cycled off as he was speaking to me. What had started as an offer had apparently turned into a mantra, maybe a daydream.

I was still standing there when Todd's Jeep came towards me from the underpass, beeping and flashing. It pulled over and Kathi hung out the passenger window.

'Watcha doin' standing in the middle of the road, Lexy?' she said.

'Have you been to the Best Western?' I said. 'Did you achieve anything?'

'We've been to Odie's Ovens,' said Kathi. 'We achieved an extra-large pepperoni and mushroom with double cheese. You?'

But I didn't get a chance to share the progress I'd made, because I had to attend to making even more. That is, my phone pinged and showed something new on Messenger, which turned out to be Press Carmichael replying to me.

I am too old and tough a bird to fall for scams like that, Lady, the message said. And she was still typing. I don't have any

cousins drowned in a canoe. These are my only cousins. Nice
try. I hope you rot in hell. Then she uploaded a studio portrait
of a middle-aged couple, guy with a fading red buzzcut, a fat
neck cut in two by his collar, and a meaty hand on the shoulder
of his seated wife. *She* had a neat cap of silver hair and a fussy
blouse that strained over her bosom and had to be scratching
her neck to bits.

You shouldn't share pictures with strangers, I texted back.

Three dots and then, Are you threatening me? Go to Hell!

'She didn't leave herself anywhere to build to,' I murmured.
'If you don't have a "Go Fuck Yourself" up your sleeve, you
have to parcel out your "Rot in Hell"s pretty sparingly.'

'What?' said Kathi.

'Nothing,' I said. 'Let's eat.'

FIFTEEN

'How would it be if we just had sex every day for the next two weeks?' I said to Taylor, once everyone had gone off to bed, leaving us with nothing but crusts and cloudy glasses.

'Doctor's orders?' said Taylor. I waited. 'I mean, that would be awesome, Lexy. Lucky me.'

'I thought that was what you meant to say,' I agreed. 'And not exactly. I've made a bet.'

Taylor was brushing his teeth, which didn't actually account for the silence. One of his most annoying habits is talking to me when he has that electric toothbrush buzzing around in there and he's dripping foam like a mad dog so I can't understand more than one word in three. I pretend I've misunderstood what he's telling me, thinking maybe I'll annoy him so much in return that he'll cut it out, but he finds this hilarious. It's like a thing we've got going now, and if I stop my bit he'll have won. So you'd imagine that the current silence, broken only by the fizzy hum of his toothbrush and the rhythmic Puck! Puck! of me pulling my floss free would be welcome. In fact, I found it unsettling.

'You made a bet?' he said, once he had spat and wiped his mouth. He doesn't rinse. He's right but it's weird and it bugs me. 'Todd, I presume.'

'Roger,' I said. It's a standing joke. It works on account of how 'Roger' means yes and how Roger could never be the man in question but someone guessed Todd instead.

'In a professional capacity?' said Taylor.

'Oh my God, what's wrong with you?' I said.

'Low sex drive, apparently,' said Taylor.

I laughed. I couldn't help it; he's funny. But there was a lot of room for misinterpretation regarding what I was laughing at. In hindsight, I should have used the same restraint I did about 'Bob Chubb', only I'm not used to having to, in my own bathroom, with my own husband, talking about our own sex life. It's true what they say about fertility treatment: it ruins everything. It was one chat with a doctor on the journey and look at us.

'I didn't make a bet with Roger about anything. I made a . . . Actually, I accepted a bet with Dr Heidi. She bets I'm pregnant in six months by the time the budget la . . . pis . . . lazuli is due and so I bet her that I won't be.'

'Laparoscopy,' said Taylor. 'What's the stake?'

'A pan of muffins,' I said. I thought that would make it better.

'Oh well, I'm glad to know you're taking it seriously.'

'Hey! I just said let's have sex every day for two straight weeks,' I reminded him. 'Anyway, how did you know that word?'

'What word?'

'You know what word.'

'Say it.'

I had forgotten it.

'Because I *am* taking it seriously,' said Taylor. 'We're trying to get pregnant and starting to worry that it might not happen. I already told you I went to get checked. And yes I looked some stuff up and learned a few terms. I'm not bragging about the huge effort of having to have sex with you, it's true. Maybe it's not such a sacrifice for me.'

'Hey!' I said again. 'I didn't mean it like that.' He left the bathroom and started to walk towards bed. '*Tay*-lor,' I shouted after him. 'Oh well, as long as you're pissed off anyway, I might as well say this: *we* are not trying to get pregnant. We are not going to get pregnant. We are trying to get me pregnant. *I* am going to get pregnant. Maybe. If both bits of *us* get on with it.'

I followed him and stood in the doorway. He was sitting up in bed, gripping a printed article hard enough to twist the paper, but clearly not reading.

'Only, right now, a bit of us is flaking on the contribution to the entire proceeding that I actually need him for. Two-and-a-half minutes of effort.'

His lips twitched.

'No one's ever going to ask if you got away without stitches after your bit,' I added.

He winced. 'So you hate that "we're pregnant" thing?'

'I'd rather you said "furbaby" and "amazeballs".'

'Nom, nom,' said Taylor, because there wasn't a blackboard handy that he could rake with his fingernails. 'Sorry not sorry. That was cringe.'

'No biggie,' I said back. 'It's just bants and you are my hubby, after all.'

'Coolio,' said Taylor. 'Still want to have sex?'

'Barely,' I said. 'And only because you didn't manage to fit in "staycation".'

'Come here then. Day one, thirteen still to go.'

'That's the idea,' said Todd, breezing in the next morning. 'You gotta keep at it.'

My eyes were still closed and I tried as hard as I could to tell myself it was a dream, that Todd hadn't worked out that I'd had sex in this room a few hours ago and wasn't giving me snaps for it. It *was* me, not us, because Taylor had risen with the dawn and gone to the reserve for . . . something.

'What's the Spanish for "cyclist"?' I said.

'Huh? Ciclisto,' said Todd. 'Wait! Ciclista. Why?'

'Nothing like "insecto sticko" then?'

'Palo. No. Why?'

'I don't think it was the Joyless Green One at the Mustang,' I said. 'God, sometimes, I think if the NSA was listening to us and transcribing it all they'd have to get counselling.'

'Some of your conversation does have an early ChatGPT vibe,' said Todd. 'We can try to find Teto and double-check. There were trucks full of ag trays going through town yesterday when we went to get the pizza. So someone will be planting something somewhere this morning. Also, we're going to the Credit Union for me to win a bet.'

'Did anyone actually take your bet?' I said.

'There's time.'

'Pan of muffins,' I said. 'I need the practice.'

'ChatGPT, the early days,' said Todd. 'I'm going to go and let you get up in privacy.' He turned, then turned back. 'You should really have a pillow under your hips, you know.'

'I'm saving it for your face,' I said. 'That came out dirtier than I thought it would. Sorry!' But he had already squeaked and run away.

Kathi had been for coffee and pastries, I saw when I joined them round the front twenty minutes later. 'Everything-seed wheat bagel and decaf for you, Lex,' she said. 'Doctor's orders.'

'Anaesthetist on long-term leave's orders?' I said.

'It's not decaf,' Kathi murmured too quietly for Todd to hear, as she handed it over. 'And there's extra cream cheese on the bagel.'

I would have forgiven him anyway because either I was going to witness genius at work this morning, as Todd wangled us into a bank and got a squint at their CCTV, or I was going to witness my most confident friend ever (including the guy in my class who believed he'd invented a new kind of glider and spent three months in traction) being smacked down in front of the two of us plus whoever was in the bank that day.

It started well. We didn't even have to hang about looking suspicious until the right teller was free. Todd managed to judge exactly when to finish his fake phone call and stop gulping cups of complimentary water from the cooler so that it was the doe-eyed kid with the silky beard and top-knot that looked up and said, 'Next.'

'Huh,' Todd said, when we were all clustered around the kid's station. 'This isn't ideal. I wanted to come and ask one of your co-workers if I could make an appointment to speak to you. I didn't think you'd be at the front on the desk. Don't you usually do kind of advanced stuff?'

'I can do,' said the kid. He couldn't really be a complete kid, but the fact that his voice was revisiting its breaking years as he took in the splendour of Todd didn't help me any to see him as a full adult.

'That's what I thought,' Todd said. 'So, is there a chance that we can have a confidential interview today? Or do they really have you out here counting quarters. Sheesh!'

'I could see you all on my break,' the kid said. God knows if he actually had been on a course to discuss loans, or online security, or long-term planning, but he was lapping the idea up. 'Ten thirty?'

'Ideal,' said Todd. 'Perfect.' He leaned in. 'Is it OK if I bring these two?'

The kid obviously wanted to say that no way were two women allowed to come and dilute this peak experience for him, in fact why didn't he meet Todd outside the bank and they could hit the road and live together forever in Puerto Vallarta. But then that would mean denying Todd something, and I took it as a good omen that all he managed to say was 'OK'.

We left the premises, Todd already crowing and Kathi and me not bothering to point out that he was ahead of the facts by a country mile. Then we started our tour of the edges of town where the fields and the real work begin. There were multiple litter-picking crews out on the verges too this morning.

'Poor bastards,' Kathi said.

'Right?' I said. 'What crimes will this lot have been duly convicted of to get sentences of honest-to-God involuntary servitude?'

'Not that you're judging,' said Todd. 'Shoplifting, graffiti.'

'Wow,' I said. 'Not that I'm judging.'

'It's a hell of a lot easier than planting peppers,' Kathi said, slowing to a crawl as we came near a work team hard at it beside the most westerly apartment complex.

'I can't tell if any of those guys is Teto,' Todd said, hanging out of the passenger window.

In the field, a woman who might have been the boss – at least, she was white and dressed in the kind of double denim that would have made bending and stretching all day a recipe for extreme chafing – took a break from trying to shoo off the inevitable cloud of gulls and strode to the edge of the field nearest us, where she gave us two heartfelt fingers.

'What the—?' Kathi said, and pulled over.

'Not today, ya bunch a racist fucks!' the woman shouted, as she stormed over to the Jeep.

'Oh!' said Kathi, and hopped down. She went to meet Rural Ripley with her hands up and out at shoulder height. 'I don't blame you!' she said. 'My God, this world! This country! But we're looking for someone.'

'ICE? Get the fuck outta my face. Lexy?'

I had hopped down too and gone to stand beside Kathi, belatedly recognising a former client who had come to me for anger management issues a year or two ago. Thank God I had failed to make any impact before her insurance ran out: she must need that anger every day now.

'We're looking for a guy called Teto,' I said. 'This is Kathi Muntz. She *is* a private detective, as it happens, but we're on the double murder and Teto was helping. We just need to follow up.'

'With "Teto"?'

'With Teto,' said Todd, coming forward. 'I'm Todd Kroger. I'm the Spanish speaker.'

'And yet either you don't know that Teto is short for Héctor, or you don't think there might conceivably be more than one Héctor planting crops in this valley today?' the woman said. I was still scrabbling for her name. Sharon? Karen? Karen! She had been angry about that too.

'We have another appointment anyway, as it happens, Karen,' I said. 'If you run across any Teto, though, would you be willing to ask if he spoke to us down at the Patsy Denoni and then give me a ring?'

'Give you a *ring*?'

'A call, I mean,' I said.

'You got any idea how angry that makes me?' said Karen. 'You been here how many years now? You make zero attempt to learn the language and how much time do you waste thinking ICE is coming for you?'

'That's a very good point,' I said. I handed her a business card in case she'd deleted my number from her contacts, or was just about to, and we all climbed back into the car and headed for downtown.

Back at the bank, the doe-eyed kid, whose name turned out to be Jake, had leaned in all the way to the idea that he was a high-flyer. He met us at the door and ushered us into a side-room, asking if we would like anything to drink and assuring us he could send someone out for 'fraps'. I reckoned he'd have to text his mum and persuade her to go on a coffee shop run if we said yes but, since we didn't want to do anything that would set him against us, we all declined and thanked him profusely for the bottles of water.

'So, Jake,' Todd said. 'Jacob? Great name. Like I said, I'm putting myself in your hands here. And I hope you – sorry, of *course* you do . . .'

'Do what?' said Jake. 'I mean, I'm sure I do. But do what?' I got the impression that if it turned out to be 'feel like jumping off a bridge', Jake would at least consider it. I shifted a little in my seat so I had a clear view of Todd. I've done it before: tried to work out why he is quite so mesmerising to strangers. He's pretty, to be sure, but lots of people are pretty in California and when you're as young as Jake – untouched by time – surely you see pretty people all around you every day. And yes, Todd looked rich, with the diamonds and cashmere, and he was good at training his focus on just one person and making them feel special, but the man was pushing forty and wore a wedding ring. Jake wasn't looking at his hands, mind you. He wasn't looking at the sprinkles of silver winking at his temples either. He was gazing deep into Todd's depthless brown eyes. Kathi and I could have practised handstands or had a game of cards and he wouldn't have known a thing about it.

'I'm sure, too, that you want to see justice done,' said Todd, in a serious voice with a throb of emotion threatening to overwhelm it but somehow held at bay. 'See a wrong righted and innocents avenged. And let me assure you, you don't have to talk to me. You could talk to Sergeant Rankinson, only . . .' He screwed his face up and waited.

He'd used this technique before and so had Kathi. I maintain that they learned it from me but they won't have any of that. The thing is, any person faced with the option of speaking to the police instead of a private individual is going to have one of three reactions. There's panic, over unpaid parking tickets, or youthful miscreance that might be on a record somewhere, or even a solid criminal background with an entry last week. Alternatively, there might be a swift nod and an agreement that the thin blue line was the best way to deal with whatever needed to be dealt with. Or, and this happens quite a lot in these parts, there could be a twist of the face as if at a bad smell and a look of affront, a look that says 'How dare you!', as in how dare you even imply that I am on the side of The Man, him with the pepper spray and the mace and the sidearm and the thirst for the tears of the downtrodden.

Jake's face twisted up in a grimace and he physically recoiled, so repulsed was he at the notion of being a good little biddable citizen and helping the cops with whatever they were up to today.

'I can see you are a man of honour,' Todd said. I thought he was laying it on a bit thick, but Jake only nodded and looked down, maybe trying to look as honourable as Todd found him, maybe showing how long his lashes were, but in either case giving Todd his in.

'Do you see your parents often?' Todd said. I'd put money on Jake living with at least one of them, but he accepted the flattery and replied that he should phone his mom more often but why did Todd ask.

'Phil and Jilly Miller,' Todd said, and launched into the sad tale of two orphans and their loss and grief and pretty much how they had to walk to school through the snow with no shoes on their feet. Then he spun off into how his friend's motel – Kathi got a flick of a glance – was where the dread deed happened and the murderers seemed to have a lot of cash on hand and so Todd was sure that they had used a Cuento bank. 'The Friday of the weekend before Easter this would be,' he said. And waited. Would Jake take the bait?

'I mean, all the banks have a camera at the ATM,' Jake said.

'And that would be something the cops would need to take care of?' said Todd, slow-blinking as if it helped him think, and knitting his brow as if this was a lot of thinking to get done all in one go.

'What? Nah. I could pull it up right now and show you,' Jake said.

'You could?' said Todd, slowly morphing into Shirley Temple before our very eyes.

'Look,' said Jake, turning to the keyboard on the desk at his side. 'Two minutes.'

'But it'll take hours of time to look at hours of feed,' Todd said, more Goldie Hawn this time, as he contemplated how this clever stuff was making his head spin.

Jake gave him a kind smile. 'Watch,' he said.

We all watched. The film jerked and hopped from one customer to the next to the next, missing out the quiet hours and freezing obligingly on the clearest frame in any visit. We saw workers on the way home give way to couples on their way to dinner, then students on their way to the downtown bars, then the same students, only drunker, on their way from the downtown bars to the late food joints, then long stretches of nothing until the first workers started up again in the grey light of dawn.

What we didn't see was a woman in a shift dress and pixie boots, a man in a coat with a leather cross on the back, a barbershop singer on stilts, or any superannuated gamers. We also didn't see Billie Miller, but then we didn't expect to. If she'd been told that she could either get her suffering husband into a room immediately or she could go trawling around town for cash and keep him waiting she would have had to be a monster to show up on this bank feed.

'So . . .' said Todd when we had watched the whole night's worth of cash grabbers, 'either people went to a different bank, or we were right that they paid with cards and the killers wiped the records and put the cash in themselves.'

'Do you know what they look like?' said Jake, breathlessly. 'The killers. We can keep checking.'

'No one seems to have seen them,' I said. I saw no reason to keep quiet now. We'd got what we wanted from Jake and my presence alongside Todd couldn't cause a withdrawal of cooperation.

'That's not right, Lexy,' Kathi said. 'When you think about it. Devin saw them. It's just that he can't remember anything useful about them. And you *might* have seen one of them. You've got no way of knowing whether the barbershop guy was one of the fake locums, dressed up, for some reason. Ditto the chick in the boots and the guy in the other boots, right Todd?'

'Except that I saw the barbershop guy on Saturday, miles after the murder,' I said. 'And what murderer would go stalking about on stilts like a—' I stopped dead.

'We saw the people dressed in black on the Friday,' said Todd. 'And not to be bigoted or anything but the man was a Nu Goth, like I said, and perhaps – just perhaps, you know – there's an argument to be made that someone beguiled by the dark side might be more likely to harbour fantasies about random killings. As art, even.'

He'd gone too far. Jake was not a square, not a khaki- and Oxford-wearing model citizen, despite working in a bank in his twenties, but Todd musing on the topic of murder as art, even without a hint of approval, had turned him back into his mother's son. He stood up and said he was sorry but his break was almost over. 'So if that's all you need, I can show you out and please don't say I showed you the feed and please let me know if the police need my help and please tell those two kids that I'm sorry about their mom and dad and was there anything else?'

'That kid is going to go home and watch an *Everybody Loves Raymond* marathon tonight,' Kathi said, when we were back out on the street. 'Todd, you have no idea how you come off sometimes. Good *and* bad. I'm telling ya.'

'You're very quiet, Lexy,' Todd said.

I was thinking furiously, trying to decide whether the thing that had just happened in my brain was a wave or a fart. Thankfully, events overtook me before I could decide it was too good to be true and too outlandish to consider and talk myself out of it. My phone rang.

'Karen?' I said, seeing the caller ID. 'You find Teto?' I nodded at Todd and Kathi. 'Where? Hang on.' I passed the phone to Todd, who was Cuento bred and buttered. He nodded a few times then hung up and passed it back to me.

'You really think it's worth talking to Teto again?' he said.

'I already did,' I said. 'Since we decided the stick insect wasn't Joyless. But now I think it might crack the whole case wide open. So where is he? Did you follow what she was saying?'

'Of course,' said Todd. 'Let's go.'

Teto, as Karen had discovered, was with a team planting peppers in a dizzyingly enormous field on the north-east side of town, closer to Madding then Cuento. It made the tomato field by the Patsy Denoni look like a market garden. Here the roar of the northbound freeway and the whizz of the southbound freeway took away any lingering sense that farming was bucolic, and there wasn't so much as a single scrubby tree to evoke the thought of a hedgerow in our minds. There was just dry brown dirt with a ditch at the edge and then the six lanes of grey road and the sun bouncing off the cars. Under a flapping gazebo at the side of the access strip, Teto stood in the shade marking off lines on the top sheet of a fat clipboard with a chubby highlighter.

'Buenos dias,' he said, when he saw who it was. Then he said something about 'Karen' too fast for me to follow.

Todd stepped forward, secure in his assumption that the Spanish meant he was in charge, but I had other ideas this time.

'Teto,' I said. '¿Insecto palo, te recuerdas?'

'Acuerdas,' said Todd.

'Jesus!' said Kathi.

'Claro que sí,' said Teto, to me, which means I won.

'¿Con . . . un . . . biciclet?'

'en bicicleta,' said Todd.

'Wow,' said Kathi.

'Nop,' said Teto. 'No bicicleta.'

'¿Y . . .' I said, 'era él . . . verde?'

'Verde?' said Teto.

'Green, right?' I asked Kathi.

'Right but—' Kathi said.

'¿Vestido de verde?' said Teto.

And God dammit I had to let Todd answer because I didn't know what that was. 'Sí,' Todd said. '¿Estaba vestido de verde, Teto?' He turned to me. 'I'm asking if he was wearing green clothes, instead of whether he was – you know – a Martian.'

'Que no,' Teto said. 'A rayas.'

'What does "rayas" mean?' I asked Todd. 'Anything to do with stick insects?'

'Oh my God!' said Todd.

'No!' I howled, because he had just realised something and this was *my* discovery and I wasn't going to be kept from my triumph by the small matter of still having only the most pitiful Spanish after all these years in California. No way. 'Kathi, what does "rayas" mean?'

'No way!' Kathi said, also mid-realisation. *My* realisation, stolen from *me*. 'Wow, we really messed up there, didn't we? But why would . . .?'

'Teto,' I said. '¿Tieno . . . ¿Tiene . . . los palos a los pies?'

'Sí,' said Teto. 'Andaba en *zancos*. Como palos en los pies. Como dije.'

'"Como dije"?' I said, turning on Todd. '"Like I said"? Like he *said*, Todd? He *told* us? But you didn't know what "zancos" were? So you just *ignored* it?'

'How the hell was I supposed to know what "zancos" were?' said Todd. 'My mom doesn't speak a word and my dad left when I was—'

'Zancos,' I said, 'if I've worked this out less than a minute after you two, even though I basically speak Spanish like a chimp . . . are stilts. Right? Palos en los pies. Sticks on the feet. Making one look like . . .'

'Un insecto palo, sí,' said Teto. 'Pero, no verde.'

'No,' I agreed. 'Not green. And this was Sunday? Domingo?'

Teto frowned. 'Fin de semana, sí. Pero Domingo, pues . . .?' He shrugged.

A careful witness, I thought, willing to agree that it was the weekend but not signing up to one day or the other.

'Gracias,' I said. 'What does "rayas" mean, by the way?'

'Stripy,' said Kathi.

'Stripy!' I cried. 'You see? I was right. Case cracked.'

'Yeah?' said Todd.

'Oh come on,' I said. 'Why else would the same person be at the Ditch and at the Mustang?'

'But why the hell would a murderer dress as a barbershop singer?' said Todd.

'And why the fuck would any murderer try to do it on stilts?' said Kathi.

'Lo siento,' said Teto, responding to the tone of dejection even though he didn't understand the words.

'No need to apologise,' I assured him, or would be assuring him if he understood what I was saying. I dug deep and found what I needed. 'Está bien.'

SIXTEEN

'This is getting weird,' Todd said. 'I was sure the fake locums got rid of the real locums so they could use the motel for a murderous rampage. But now I'm sure it was the stripy stilts guy.'

We were parked back on the forecourt of the motel, since I had clients to see and Kathi had a laundromat to run, and we couldn't think of anything else to do anyway, beyond bugging Winebox Winnie at the Best Western.

'This was born weird, Todd,' Kathi said. 'Whether the random killing of a pair of tourists was by a pair of fake locums in a motel full of Goths and geeks *or* by a circus freak who revisited a Mustang full of blood and no bodies.'

'Blood and scalp,' I reminded her.

'Oh, pardon me,' said Kathi. '*So* normal. If things ever start to feel strange, adding scraps of scalp always helps.'

'Tsscht!' said Todd. Jilly Miller was approaching the car and we had the windows down. She didn't seem to have heard anything, though, since she hoisted a brave smile on to her face as she caught our eyes.

'Sergeant Rankinson called us,' she said. 'They got the DNA results back. It's Mom and Dad's blood. And they've got a pretty good estimate of how much was lost too. Phil took the call. She went into a lot of detail about how they calculate it, so he took it off speaker. But, anyway, there's no chance they could have survived it. I knew that. But now I really know for sure. Not that I didn't.' She heaved a breath. 'And I'm glad.'

All of us took a moment to find a response.

'Gl–glad?' was what I came up with in the end.

'Sorry,' said Jilly, scrubbing at her face. 'Just that the bit of . . . hair . . . you know? Do you remember?'

'We were just talking about it,' said Todd gently. 'I'm so sorry.'

'So I was thinking how painful it would be, if she was still alive. If they were being held somewhere. So I'm glad they're not.' She knuckled hard into her eye sockets, as if she was trying to drive away the images her words conjured.

'Honey,' Todd said. 'Don't drag your under-eye skin like that. Come with me and let me get you some serum. I got samples. I'll let you try this one kind that there's a waiting list for, but you have to promise not to snarl your knuckles into your sockets any more, OK?'

Kathi was looking at him as if he had lost his mind, but then she's not so much with the pampering. I was a bit *less* surprised that Jilly's shoulders dropped and she nodded. Todd hopped out of the car and put an arm around her, guiding her to his room and his bottomless cosmetics case.

'That is the saddest thing I ever heard,' Kathi said. 'She kind of half-hoped they were being held captive somewhere, all drained of blood and missing a bit of scalp?'

'I'm thinking about Phil, who heard all the details,' I said, checking the time on my phone. 'Can you go round to the boat and tell my noon appointment that I'm running late? Let me quickly go and check Phil's OK? Molly should know better than giving him chapter and verse on methodology, wouldn't you say? Tell her that from me.'

'What like after I go and deal with your client, I go and deliver your message to Molly?'

'Well, mention it while you're there anyway.'

Kathi frowned. 'Why am I there?'

'What?' I said. 'To tell her about stripy drawers. To say one of the guests from the motel was seen at the Mustang. I didn't think we even needed to discuss it. Of course we're telling Molly.'

'Of course we are,' Kathi said. 'Eventually. When I can work out how we know without using Teto's name.'

I couldn't argue. These days, it was up to all of us to make sure no one who might not want to deal with the cops didn't have to deal with the cops. 'Maybe Yuzula or Fern would be willing to say they saw him?'

'I'll think of something,' Kathi said.

'But will you go and have a word with my client? His name's Michael.'

'Is he a gibbering nut job?' Kathi said. Sometimes it occurs to me that I have learned a great deal more about professional de-cluttering and make-overs than the other two prongs of our little trident have ever learned about therapy.

'Bereaved with a chance of house-clearing,' I said.

She practically broke into a trot, leaving me to cross the forecourt to the Millers' rooms nice and slow, give myself time to work out what to say.

I didn't need to say anything, as it turned out. When I lifted my hand to knock on the door I heard a burst of soft laughter and the murmur of a voice, presumably Phil's. He hadn't mentioned a partner but this was definitely a conversation between intimates. He'd be ashamed to sound so cheery in front of anyone else. I wondered if he was sticking around in Cuento purely for Jilly's sake, and hoped he wasn't setting his own well-being at too low a price or even jeopardising this relationship, which sounded as if it was a close one, as far as I could tell from the tone of voice. Which is quite far. The other party – a woman, I thought – was on speakerphone, so I could hear the easy back and forth between the two, no worries about awkward silences and no attempt to jump in and score points. I can always tell whether a couple is happy deep down, even if they're warring, after I listen to them talk about small matters or shared memories for five minutes or so. It works for families too, but I've tried to steer clear of the *American Horror Story* freakshow that is the average aspirational California nuclear family these days, ever since my trademark, 'Couldn't you just say no? She's nine' and, 'Why not go out for a walk and scream at a lake?' etc., etc., were met with such stony stares.

'Forgot the freaking yoghurt!' I caught, as Phil's voice lifted briefly. I smiled to myself and left him to better comfort than I could offer any day.

I passed Kathi halfway round the motel and tried not to interpret her look. I'd find out soon enough and, indeed, Michael was standing on the porch, hands on hips and frowning.

'Who was that?' he said. 'I know I agreed to this "grief

counselling" to stop my children from nagging me to death but I won't be bullied. Why is everyone so determined to sweep my wife away and relaunch me on the world?'

'Kathi runs the laundromat,' I told him. 'She was only supposed to say I was on my way.'

'Oh, not "I can clear out your closets in one morning as long you give me a free hand" then?'

That was my fault, but he wasn't to know so I shrugged. 'It's like care-home etiquette has taken over,' I said. 'You know, how you have to get all your loved one's stuff out before the wake or pay another month? I say none of Lillian's treasures are doing any harm right where they are. If her hairbrush is still on the countertop in the bathroom in ten years, so what?'

'I'm not sure I agree,' Michael said. 'Ten years is too long for a hairbrush.'

'Huh,' I said. 'What's the shelf life of a hairbrush?'

'Two months.'

'And clothes?'

'Hanging or folding?'

'Both.'

'Hanging, a year. Folding, six months.'

'How about the Chex Mix in the top dressing-table drawer?'

'I could do that in the months between the hairbrush and the folding clothes. I see what you're doing here, you know.'

'You're very quick on the uptake,' I said. 'How come? Sudoku?'

'I'm only sixty-seven!'

'Is that so? Sounds quite young to sink into permanent grief.' He flashed me a look. 'See? You didn't know I was doing that bit, did you?'

'Touché.'

'Tell me about when you realised Lillian was the girl for you,' I said.

He started back. 'Really? That doesn't sound very brisk and healthy. I thought the whole point of this was to drive me past all feeling as quick as possible.'

'That's army basic training,' I said. 'An easy mistake to make. Go on, tell me.'

The rest of the afternoon after Michael, though, was spent on common-or-garden unhappiness. I still had the rump of election dismay and the follow-on existential dread on my books, but most of Cuento's well-heeled and/or well-insured had reverted to their usual state of ennui and formless dissatisfaction. If it wasn't for my pro bono evening slots, some days I think I'd tip them all into the slough. Today, though, Michael's gentle fondness for his dead wife was still hanging round me when Taylor came home. He had talked about her snoring, her refusal to accept that she snored, the time just after they got their first smartphones that he had recorded her snoring and she had gone to stay at the St Regis in San Francisco for a long weekend of sulking. He remembered how she had never been able to remember a password or forget a birthday, how she would eat anything that anyone cooked for her, even to the point of having to stop on the way home to pick up Tums. What struck me was that all his wonder and still-half-disbelieving gratitude was clearly for a deeply ordinary woman. So, I decided, I could feel just as amazed and anointed at being married to my deeply ordinary man.

Just as well, because Taylor was about to test my patience like never before since the wedding – when I had morphed into a lace-edged, cake-tasting super-villain and couldn't stand anyone much.

'I wish the cops gave you a copy of your statement to keep and not just to sign,' I said, after he had peeled off his disgusting bird clothes, tied them in a bag for Kathi and padded out on deck in clean shorts and T-shirt. 'Are we dead sure what day it was we saw the barbershop singer? Saturday, right?'

'Could have been,' said Taylor. 'Certainly could have been Saturday.'

'He was coming downstairs, on his stilts. I was worried about him slipping. Did I say anything?'

'Um,' said Taylor.

But it wasn't his 'can't remember' um, or his 'wasn't listening' um, or even his 'can't work out what the best move is here' um. This was his 'dammit I thought I got away with it but here it is again come back to bite me' um.

'Um?' I said.

'Yeah, see, you couldn't have said that to me, about him slipping, because I wasn't there. You might have been there when I saw the guy, but I definitely wasn't there when you saw him.'

'OK.' None of that seemed um-worthy. 'Well, I only saw him once.'

'Right,' said Taylor. Everything about his tone and expression was screaming *wrong*.

'Are you OK?' I said.

'Yep,' said Taylor, even his body language joining in now to scream *no*.

'OK,' I said. 'How about coming to bed for half an hour before we start the evening.' I managed not to say 'and get it over with', since it was only day two, with twelve to go. But I don't think I conveyed any sense that I couldn't wait till bedtime. Certainly, I watched Taylor decide that he'd rather broach an awkward subject after all, than oblige with a contribution to a family expansion plan that clearly had nothing to do with desire.

'I don't think it was the same guy!' he said. 'I know I'm hopeless but I really and truly don't think the guy I saw was the same guy you saw. That tomato guy—'

'Teto?'

'Right. Teto said "stick insect", you told me.'

'No, I didn't!' I said. 'Teto told us someone who went to look at the *Mustang* was a stick insect. Not the barbershop singer. You never bloody listen to me! Except, actually, yes in this instance it was the same guy. Sorry. But my God, that's a technicality.'

'What?' said Taylor. 'Never mind. But you said this guy was skinny, right? To Molly? On Saturday? Long legs, because of stilts, sure, but also skinny? And the thing that's been bugging me is that my guy that I saw was kinda chubby. If he wore stilts he'd look like a taffy apple.'

'*If?*'

'Yeah, but by then I'd been agreeing that we saw the same guy, and it would be weird to start backtracking and then there's that thing you always say – and I really do agree – about correcting each other in public. You hate it when couples do that.'

'But when we're talking to the cops about a murder, Taylor!'

'I didn't know there were exceptions! And I hate it too. I mean, yeah, I suppose it's funny when Kathi and Noleen really get going. And it's sweet that Roger doesn't mind when Todd does it, but when Della picks Devin up on stuff, it always strikes me as kind of . . . quelling. Is that the right word? And you know what you're talking about, being a therapist. And I know your parents bicker incessantly but they've got the years under their belt, right? Solid as a rock. Anyway, lot of reasons but in the end I decided to go along with what you said. Happy w—'

'If you say "happy wife, happy life", you will have neither.'

'Devin says it.'

'No, he does not. I've *never* heard Devin say that.' Taylor's eyes grew as round as the facial disc of an owl out hunting. 'Oh my God!' I said. 'Do you and Devin talk to each other about Della and me?'

'Um,' said Taylor, and this was his 'Abort! Abort!' um, no mistaking it.

'Because you're both two princelings lumbered with older women who hound the life out of you?'

'Della's only four years older than Devin,' Taylor said, because he is the stupidest man who was ever born. Luckily for him, though, I have a very edgy sense of humour and the expression on his face as he heard these words coming out of his mouth cracked me up into tiny pieces.

Once I had stopped laughing, I said, 'So you *didn't* see the barbershop guy with the stilts, who *does* actually happen to be the stripy stick insect Teto saw too. But you *did* see another guy. But you *didn't* tell the cops.'

'Well, that sounds bad,' said Taylor. 'But, when you think about it, everyone saw everyone anyway. So it doesn't matter who I saw.'

'You don't think it would matter if you saw one of the fake locums we thought were the killers?'

'Devin saw him!' Taylor said. 'Devin saw both of them.'

'And can't remember a damn thing about either of them.'

'Oh shit, Lexy,' Taylor said. Then, 'Nah, I'm pretty sure I saw one of the guests.'

'Right,' I said. 'Let's narrow it down. We've established that he wasn't in stripes on stilts. Was he dressed all in black?'

'Nope, just dressed in . . . whatever. A shirt and khakis. Just a kind of chubby guy, not obese, just middle-aged. And I can't remember when I saw him. I wouldn't have said Friday, because we weren't around for most of it, and I wouldn't have said Sunday. But it was definitely that weekend when Kathi and Noleen were away, because I remember thinking it was different having strangers around when strangers had booked them in, instead of Noleen giving them the once-over and thinking they looked OK. Maybe it was because Diego was in the pool and there was this guy on his own nearby.'

'Did you get a vibe off him?' I said. 'Sounds like it.'

'I think I must have,' Taylor said. 'I don't think I would have had all those thoughts if I hadn't. You know?'

'So it's not even that you agreed with me that a chubby, middle-aged guy in unremarkable clothes, sometime last weekend, was a skinny guy on stilts and fancy dress on Saturday and told the police that, but that you agreed that a creepy, *suspicious*, chubby—'

'Cut it out, Lexy. Even though he wasn't all in black, it could still have been Todd's guy. Un-Gothed for work.'

'Seriously?' I said.

'You're right,' said Taylor. 'Todd would have said the person he saw was on the heavy side, wouldn't he? Even if he only saw them in the dark, from a distance.'

'To be fair,' I admitted, 'I might have remarked if a Goth was plump too. You don't think of corpulent Goths, do you?'

'No,' said Taylor, perking up. 'But he had just the figure for a serious D&D habit. I think he was probably one half of the couple Della and Devin saw, but again straight from work, before he had put his merch on.'

'At the weekend?'

'Or church?'

'I thought you said it wasn't Sunday.'

'No, I just didn't say it was. Maybe he was Jewish.'

'Was he?'

'Nah.'

It's not really fair how Taylor gets to say that *and* gets to jump down anyone else's throat who says it. To prove I'm right, I said, 'Maybe he was Muslim.'

'How could we know?' said Taylor, the King of Woke. 'So do we have to go and tell Molly?'

'Who's *we*?' I said. 'You might.'

'Fuck,' said Taylor. 'She'll eat me alive.'

'And you might not,' I went on. 'Or at least it might not matter too much. If he was one of the fake locums, then she'll chew you up and spit you out. But if he was one of the D&D oldsters, not so much. And, luckily, I might know how to find out.'

I took my phone out and texted Della, which is not easy to do with crossed fingers. **Body type fake locums?**

The three dots began dancing and in another moment the reply appeared: **Unsquandered ecto.**

I smiled. Della has a lot of thoughts about body types and lifestyle. She is slender herself, bordering on willowy, but she has seen too many of her country-people bring their endomorphic genes north of the border and meet the modern American diet in a head-on collision. She is vociferous about her husband – much given to slumping on a couch, eating 'family sized' bags of bright orange dusty things, and slurping on sweet drinks that nobody even pretends are family-sized, while he zaps invaders from other planets – not squandering the ectomorphic head start his genes have given him.

'Good news,' I said to Taylor. 'It wasn't a fake locum. Now then: belt and braces.' I texted Devin.

Body type D&D merchmeisters?

The three dots danced and the reply came even quicker.

DK Y.

? I texted back.

dunno why

Why what? I texted.

Dear Lexy, he texted back. **I don't know the answer to your question. Why are you asking?**

I punched the button to speak live. 'Well, that saved a ton of time, didn't it? Never mind. Devin, you must know. You saw them, for God's sake. And as for why: murder? So come on. The people in the merch. What sort of shape were they?'

'H-human?' said Devin.

'Della deserves a medal,' I said.

'I know, right?' his voice leapt with love. 'She's so great.'

'Devin,' I said, 'think hard. Were they fat?'

'I wouldn't say that.'

'Because . . .'

'It's mean.'

'Jesus. Were they thin?'

'I wouldn't call them thin.'

'Because . . .'

'I have a daughter, Lexy. And body dysmor—'

I sighed so loud I didn't hear the rest of it. 'OK, tell me this. What size were the hoodies? The Ace Ventura and Tia Maria sweatshirts?'

'Venger and Tiamat,' he said. 'XXL. Perhaps XXXL. Big.'

'Thank you Devin,' I said.

'Welcome, weirdo,' he replied. He meant it too.

'Even better news,' I told Taylor, when I had hung up. 'Chances are the guy you saw was one of the XXL D&Ds. So it doesn't matter that you didn't tell Molly.'

'Phheee-ew,' Taylor said. 'Any day I don't have to face Sergeant R is a good day in my book.'

'Oh no, you're still going,' I said. 'But I'm coming too and I'll protect you.'

'Oh?' said Taylor, so suspicious. And, on this occasion, right. 'Why the change of heart?'

'Because we found something out earlier that she needs to know,' I said. 'And I think I've worked out how to tell her. Or how you can, anyway.'

'Oh?' said Taylor again, even more suspicious and just as right.

'You know when they plough the fields and make planting furrows? And it attracts gulls?'

Just like that, Taylor forgot all about murder. 'Oh, Lex! I knew it was only a matter of time!' I had no idea why he was so excited. I gave him a bright non-committal smile and waited to find out. 'Gulls!' he said. 'I know what you're thinking. Fascinating, right?' I didn't argue. 'We are seventy miles from the coast as the crow flies, and yet when they turn the earth to plant in spring, what follows the tractor?'

'Gulls?'

'Gulls.'

'But you wouldn't be able to solve the fascinating mystery of why they come so far inland by going and gawping at them, would you? So what other reason would you have to . . .?'

'Well, no,' Taylor said. 'But how could you not stand in wonder? It's like the Great Pyramid at Giza.'

'Is it?'

'You can't learn how *they* did it from gazing, but you can't help gazing and wondering anyway.'

'Right. And you do, don't you? Go and gaze at gulls? Where they're planting? Which was how Teto and Co. knew you?'

Taylor looked quickly to one side and then the other. 'Um, yeah, I do,' he said. His tone would fit trying on my undies when I was out but seemed a bit over the top for this. He took a big brave breath and went on. 'Sometimes, in spring, in the morning, when I'm going to the wetlands, I leave a bit early and go wherever they're planting first.'

'Huh,' I said. 'I knew you left early but I thought it was to avoid Todd, or maybe to stop at Swiss Sisters and not have to get me something too and bring it back.'

'I would never do that!' said Taylor. 'Go for secret coffee and not get one for you, I mean.'

'It's not an issue,' I said. 'Todd brings it anyway.' Then I remembered. 'Or he did. Before he decided he was my obstetrician and cut me off.' A cloud passed over my heart and it must have crossed my face too because Taylor saw it. 'Anyway, this is all good. For Molly purposes, anyway. You can say you got mixed up. You *did* see the same guy as me, but you were concentrating on the gulls – who wouldn't? Pyramids and all that – so you forgot where you saw him.'

'Will she buy that? And why am I selling it?'

'Teto,' I said, and didn't need to say any more. But said more anyway. 'All she'll care about is getting the gen, "from whatever source derived, without apportionment among the several . . . witnesses".'

'You are a dead cert for this citizenship, babe,' Taylor said. Then he frowned. 'But why didn't I mention the chubby guy?'

'Say you only just remembered. Don't tell her you didn't want to argue with me in public. That really is weird.' Then I considered it. 'Or, if she's had the chance to hear the rest of them arguing, maybe it won't seem that way. Play it by ear when we get there?'

'Wait, *who's* arguing?' said Taylor.

'All of them,' I said. 'Todd took a huff about whether or not he can do Goth taxonomy – hang on no, it was gender presentation. And the truth is it was two separate people all along. And Devin went through Della for not knowing which swamp monster had the pink claws in the reboot of the offshoot of some mad crap he loved when he was a kid.'

'But they were two separate people too?'

'Four,' I said. 'But even if they hadn't been, she blocks all that out now. I think she's trying to keep the hope alive that Diego and Hiro are never going to start mooching around looking like big honking American kids, once she stops buying their stuff and they choose their own.'

This time the cloud passed over Taylor's face first and then my heart. He really did want to have a couple of big, honking American kids of his own to roll his eyes at when they mooched about in terrible clothes one day. 'Bed?' I said. 'Then Molly? Or Molly then bed? Or just Molly? Or just bed?'

'Well, not bed now that you've said Molly ten times,' said Taylor. 'Jesus, Lexy.'

And, in the end, she wasn't even grateful that we laid our dwindling fertility at her feet. Well, mine. We did the brave thing, too, and went to see her in person, rather than hiding behind a text or an email. To give her her due, she did come out to see us in the front bit of the PD when they buzzed through to tell her we were there. But she took the news of another stranger sighting at the Last Ditch Motel the weekend before Easter without a flicker of interest. Taylor even said the guy seemed creepy, but Molly shook her head.

'After the fact,' she said. 'You didn't tell anyone at the time that he seemed creepy, right? Right. You didn't alert the parents of the young children. You didn't stand and watch where he went or take a licence plate? This is why eye-witness accounts are so notoriously unreliable.'

'Surprised you spend so much time with people stuck in that tiny interview room dying of your coffee machine poison while you grill them to give you these useless accounts, really,' I said.

'Does he want a lollipop?' Molly said.

The diss was so subtle that I couldn't even get a square look at it, but I was sure it was there: something about talking to me like I was Taylor's mum, reflecting back at me the fact that I'd just leapt to his defence, exactly as a mother would. So it was Molly's fault that we kept the real news – about the stick insect being seen at the Mustang – to ourselves. Let Kathi work out how to get the information to the good sergeant without putting Teto on her radar; I had changed my mind about making my husband look like a bird-obsessed weirdo, just to help her out.

Instead, I curled my lip and left.

And almost immediately made another discovery, leading to another theory, both of which Molly would have loved a share of. It's her retrospective fault that I didn't tell her about them too.

SEVENTEEN

Here's what happened. We were having a familiar, well-worn – almost to the point of being ceremonial – conversation as we made our way hand-in-hand back to the Ditch. The prep work for this particular example of the conversation had been done in the Lode supermarket the previous weekend. We had stocked up on fresh veg, brown rice, oily fish, the good beans in the jar (not the cheap beans in the tin), and brought it all home to make nutritious meals for the week, seasoned with a spritz of lime, not salt, and sprinkled with herbs, not ketchup.

Only now it was Thursday and it was eight o'clock and we were both tired and ready to eat.

We skipped the bit where we beat ourselves up for having been in a huge shop full of cheese and bacon and frozen meatballs and squandering our chance again. There was no point. Instead, we went straight to discussing the ease, cost, health and tastiness of all the purveyors of ready-made dinners in and around Cuento.

'We could have lettuce wraps, black instead of refried and no sour cream,' said Taylor. 'Mexican doesn't have to be unhealthy.' It was lovely when Todd wasn't here, because we didn't have to acknowledge that the food in the Mexican restaurants in Cuento wasn't Mexican.

'We won't though,' I pointed out. 'Not once we get there. We should just go for a double bacon cheeseburger extra fries and be done with it.'

'Or Japanese?'

'Tempura. I'll say I won't, standing here, but I know I will.'

'And we had pizza last night.'

'Italian people live forever,' I said. 'All the tomatoes and olives and wine and sardines. We need to stop saying pasta isn't a great choice.'

'Yeah, but Italians eat that every day,' Taylor reminded me. 'Not as a healthy break from fried chicken.'

'Oooooooo,' I said. 'You've done it now, Tay. Fried chicken!'

'No one starts a clean eating regimen on a Thursday anyway,' he said. 'Let's pick up the car and go. Don't tell the rest of them. I want you to myself for a change.'

'Right,' I said. 'Nothing to do with the fact that we'll ditch the wrappers in a public bin and wipe our faces before we get home again then? Gotcha.'

The chicken shop on the northern edge of town was doing a brisk trade this fine weekday evening. It was a local chain, slowly creeping out from San Francisco and well-bedded into Cuento, where students of all stripes eat all day long and through the night, and bros like to outdo one another with the hot sauce collection too.

Tonight there was a queue of eleven people ahead of us, in three groups. Five women, ruddy and muddy, must have just come off a sports field of some kind: they had those baggy socks that, stretched out from having pads stuffed down them, sagged around the girls' bruised ankles. I wasn't worried about them: they were in high spirits but they were a team, meaning that they would have their order all ready to go when the time came. Ahead of them, though, were five male students of a very different kind. They were each bent over their individual phones and all wearing two earbuds so I could already see how it was going to go when they shuffled to the counter. The server would speak. Student One would remove one earbud with a bewildered frown and say 'Huh?'. The server would break the jaw-dropping news that she had asked what Student One wanted to eat. Student One would lift his head for the first time and start reading the menu board above the counter. He would put his earbud back in once the process of ordering food was complete. The server would speak. Student One would take his earbud out with a look of actual annoyance this time. The server would blow his mind with the news that she was asking what he wanted to drink. Student One would look over at the fountain and begin to ponder.

Leaving four more of them to go.

Unless, of course, the single man standing directly in front of Taylor and me started kicking them. He had on Dr Marten's boots with many, many lace-holes and they might well have had steel-toecaps too. Tucked into these with no need for any folding was a pair of sprayed-on black jeans. I reflected that it was just as well they were so tight or else the belts and chains at his waist would have brought them down like the vicar's trousers in a bedroom farce. The reason we could see the chains was that his Dennis the Menace stripy jumper wasn't the baggy, stretched-out comfort blanket that Robert Smith went in for. Or maybe it was but he had washed it on the wrong setting and now it hugged his ribs, skimmed his waist and surely cut off the circulation in his armpits. His outfit was topped off by a stiff leather dog collar, bristling with spikes, and above all that his hair was backcombed, teased and sprayed into a jet-black pineapple that gave him an extra foot of height.

If he'd been the London punk he looked like to me, he'd at least have spat on the students if not actually gone in with the Docs. But when I gave a loud and passive-aggressive British sigh, he turned round and stared at me out of heavily kohled eyes and said, 'Take a chill pill, lady. If you're headed to the airport, there's a KFC at the gate.'

I didn't answer. I was mesmerised by his neck, or rather by his spiky dog collar, or rather by the fact that one of the spikes on his spiky dog collar was missing, leaving a little hole in the leather that showed the skin of his throat, or rather by the fact that I was pretty sure I knew what one of those little spikes would look like when detached from the leather where it belonged.

'Are you a Goth?' I said.

He wasn't as patient with me as he was willing to be with the clueless bunch of mouth-breathers still trying to cope with having to take out an earbud to get their dinner.

'Lexy?' said Taylor.

The Goth merely rolled his eyes.

'No but I mean, what kind of Goth would you say you are? If you *are* a Goth. Or are you a punk?'

'I'm a med school student going to a costume party,' the guy said. 'Why?'

'Doesn't matter,' I told him. I had a Goth taxonomist at home anyway. 'So you don't normally wear your hair like that? Cos, if so, you need to put some heavy conditioner on it before you try to comb it out. Maybe sleep in a shower cap and attack it in the morning?'

'Are you nuts?' the guy said. He lifted the edge of his wig and showed me a neat medical student haircut underneath.

'Just as well,' I said.

I was still wondering why someone would buy fried chicken on their way to a party when he got to the head of the queue and started reeling off a monster of an order, because it was his party and he was letting the chicken shop take care of the catering. Which was OK because it gave me time to call Todd and ask him if he fancied chicken for dinner because I needed to talk to him and to Kathi too.

'Is no one in this line just getting a chicken sandwich for themselves like an American?' came a plaintive howl from behind us when I started relaying Todd's order to the server: *grilled* chicken, *brown* rice and peas, *undressed* salad.

'Looks like our happy hour's going to be an early night then,' Taylor said as we climbed back into the car with our fragrant parcels. I had completely forgotten about Day Two of Get Lexy Pregnant, which was not great in one way but from a different angle it was just what Dr Heidi had advised me to do. As long as I set an alarm on my phone to remind me about the other bit too.

'OK,' I said, when we'd gathered on the porch twenty minutes later, with fried chicken, chips, rice and peas, mac and cheese, the pile of pork chops Noleen had been grilling when Kathi told her of the change of plan and four bottles of red wine. This was Todd's version of being kind because I wasn't nuts about red wine recently, following a Christmas incident that could still make me shudder. He thought it would make it easier for me not to drink if nothing I liked was available. He has *been* to Scotland but it didn't take.

'So do you want the end result or do you want me to show my working?' I said. 'Oh hey, Kathi, did you think of a way to tell Molly about the stick insect without dropping Teto in it yet?'

Noleen filled her wine glass to the rim so that only the surface tension of the liquid kept it from spilling.

'Walk us through it for me,' said Todd. 'I can still appreciate the accent even if I'm not interested in the content.' He was scrutinising his skinless breast of grilled chicken, God knows what for.

'Right, so you know how we pivoted to the idea that the barbershop on stilts guy was the murderer, because he was seen here at the motel *and* at the Mustang?' I said. I took a big bite out of a crunchy drumstick and chewed while they were all nodding. 'Well, how about if I had evidence that one of the *other* people who was here was actually the murderer?'

'Hang on,' said Noleen. 'I missed something. I thought you had decided the locums did it.'

I waggled my eyebrows at her. 'Todd, did you see the locums at any point?'

'Aaaabsolutely not,' Todd said. 'I made sure I didn't. I didn't want them to find out I was permanent and start asking me all sorts of questions about motel protocols. No, I did not.'

'I say you did,' I announced.

'I don't follow any of this,' said Taylor.

'Really?' I said. 'And you just gave up . . . our planned evening . . . anyway? Wow.'

'Your planned evening better not have been conception,' said Todd. 'Because—'

'I'm eating!' said Noleen. 'God Almighty.'

'Because we can wait twenty minutes,' Todd went on, ignoring her. 'Put that chicken in the oven to keep warm and we'll see you back here after.'

Taylor bent low over his plate and concentrated on shovelling macaroni into his face.

'I don't know what *your* problem is, 'I told him. 'Twenty minutes is not an insult.'

'I was including fifteen for you to lie with that pillow under your hips like I advised you,' Todd said. 'But if you promise to get right to it after we leave, go on with your story now.'

'Yes, please, carry on with the story of blood and scalps and murderers,' said Kathi. 'Before I puke my leg portion back up again and waste it.'

'I will go on with my story,' I said, 'but right now I need to break off and get some information from you first,' I said. 'Do Nu Goths wear dog collars?'

'Like pastors?' said Noleen.

'No, like buckle chokers,' said Todd. 'I assume anyway. They might do. Why?'

'Did you happen to see anything glinting at the neck of the . . . which one did you see? . . . that night.'

'I saw the guy,' said Todd. 'No. Why?'

'Because I worked out what the thing was that wasn't an earring, on the floor of the Millers' room,' I said. 'It was a stud from a spiky . . . buckle choker? That sounds painful.'

'Sometimes that's the point,' Todd said.

'Scalp and blood, scalp and blood,' Kathi intoned as if it was a mantra.

'Which suggests to me that the Goth was the killer.'

'I thought the locums were the killers,' said Noleen again.

'And who was the barbershop singer?' said Kathi.

'So . . . the barbershop singer and the Goth guy were a couple?' said Taylor. 'A skinny couple. In which case who's my guy?'

'What guy?' said Kathi.

'I have absolutely no clue,' said Taylor.

'Me either,' said Noleen. '*Why'd* Jilly try to take the stud away?'

Bugger.

I took another bite of chicken to give myself some thinking time. By the time I'd swallowed, I'd come up with, 'That is a very good question.'

'And here is the obvious answer,' said Todd infuriatingly. 'The locums are the killers. The stud was from the victims. And Jilly thought she was finding out more than she ever wanted to know about how her parents rolled. Which she didn't want Molly to add to their file.'

'There wasn't any fetishwear in the duffel bag or the rest of the luggage,' I said, not ready to dump my theory.

'You've missed the point,' said Todd. 'I said, Jilly *thought* she'd discovered something. And now we know what the corpses are wearing.'

'But how did Jilly Miller know what the stud was?' I said. 'Is *she* . . .' I couldn't pick a word.

'Kinky?' said Todd. 'I didn't get that from her. But she must be, huh?'

'Not necessarily,' Kathi said. 'She also knew plastic tarps come from the factory dusty. That impressed me and I remembered it. People know stuff. All of us know completely random stuff.'

'I can identify the three major types of Roman columns,' Noleen said. 'Doric, Ionic and Corinthian.'

'I can name all the parts of the ear,' I said. 'It never comes up in a pub quiz and that bugs me.'

'How many parts of the ear are there?' said Taylor.

'Lobe, helix, rook, daith, conch—' I began.

'Everyone knows that,' said Todd, pinging one of his piercings, the tragus.

'OK, you asked for it,' I said. 'I know it's unconstitutional to—'

'No!' said Noleen. 'I cannot sit through another firehose of ratified gobbledegook.'

'What? Like "Doric, Ionic and Chrysanthemum"?' I said.

'That's four words,' said Noleen, holding up that many and waggling them. 'If you can say your thing in four words . . .'

'Challenge accepted,' I said. 'That's not two of my four!' I added, as she started making a fist. 'Get them up again, you chancer.' I cleared my throat. 'It is unconstitutional to . . . levy a poll tax.' I finished off with a raspberry.

'Anyway,' said Kathi.

'I didn't get one yet!' Todd said. 'I know the Kings of England. But don't tell Roger. I don't want *that* can of worms opened up again.'

We all leaned hard towards prising the lid off this then we all resolutely turned back to the matter in hand at last.

'Kathi?' I said.

'I know six ways to open a bottle of wine without a

corkscrew,' Kathi said. 'All without driving the cork inside. Because that's nasty. And we haven't done Taylor either.'

'Birds,' said Taylor. 'Mostly.'

'I meant,' I said, once they'd all stopped laughing, 'Kathi, do you want to tell Molly we worked out what that stud is?'

'Why me?' Kathi's place at the head of this operation blinked on and off like Vegas neon sometimes.

'You already need to tell her about the stick insect,' Todd pointed out.

'We've got that covered,' I said. 'Right, Taylor?'

'I remember you said we did,' Taylor agreed. 'I can't remember now what it was you were planning. This is all very confusing. There are too many people and nobody saw all of them and the wardrobe changes are over the top. Vampires? Stick insects? Fake locums and real locums and skinny dudes and chubby dudes and more grandparents than any family needs, if you ask me.'

We all stared at him. I've got clearance to stare at Taylor. He's my husband. I can look, touch, lick, whatever I want to do. But Kathi was staring at him too, with a faraway look in her eyes. And Todd was staring at him with his head tilted over to one side. So I think we were all having the same strange experience, that of wondering if he was on to something.

'Do we need a spreadsheet?' he said. 'I know how to do that. Mostly for birds, but it's the same thing, right? Migration to and from the Ditch, changes in plumage, mating pairs? I can nail it all down for us.'

'But first come back to see Molly again and tell her about the stick insect,' I said. 'And I'll tell her what the spike is. Oh! Should we tell Jilly that we don't think her parents are into all that?'

'It might help her to be prepared for when the bodies turn up,' said Kathi. '*In* "all that". God, those poor kids. It never ends for them.'

'But not tonight,' said Todd. 'None of this is for tonight. Right?' He glared at Taylor and then at me.

'Would you like to select a playlist?' I said. 'Spritz our sheets with all the perfumes of Arabi— Oh my actual fucking God,

Todd! I'm kidding.' Because I swear he was thinking of what tracks would help and what scents he had in his bathroom that would put us in the mood.

'Todd,' Taylor said, standing up and putting out his hands. 'I love you, man. And I wouldn't change you even if I could. But I got this. Seriously.'

'Wow,' said Kathi. 'I guess a man's gotta do what a man's gotta do.'

'When the going gets tough, the tough get going,' said Noleen.

They laughed themselves off the boat, and I could still hear them cackling all the way round the side of the motel until they clamped it because they knew Hiro and Diego would be sleeping.

'I got this?' I said, through my clenched teeth, once we were alone. 'I *got* this? Like you're picking up the bill or changing a tyre?'

'Right,' Taylor said. 'Obviously, I don't got this. Any of this. I don't know what to say or do or how to say it or do it and I'm sick of getting it wrong but I don't want to give up and I think you're being really mean to me most of the time and I get that I need to suck it up when you have your period and I'll have to suck it up when you are pregnant – you and you alone; got *that* loud and clear – and obviously during the birth and afterwards, if you're tired or people are the way they are because you're a *mom*,' He took a breath. 'But I no way in hell see why I have to suck it up right now. So. Shoot me.'

'Or . . .' I said, standing up and turning my back on him then dropping the neckline of my T-shirt so he could see my bra strap. 'I could make it up to you. Because you're right, and I'm sorry.'

Which I did. Because he was. And so I should be.

EIGHTEEN

We never made it to Molly's the next day. Personally, I almost never made it through breakfast without crawling back under the covers and curling up into a ball until the world went away. That's how excruciating it was to tell Phil and Jilly Miller what we knew about the nature of the spike. It would have been fine if I'd done it alone, or even with Taylor squirming at my side, and I could have lent moral support to Kathi if she could have been persuaded to take on the task – perhaps if drinking bin juice was her other option – but there was only one person in the world confident enough and oblivious enough to broach this topic of conversation and so it fell to him. Kathi and I were powerless to stop it unfolding.

He had invited them to breakfast by text and they had both accepted. So the siblings were side by side at the trestle table on the forecourt when Todd came downstairs from his room carrying his big cast-iron frying pan in both hands. He's very proud of his frittata and this was a beaut, perfectly browned on top with the cheese still bubbling, fluffy inside, bursting with al dente vegetables, and leaving the pan without a single morsel sticking.

'Tuck in,' he said, when the whole thing was divided among the six of us – about half a pound of food each, I reckoned, except for Todd's portion which was a sliver he still wouldn't finish. 'I'm going to talk,' he went on, 'but you just listen and enjoy your breakfast. You need to keep your strength up and I've added nutritional yeast and fresh ground flax. Now then.' He smiled at the Miller kids. 'We know that the little spike the cops found on the carpet wasn't an earring, but there's no need to worry.'

Jilly had been chewing her first mouthful of egg, but she stilled now with a lump in her cheek and dread in her eyes.

'What?' said Phil. He looked between his sister and Todd. How much did he know?

'And we understand entirely that you wanted to shield your parents from gossip and ridicule,' Todd said. 'Don't look like that,' he added. Jilly was still turned to stone except that she had started to drool where her mouth was threatening to drop open around her half-chewed lump of breakfast. Todd handed her a napkin. 'We don't judge,' he said. 'I don't judge anyone who does anything with any number of other adults. And even these two' – he jerked a thumb at me and Kathi – 'who are, as you see, pret-ty vanilla don't care enough to form a view.'

'What?' said Phil again.

'You love your sister, don't you?' said Todd. Phil frowned, probably on his way to a nod. Todd sailed on before he got there. 'You probably don't even think about her bedroom preferences and proclivities, right? Of course not.'

Kathi, beside me, was practising deep breathing.

'So, *no one* here cares how you knew what the spike was, Jilly.'

'Proclivities?' said Phil. He had a point. Strictly speaking, the word was neutral but you never hear it used about knitting blankets or breeding parrots.

'The point is that it didn't belong to anything that your parents owned.'

Jilly and Phil shared a look but said nothing. At least Jilly was chewing again. She got the mouthful down and pushed her plate away, taking a sip of water. I noticed that her hand was shaking.

'So you need to prepare yourselves for when their bodies are found,' Todd went on. Jilly Miller slumped back, forgetting that she was sitting on a bench, then grabbed the edge of the table with both hands to keep from falling over backwards. Phil gave a shaky laugh. If it hadn't sounded too absurd to suggest it, I'd have said they were relieved. I made a mental note to point out to Todd that when the orphaned children of murdered parents are relieved to talk about their mother and father's corpses, that should tell him something about what he'd been saying previously.

'We suspect,' he said, 'that your parents might have been dressed up in the clothes in question as part of an attempt to belittle them.'

'What clothes?' said Phil. Maybe he wasn't a morning person. His contributions had been minimal so far, certainly, and he wasn't joining any dots here.

'Belittle them?' said Jilly.

'*I* don't think it belittles the people who choose to put it on,' Todd said. 'I don't believe in shame, as I said. And if you decide not to buy into what the murderers think, then they have no power to affect you.'

'*What* clothes?' said Phil.

'Fetishwear,' said Todd.

'You think the killers – what makes you assume there's more than one, by the way? – but you think they dressed my mom and dad up in . . . what do you mean by "fetishwear"?' said Jilly.

'Thigh boots, ballet boots, pasties, chaps, clamps, rings, straps, obviously something studded.'

'Stop speaking!' said Kathi.

'I will, but only to repeat to Jilly: you don't need to pretend to us. You're a healthy young woman, having fun. I hope you stay safe, but apart from that—'

'Seriously, 'said Kathi. 'Just close your lips and let your larynx be at rest.'

But I was watching Jilly and Phil and, unbelievably, they were only just managing not to laugh.

'Glad we cleared that up then,' Phil said. 'What the hell is a ballet—'

'Don't encourage him,' said Kathi. She wheeled round to Todd. 'Seal your lips around that thought!'

'Everything sounds filthy now,' said Taylor, speaking for the first time. This was too much for Jilly and she started to giggle. Then she pulled her frittata close again and took a second bite.

'Anyway, it might be moot,' I said. 'The clothes mightn't be publicised even when your parents are found. And I'm sure they will be.' It was a stone-cold meaningless platitude but both Millers looked grateful.

'Why not?' said Jilly. 'Publicised, I mean.'

Would the police let this detail be publicly known? I wondered. 'Well,' I said, not quite such a total platitude, 'I would have thought they'd keep it up their sleeve as a way of getting rid of time-wasters.'

'Does that really happen?' Jilly said.

'False confessions?' said Kathi. 'All the time. Massive waste of police time. My time too once or twice, but you get pretty good at sniffing them out. We got one guy in Cuento who's the town confessor like you'd have a town drunk.'

'But he won't know where my mom and dad are or what they're wearing?' said Phil. 'Yes, I see.'

I wondered what it was he did for a living; he really didn't strike me as very bright.

'Well, they wouldn't be able to keep it quiet *where* they turn up: two . . . departed loved ones,' Todd said, stopping himself saying 'corpses' or worse. 'There will probably be a certain amount of hoopla – TV units, and the like. You should prepare yourselves for that too.'

'How?' said Jilly. It was a very good question and she looked to me – the therapist – for the answer.

'Rest, good food, fresh air, kindness to yourself,' I said. 'Comfort if you can find it and also . . . keep your expectations reasonable. You will be tired and you might be angry. Just sit with it and don't judge yourself. Are you sure you're still OK to be here?'

'Where else would we be?' said Jilly sadly. 'Right, Phil?'

'Comfort if we can find it,' Phil said. 'That *is* here. Knowing you're trying to help, knowing you're all rooting for us. Jilly's right: where else?' He had cleared his plate and, after speaking, he looked around as if at a view of hills or meadows, not at all as if at a view of parked cars, the chain link round the pool, the edge of the self-storage facility and the start of the dusty fields. Either this guy had a real talent for what I still refuse to call self-care, or he had got his doctor to prescribe something amazing in the last few days. Or gummies, I suppose. Whichever it was, I was happy for him.

As the party broke up, Todd to do his dishes, Kathi to get

the Skweek open and Taylor to stroll up through town for his regular stint on the 'ask me' table at the public library, the Miller kids seemed content to sit together over the last of their coffee and watch the world, such as it was, go by. The world going by on a Thursday morning in April was mostly travellers checking out and Noleen starting to clean rooms, although Leo, the construction guy, sometimes came back for his morning break, something Diego and Hiro found fascinating when they were around. With his hard hat, Hi-Vis and toolbelt, he was Rubble, their favourite Paw Patrol pup, sprung to life, only with heavy boots too.

'I'll walk as far as Second Street with you,' I said to Taylor. 'It's Janine this morning.'

Janine was a long-term client who grew new phobias like other people collect recipes, clipping them out of magazines and practising them until they become second nature. Her latest was a fear of tunnels, which made getting to the Ditch from downtown a bit of a rigmarole. She could have come over the footbridge along at Turkey Trot Road and round, but she had a fear of heights too. My solution was to meet her on a bench in the park, thanking my stars we lived in California and wondering what she'd do if she lived in some blizzard-blown square state, although since this entire country insisted on making old men stand outside freezing their hands to a bible every fourth January, Janine would probably just sit in the park anyway and get hypothermia.

We passed a pleasant therapeutic hour – i.e. fifty minutes – at the park, Janine and me, ordering her phobias like a doll collection, first by severity, then by frequency of attack, then by avoidability of trigger. We finished off with some relaxation exercises. She lay flat on her back on the picnic table gazing up into the tree canopy overhead, while I guided her through a sequence of soothing imaginary events. She was so relaxed by the end that I thought the man staring over in our direction was concerned for her health, like I might have drugged her. Maybe he just had a stick up his arse and thought it was unhygienic to lie on the picnic tables, the same ones bird shit on all day until the rats come out in the evening.

I stayed on after Janine left, claiming that I had to answer some emails. In fact, it was so that we didn't end up walking up the street together like pals: there are limits to the loosening of professional boundaries, even for me. Once she had gone, though, I didn't even take out my phone. Taylor and I had more or less given up on our digital detox after catching each other multiple times, him on YouTube, subdivision birders, and me on Realtor.com, subdivision Hollywood Hills, but I could still decide to sit and stare into space, feeling the breeze and listening to the helium quacking of a nursery school on a field trip. If it wasn't for that guy glaring at me I would be having a quality interlude in my day.

I could have left by another route and not gone past his table – of course I could – but I was curious to see if he'd speak to me and reveal what I'd done to offend him so. As I approached on a trajectory to miss him by three feet and with my sights set on my exit from the park, I was astonished to see him cringe away from me, scooting along the picnic bench in a way all but guaranteed to get him a splinter or two in the backs of his thighs.

'Are you OK?' I said. I didn't really have time to deal with someone clinically upset but he looked as if he could do with a friendly word, at least.

'I am if you leave me alone this time,' he said, getting his phone out of his pocket and brandishing it at me. I had no idea what I was supposed to understand by the gesture. He hadn't dialled a number or started recording. Then I processed his words.

'This time?' I said. 'I've never clapped eyes on you in my life before.' Even as I said it though, searching his face like you would after such a not quite accusation, a faint bell began to ring. That look of anxious outrage, that uncomprehending grievance. The last time I'd seen this guy I was feeling it too, though.

'When was it . . .?' I said, searching my recent past.

'Oh Miss Innocent?' said the guy. His voice and face was bringing it slowly into focus but I still couldn't quite get the memory to form. I stared at his sideburns and at the

Lego-esque snap-on look of his hair. 'It was Easter,' he said, at last. 'As you well know.'

'Yes!' I agreed, everything suddenly clicking. 'You're the barbershop soloist, aren't you? Look, I told you at the time that was a misunderstanding. And you know, this is a small town. We're going to run into each other – we just have. There's no need for the dagger looks, OK?'

'And *I* told *you* at the time that I am not a barbershop singer,' he said. 'It was a costume for the parade.'

'No, you didn't,' I said. 'You didn't say anything to me. You just scuttled off.'

'Well, I'm not,' he said. 'I merely dressed up for Easter in a costume like a hundred other people that day.'

'What a weird costume to hire for Easter though,' I said. 'You can understand why I thought you *were* one, since you had all the clobber.'

'I didn't hire it,' he said.

'So you own a barbershop singer's outfit but you're affronted if someone thinks you might be a barbershop singer?' I said. 'That seems . . .'

'That seems like absolutely none of your business,' he said. He was getting more prissy by the minute. 'But, if you must know, I found it at a Free Stuff corner a couple of days before Easter. And I put it back there a couple of days after. I meant to keep it until you assaulted me but, as I'm sure even you would appreciate, you permanently soured it for me.'

'A Free Stuff corner?' I said, ignoring the rest of it and letting my gaze rise until I was looking into the distance. 'A . . . Free . . . Stuff co—' I snapped my eyes back to meet his. 'Which one?'

'Why?' he asked me. 'Why should I give up a good tip to someone who's treated me the way you treated me.'

'It. Was. A. Mistake,' I said, clapping along. 'And, you know, hoarding a Free Stuff corner for yourself is the sort of thing that bothers men of honour.' I put Devin out of my thoughts as I spoke, still chasing a notion that was so far eluding me.

'It didn't last anyway,' he said. 'It peaked early and fell hard. Too good to be true, I suppose, finding an almost complete barbershop quartet outfit just sitting there.'

'So if it's dormant, why not tell me?' I asked him.

'If it's dormant, why do you want to know?' he demanded. 'As if I can't guess. You're planning to keep an eye on it, in case it picks up again, aren't you?'

'Whereas you wouldn't dream of such a thing?' I was tired of this guy. Even in these days of bottomless victimhood he had a talent like few others I'd ever met in real life. Besides, I had too many half-formed thoughts and semi-invisible wisps of possibility whirling around my head for me to carry on talking to him. I needed to concentrate, because this must be something. It *must* be. But I couldn't begin to work out what, with him wittering on. He flung a few more huffy remarks at my back as I walked away, but I kept moving.

On the corner of Eleventh Street, I stood under the shade tree and stared down at the sad remains of a burnt-out Free Stuff corner. They never really die, but this one was far from thriving. There were two battered cardboard boxes, one with a few stray beads in the bottom and one with some loose pages from a textbook. Up against the side of one box was a pair of well-worn trainers and what looked like a red flannel onesie. Pretty much textbook moribund Free Stuff for a college town. But if I was right – and I was almost sure I was – and if the guy in the park was to be believed – and why not – then a few weeks ago this corner was a hot zone, where he had found pretty much all of a barbershop quartet costume, the trousers far too long. And Bill and Billie Miller had stopped off right around here for no purpose anyone had been able to discern. If I was right, and I really was pretty completely sure I might be, then it must mean something. I raised my eyes to look up through the tree to the sky above, hoping for inspiration, and had to take a staggering step out to the side as I reeled at what I saw.

I fished my phone out and texted Todd and Kathi. Should have been Molly. Wasn't.

Meet me on the corner of 11 and G. Now. Drop everything.

They were there before a resident in any of the nearby houses had had the chance to come out and ask me why I was loitering. Todd pulled up and leapt out. Kathi descended at a more measured pace but with an avid look in her eye.

'Well?' she said.

'I think this Free Stuff corner is significant. First, the Millers were here.'

'Somewhere near here,' Todd said.

'And I've just found out that the guy at the Easter parade in the barbershop outfit found it – *most* of it – at a Free Stuff corner.'

'Right,' said Kathi.

'And I didn't tell you this but I ran into a medical student at the chicken shop the other night and he was dressed as a punk or a Goth or something,'

'Big difference,' said Todd.

'Not relevant,' I said. 'The point is he was dressed up for a party and I think maybe he got his clobber at a Free Stuff corner too.'

'That's a stretch,' said Kathi.

'His buckle collar had a spike missing. *That's* how I worked out what the spike was, see?'

'You didn't say that,' Todd pointed out, reminding me of the guy in the park for a minute.

'No, I took the glory for a deduction I didn't deserve,' I admitted. 'But that's all by the by. I'm right. The medical student got a discarded Goth outfit – almost complete – right here on this corner. And that twat from Easter got a barbershop quartet outfit with too-long trousers – almost complete – here too. And there was a minstrel on stilts at the Ditch where the Millers were murdered, and a "stripy stick insect" at the Mustang full of their blood and the Millers were near this corner.'

'Why do you keep saying "almost complete"?' said Kathi.

I pointed up with both hands. They raised their heads and saw what I had seen: a red and white bowtie and a black strap with silver chains hanging from one of the branches of the shade tree.

'Oh my golden lamé hotpants!' said Todd. 'We need to speak to Teto again. Because remember who else he said he saw at the Mustang?'

'Vampires?' I said.

'Who look a little like . . .'

'Fuck me, Goths,' said Kathi. 'Todd, you know how you didn't know the Spanish for "stilts"? Is there any chance you don't know the Spanish for "Goth" either? Is there any chance that the Spanish for "Goth" might be "vampiro"?'

'I reckon *Teto* doesn't know the Spanish for Goth,' Todd said.

'So . . . the Millers stopped off here,' said Kathi. 'To see someone, and that someone killed them. And that someone impersonated the locums all weekend afterwards, *perhaps*. Or, perhaps . . .'

'Kathi,' I said. 'I've known you for a lot of years and I can tell this is no short thing you're gearing up to say. Should we really be standing right here, on this very significant corner, possibly visible to a murderer, while you hash it out?'

'Yeek,' said Todd, spurting towards the Jeep. We bustled after him, only pausing – in Kathi's case – to snap a couple of shots of the tree branch with its adornments.

Todd took the wheel and headed due north out of town to the big road that swoops back round to the Ditch. It's got a forty-five miles per hour speed limit and might not be any quicker, given the distance, but certainly gets you away from murderers faster than the short blocks with stop signs at the end. Today, it ended up being a great idea for another reason too.

'OK, here goes,' said Kathi, as we swung round the far north-eastern corner by the Lode supermarket and turned towards the mega-church on the eastern edge of town.

'Teto!' Todd shouted. He hit his indicator and swerved to the hard shoulder, earning a long horn lean and a hand gesture from the car behind him. He blew a kiss back and parked with lights flashing.

We were having a break to get on the trail of a vampire, it seemed. Never a dull moment.

NINETEEN

'Sí,' Teto said. 'El vampiro. Sí. Música punk. Gótico.'

'So not a real vampire?' I said.

Todd translated.

Teto asked a question I didn't quite follow the words of but had no trouble understanding, and the answer would be something like 'Yes, I know there are no real vampires and no I'm not insane', but I didn't trust Todd to translate for me so I kept schtum.

Todd grilled him a bit more and, on account of now knowing the Spanish for stick insect and various types of music sub-culture, I followed along. At least to the extent of getting that he was asking about the other people who had been there, besides the two we knew about. Teto shook his head and spoke quite decisively about there being nothing unusual about them which I understood completely on account of the Spanish for normal being 'normal'.

Then he took off his hat and wiped his head with a spotted handkerchief while looking over at his workers all standing looking back at him, which was basically Esperanto for 'It's boiling hot and I'm out in the sun here, plus we'll never get this field the size of Wales finished if you keep me here much longer'. We thanked him profusely and clambered back into the Jeep, Todd earning another horn blare and middle finger for the way he pulled back out into the traffic again. He puckered up and gave a theatrical 'mwah' out of the side window as we overtook the car in question on the inside and left it in our dust.

'This is a small town,' I said. 'You're going to get followed home and punched one of these days.'

'I would run towards them, calling them "Captain",' said Todd. 'I've done it before. They took off like startled bunnies.'

'But on a related point,' Kathi said, 'since this is such a small town where will we go to discuss what we need to discuss? Home is the obvious choice, but I'm hungry and we did that aspirational grocery shopping again so there's only salad in there. Todd?'

'Me too. Taco stand?' It never takes much to get Todd to the taco stand at that edge of town. It is so-called because its name is 'Top Tacos', but it serves the full enchilada, pun intended. I'm a particular fan of the nachos Mexicanos, a giant platter of puffy homemade triangles heaped high with meat, cheese, beans, sour cream, salsa, avocados (it's state law) and lime wedges. I ordered it today. Todd ate two tacos with salad and beans, but sucked down about a pint of horchata. Kathi went for her traditional two-hand burrito with everything. We had to wait a while before she said a word. When she had re-wrapped the half she'd be having for dinner, possibly with Noleen if they added some of that salad, she wiped her mouth with one of her personal supply of napkins from out of the zipped pouch on her belt and began.

'So,' she said in opening, another state law, 'there were a couple of very memorable individuals at the Ditch that fateful weekend and they tried to draw attention to the Mustang too. Plus there were fake locums. We're looking at four people, minimum. The . . . I can't keep saying barbershop singer. What did you call him, Lexy?'

'I can't remember,' I said. 'A minstrel?'

'Racist but shorter,' Kathi said. 'The minstrel, the Goth, and two locums. And there were others there too. The UCC parents, the big family . . . but none of us were there all weekend and the fake locums messed up the billing so we can't be entirely sure who was where when. It's a classic shell game.'

'What's a shell game?' I said.

'This is getting really old,' said Todd. 'You've been here how many years? "What's a *pop* tart?" "What's a *shell* game?" "What's a *mitzvah*?" It's not cute any more.'

'What's your *problem*?' I said, mimicking him mimicking me. 'I never asked what a pop tart was. I just said I'd never eaten one. As opposed to you having gorged on . . . Eccles cakes during your California childhood, I presume. And I never asked what a mitzvah was either. I just said it was odd to hear it without the "bar" bit for the first time. Like a henge.'

'A henge?' said Todd. 'Like *Stone* Henge?' Then he said, 'Fuck,' because he'd made my point for me.

'So,' I said, smiling sweetly, 'what's a shell game?'

'Welcome back,' said Kathi. 'Shut up, the both of you. OK, we don't know why these people went to the Mustang – to try to get bystanders interested enough to report it? – but we know why they went tramping about the Ditch, don't we? To confuse witnesses and distract from the actual murderers. Right?'

'Or they were the actual murderers,' said Todd.

'And the fake locums just . . . what?' I said. 'Delivered the victims?'

'And anyway,' said Kathi, 'we still don't actually know why the Millers were up there at Free Stuff corner on Friday night.'

'I say we do,' I said. 'I say they knew someone there. We all said this already actually. They came to see if their friends . . . Wait.'

'They came to see if their friends would let them crash and, most unfortunately, their friends not only didn't have a spare room but were also kinda busy planning a murder in a motel?' Kathi said.

'But it worked out well for the dream-streets pals in the end,' said Todd, 'because they'd gone to all that trouble to get the gig and lay in a lot of costumes, but they forgot to choose a victim!'

'Why if their old friends the Millers hadn't knocked on the door, it would all have been a big waste of time!' Kathi supplied.

'Phew!' said Todd.

'OK, OK,' I said, holding up my hands. 'Enough with the sarcasm relay team. Maybe the dream-streets pals aren't the fake locums, but I still say someone from Cuento would be in a better position to be a fake locum than someone who didn't know the town at all.'

'Or there's secret option C,' Todd said. 'They've been to stay at the Ditch on recon. We might have seen these people. Multiple times.'

'If we'd seen them multiple times, we'd have started recognising them,' Kathi said. 'Noleen would.'

'Maybe they're masters of disguise,' I said. I was being flippant, but as I spoke I had that odd sensation I'd come to know

so well over my years of assistant detecting: that of hearing
something come out of my mouth before it had lodged in my
brain, so it felt more as if I was learning it than sharing what
I knew. 'Oh my God,' I said. 'Taylor was right. We should have
done a spreadsheet.'

'Go on,' said Todd.

'I think I know why they used cash and – apart from one
loose end – it explains everything.'

'If we're allowing loose ends, though . . .' Kathi said.

'Real life has *got* loose ends,' I said. 'What I was thinking was
that maybe we don't need fake locums *and* a minstrel *and* a Goth.
We already know the minstrel and Goth weren't real, because
what lifelong Goth or punk or vampire gives his clothes away for
no reason? Ditto the stripy blazer. So what's to stop us saying the
fake locums and the two in costume weren't the same people?'

'How would a spreadsheet help?' said Todd.

'Are you kidding? It would show who was where and when
and who saw who and – crucially – who was never seen in the
same place at the same time. Like . . .'

'Sheldon Cooper and PeeWee Herman,' said Todd.

'David Hyde Pierce and Tilda Swinton,' said Kathi.

I never join in with any of this because they never know who
I'm talking about but, if I felt like wasting comedy gold on them
again, I'd have said Pat Butcher and Bake Off Nelly. Instead, I
said, 'There's only two people. The fake locums, the murderers,
and the barbershop punk mash-up are all the same single couple.
I bet no one saw more than two of them at the same time.'

'And what's the loose end?' said Todd. He was prising the
lid off his Horchata cup to drain the dregs that he couldn't
get to go up his straw.

'One of the lots of people who looked in the Mustang were
nothing to do with the Ditch.'

'The normals,' said Todd.

I sat up again. He had sparked another idea. He knew he had
and he really hated that. And it was worse this time because Kathi
sat up poker straight too. 'That's not what Teto called them the
first time we spoke,' she said. 'Remember what he *did* call them?'

'Los abuelos?' said Todd. 'So?'

'So?' said Kathi. '*So?* That's the other guests that were seen at the Ditch that weekend! The Dungeons and Dragons grandparents!'

'Hardly normal,' I said.

'But what if Teto saw them out of their merch?' Kathi said.

'Devin thought he'd seen the same people in and out of it,' I reminded them.

'No,' said Todd. 'You're both totally reaching. It really is just a loose end. They definitely weren't the locums. They were with the big family who checked in late on Sunday, only they came a little early.'

'Oh come on!' said Kathi.

'No, he's right,' I said. I rubbed my temples as I spoke, because all of this was making my head hurt. 'The D&D abuelos definitely aren't the same people as the fake locums and the other two. They were fat. Devin said so. And I think Taylor saw one of them too. He said "chubby". Dev said "triple X". Anyway, there's no reason at all to suppose the old people who looked in the Mustang are anything to do with the old people who checked into the Ditch, is there? The only people with the time and money to go on trips and look at art in this country are retired boomers.'

'And so why didn't they report the blood then?' said Kathi.

'Because they thought it was "art"?'

Kathi gave a huffy little shrug. 'Hardly "normal",' she muttered, quoting me. 'OK then. Can we go to Molly with what we *have* got? We can tell her there might be DNA on the bowtie and the whatever that was with it.'

'Section of bondage webbing,' said Todd.

'I wasn't asking!' said Kathi. 'Jesus, Todd. We've just had lunch.'

In the end, we decided to stop off at the Ditch first to tell the Millers to brace for developments. It was a two-part plan. We would give them some comfort and we would pre-emptively manipulate Molly into taking us seriously when we went to lay all this on her crowded desk. She wouldn't dare blow us off if the Miller kids were in the wings all set to pester her to death about where our brainwave had led to.

But they were out.

The three of us had trooped over and tried first one door and then the other, getting no reply, then trooped back again and gone to ask Noleen if she knew where they were.

Thus we were right on the spot for the next instalment of proof that spreadsheets are the dog's bollocks, as Taylor put it that evening while we raked it all over in our very particular kind of post-coital glow. I would call it more of a gift from the gods. Or from God, perhaps. *The* God, since it was the early moral teaching of one of His churches that handed it to us. Todd called it karma. He didn't go into any detail about what exactly he had done to earn it. He just nodded quietly and took it as his due. Kathi called it the kind of random occurrence that keeps detectives humble and realistic. She glared at Todd who smiled back beatifically. Noleen called it the easing of a logjam. She expanded by saying that the worst constipation in the world frees up in the end if you keep on eating.

It's a wonder the bringers of the gift, the karma-mongers, the randos, the spreadsheet cell- fillers didn't turn on their heels and leave. Noleen had basically called them shit. And she was wearing a sweatshirt with a picture of a pricklier-than-usual saguaro cactus that said 'Go climb a tree' underneath.

I hadn't seen them last time so I didn't recognise them now, but I've been here long enough and encountered enough midwestern tourists passing through to know what the dowdy, calf-length skirt on this motherly looking woman and the buttoned-up-to-the-collar shirt on the central-casting-dad of a man meant. These were heavy-duty Christians of some kind. They weren't Amish – they'd come bare-headed in an SUV, for one thing – and they weren't the ones with the nun-type scarves either, but they certainly weren't chortlers at rude sweatshirt slogans.

'Hello,' said the man, choosing me as the safest person on offer after dismissing Noleen, lumping Kathi in with her somehow – perhaps a better gaydar than you'd think, and taking a physical step backwards upon glancing at Todd.

'Hi there,' I said. 'Checking in?' His brow twitched at the accent, but he'd take a foreigner over these denizens of Sodom and Gomorrah, apparently.

'No,' he said. 'We came back to apologise and put something right.'

He can't have been expecting the reaction he got. I know my face drained of colour. I've learned how that feels from the inside over my years in Cuento. Todd gaped and put a hand over his heart. It looked performed but that's just his way; he meant it. Kathi widened her stance and took her phone out of its clip. And Noleen said, 'I'm calling the cops and they're real close. Even if you kill us, you'll never get away.'

'There's no need for . . . We came to . . . *Kill* you?' the man said, like a Rolodex of disbelief. He was shocked to his marrow but he was also scrabbling about in the baggy pockets of his khaki trousers, and the thought flashed through my mind that my parents would be devastated and that it's really stupid to have only one child and that they wouldn't even get the chance to tell me they told me so for living in this gun-nuts hellhole of a country.

Then I noticed that what he had plucked out of his pocket was a wallet and I realised that no one in their right mind walked about with a gun in that kind of pocket anyway, all set to blow off a testicle any time he sat down.

Noleen was shouting now. 'You think you can *buy* us?' she yelled, still jabbing at her phone buttons. How long did nine-one-one take, for God's sake? 'You think we look like the kind of people you can *buy*? Well, if that ain't every last damn thing that's wrong with this land I used to love. You and your Sundays-only bullshit and then you worship the God Almighty dollar all week long.'

'Hon?' said Kathi, the first of us to get a clue that what we all thought was going on here couldn't possibly be.

'Now look,' said the woman, stepping forward, all red in the face. 'We are sorry. It was a simple mistake. We are willing to pay a forfeit either to you or to a good cause of your choosing.' She took a breath. 'Within reason.' Todd snorted and the woman flushed a little deeper. 'But kindly stop speaking to us in that un-called-for manner right now. We can still go on Tripadvisor, you know.'

Noleen blinked a couple of times, said, 'Butt dial' into the phone and hung up.

'So you didn't murder two people and hide their bodies then?' said Todd.

Now the stepping back, draining of blood and pressing of hand to heart happened on the other side of the desk. Thankfully neither of them took out a phone to call the police. We all just stood there breathing raggedly and waiting for some of it to start to make sense.

'So . . . who are you?' said Kathi.

'We're the Millers,' the man said. He held out a hand to shake, then switched it up when he saw Todd swaying, and grabbed him by his elbow instead. 'Are you OK? Are all of you intoxicated?'

'You're . . . the . . . Millers?' said Noleen. 'Do Phil and Jilly know you're here?'

'Who?' said the woman. 'What's going on here? Are you all drunk on cannabis? Terry, we should never have come to California. It's been one thing after another.'

'Who's Terry?' said Todd.

'Phil and Jilly, your son and your daughter,' said Kathi.

'You're not the Millers,' I said. 'Jesus Christ, Kathi, I know you said there's always a nutter or two pretending they're the perp, but is *this* normal? Have you ever heard of people pretending to be the victims?'

'Maybe we are "drunk on cannabis",' said Noleen. 'This is as freaky as fu—'

'Stop swearing!' said the woman, sounding genuinely pained. 'What is wrong with everyone in this Godforsaken state?'

Her husband was wrestling something out of his wallet. 'I don't know what you think is going on here,' he said. 'I don't know what your game is. But I am Terrence Miller. This is my driver's licence and I have two sons, called Terrence Jr and Malcolm.'

While he was angrily pulling out his ID, I was just as angrily calling up my saved photos with shaking fingers. And while he was saying his piece, I was saying mine. 'These are the Millers, Mr Whoever You Are. Wait, not them. That's the wrong Press Carmichael's brother.' I scrolled. '*These* are the Millers, Mr Man. In their kayak. Do you do much kayaking? Did you, when you were alive? Hm?'

Which is how come we both said, 'What?', at the same time, like we'd been practising.

'We stayed here,' the wife said. 'Over a Sunday night, the weekend before Easter.'

'No way,' said Todd.

'Huh,' I said. 'Are you by any chance half of a barbershop quartet?'

But the Millers – these new Millers – had had it with me and my nonsense and neither of them answered me.

'We stayed here,' said the wife, trying again. 'With Terrence Jr and his wife, Betsy, and their children. Just one night.'

'You're the big family?' said Todd. 'Oh my Go-tterdammerung revival!' It was a nice swerve and very kind of him to try, but I'm not sure it helped. *Götterdämmerung* always sounds like swearing to me.

'We don't judge the fruitfulness of our children,' said the husband. He so did, though. I could tell.

'We left early,' the wife went on, with a severe look at her husband for judging. Whatever sect they were in, it wasn't full-on surrender for the womenfolk. 'To get back on the road. After our unscheduled stop. And somehow . . . we didn't pay.'

'Yeah, we know,' Noleen said. 'We thought the locums had comped you. But you're saying you pulled a fast one?'

'The who?' said the man. 'Why would someone comp three rooms?'

'*Three* rooms?' said Kathi. 'What?'

'And because we didn't pay,' said the wife, 'we didn't have paperwork, and we couldn't remember the name of the motel – it was dark – and actually we couldn't remember the name of the town except that it was something exotic, so the only way we could put it right was to come back. Which is what we did and I can't for the life of me understand why we're being cursed at and threatened and ridiculed and I wish we had kept the money and saved our time.'

'Or given it to a good cause *within reason*,' said Todd. 'Exotic! It's Spanish.'

'How the he-eck do you check out of a motel and forget to pay?' said Kathi.

'It seemed a little disorganised,' said the man. 'Your weekend managers – the Locums? Was that the name? – seemed young and inexperienced . . . and they weren't really focussed on customer service, we found.'

'No shit, Sherlock,' said Noleen, giving no quarter whatsoever. 'The locums were focussed on murder. The thirteen of you were lucky to get away. Bet you wouldn't of come back to settle up if you known that, huh?'

'Eleven,' said the woman, who we were going to have to start calling Mrs Miller, no matter how confusing it might turn out to be.

'Five kids?' I said, thinking if Noleen had rounded up out of disapproval over their fruitfulness, the Miller dad wasn't the only one judging.

'Seven,' he said. 'Fine by me.' It so wasn't. 'They started at eighteen, see.'

'Eighteen,' I echoed. 'Old enough to vote, serve and procreate. But not drink.' Both Millers frowned at me. 'I'm studying the constitution,' I explained.

'But to get back to the point, Lexy,' said Kathi, 'seven children plus parents and grandparents makes thirteen.'

'Seven plus two plus two makes eleven,' said Mrs Miller.

'You forgot a plus two,' said Noleen. 'The other grandparents. The ones who came separately.'

'Jed and Elias and MaryBeth and JoLouise and Benjy and Mitzi and Cameron's other grandparents?' said Mrs Miller. 'When were *they* here? You getting this, Terry? They were too busy and important to join us on our trip and they came here anyw— How did you know they were related to us, though?'

'What?' said Kathi. 'They were here at the same time as you. They came a night early and left with you. Right?'

'Wrong,' said Mrs Miller. 'They were invited, sure. But they had *plans*. In the *city*.'

'Which city is that?' said Todd, all innocence.

'Columbus,' said Mr Miller, in the tone of voice you'd more usually hear saying 'Vegas' or 'Miami'.

'So . . . the other grandparents,' I said, thinking it through, 'the ones who came on Saturday, were nothing to do with you?

And you need to pay for three rooms? For one night? So the money we got' – Noleen stirred – 'sorry, *you* got . . . was for a Goth that Todd saw on Friday, and a barbershop singer that I saw on Saturday, and a Dungeons and Dragons pair of abuelos that Devin saw . . . sometime. Three rooms. Nothing missing.'

'Roger saw Miss Pixie,' said Todd. 'If she's not the Goth guy, one room was comped.'

'Is "Miss Pixie" a drag queen?' said Mrs Miller.

'Thank you!' said Todd. 'That's ballpark what I said.'

'It's nothing like what you said,' said Noleen.

'And are we three for three at the Mustang full of blood after all?' said Todd, ignoring her.

'Uhhhhhh,' said Mr Miller, 'if it's all the same with you' – he swivelled his eyes around, searching in vain for somewhere to rest them – 'we'll just settle up and get on back to Idaho. We won't say a word on Tripadvisor. And we won't be back.'

Noleen started clicking at her keyboard, generating a bill for the too-honest-to-live Millers. I flashed my eyes at Todd and Kathi, drawing them away. I had thought of a way to tie this all up in a bow for Molly.

'Devin isn't ageist,' I said, once we were outside and away from all ears. 'So why did he call the D&D couple grandparents?' It was all just about to fall into place.

'Duh,' said Kathi. 'Kid stuff in their car.'

'Correct,' I said. 'How about Teto? Ageism or some other reason he said "abuelos"?'

Todd whistled.

'Follow me,' I said. 'I can explain everything.'

Except where the bodies were or who had killed them or why, that is.

Baby steps, though. Pun, once again, fully intended.

TWENTY

'And I think I even know why the murderers used a Free Stuff corner,' I said, hustling out of the office and along to Devin's work room. 'Cross everything you can cross without fractures,' I added and rapped on the door.

'Sopen!' came Devin's voice.

The rooms at the Ditch are all pretty much the same. If you've been in a traditional roadside motel, you've seen them. But when people live in a place permanently, they make it their own in subtle and not-so-subtle ways. Della had made *her* place her own back when she shared it with Baby Diego. Nice wooden furniture, bright blankets and throws, colourful pottery plates and cups displayed on the shelves in the kitchenette. When Devin moved in, the only thing that changed was that he got space in the drawers to keep his clothes and one hanger in the wardrobe to store his only suit.

In this room, Devin's old place, now his workspace, it was a different story. He had lived amongst a chaos of skateboards, discarded clothes, unneeded power cables and actual litter, never changing his sheets or pairing his socks or caring about crumbs. These days the only thing that looked the same was his desk with its screens, wires and fans. The rest of it was still cluttered, but with Diego's fishtank, Hiro's playpen, boxes of the family's out-of-season clothes and a jetsam of toys that looked like a mid-sized Target had exploded. I gave the place a good once-over and felt my heart sink. The wardrobe was open and plastic storage tubs were stacked in there up to the hanging rail. There was no other place to stash anything.

'Did you sell it?' I said.

'Sell what?' said Todd and Kathi. They didn't have Terrence Miller's and my perfect timing but it was still a chorus.

'No,' said Devin.

'Did you put it back?' I said.

'I went by but that corner burned out *fast*.'

'What are you talking about?' said Todd.

'Did you donate it?' I asked.

'Not yet,' said Devin.

'Cross your digits, folks,' I said. 'Devin, is it by any chance still in the boot?'

'What are you talking about?' said Kathi.

'I couldn't work out what to do with it,' Devin said. 'I'm waiting for Dell to find it and tell me what's best.' That poor woman, I thought, and not for the first time, even though Devin's over-reliance on his wife, slacker passivity and general hopelessness was working in my favour today.

'The baby seats from the D&D abuelos got put at the Free Stuff corner on Eleventh, just like the minstrel get-up and the Goth gear,' I said. 'And Devin found them there.'

'Huh?' Devin said.

'Car keys,' said Kathi, with the universal gimme gesture.

'But don't touch anything,' I said, scampering after her once Devin had chucked his fob her way and she'd headed back out again. 'Because I reckon they put it all at the corner to make sure it disappeared and got covered in a DNA smorgasbord on its way, but because Devin scooped his portion pretty much immediately and marooned it in his boot, there might be lift-able prints somewhere.'

'But every mad salivating murderer knows to wear gloves,' said Todd.

'Not if they're pretending to be a pair of harmless Dungeons and Dragons-loving grandma and grandpa on a sunny spring weekend they don't,' I said.

Kathi popped Devin's boot and we stood in an arc gazing at the haul.

'But none of the actual D&D stuff?' Kathi said. 'The merch?'

'Are you kidding?' said Todd. 'That would be long gone. The first UCC student to mooch past the corner after it dropped would have that plucked and on his own back, head and feet before you could say "cash-free economy". Pfft.'

'Shame,' said Kathi. 'Maybe Molly has the manpower to

ask around town for who the hardcore Free Stuff corner boys are and find out that way. It's not one of my regulars.'

'I don't think it's one of anyone's regulars,' I said. 'I reckon what the Millers' killers – the other Millers, I mean, the first Millers—'

'The skinny Millers,' said Todd. 'We know who you mean.'

'The dead Millers,' Kathi said. 'That's their main feature for me.'

'Right,' I said. 'Bill and Billie. I reckon their car was up at Free Stuff corner on Friday night *after* they were killed. I reckon their murderers – locums, vampire and minstrel—'

'Also skinny, as it happens,' said Todd.

'God almighty,' said Kathi. 'Lexy, can't you do something about his body fascism? Is it in the DSM-5 yet? Also "the murderers" picks them out of a crowd all on its own, ya know?'

'Right,' I said. 'No, it's not. Body dysmorphia and all the attendant eating disorders are in there, but Todd is a healthy weight.' Kathi smirked; he would worry at away that 'jibe' all day. 'I think the murderers stocked the corner of Eleventh with a loading dose of excellent Free Stuff to get the word out about a new hotspot and ensure that all the discarded distraction clobber got picked up and taken away in good time once the plan was up and running.'

'Although if the Millers were already dead, that plan was all the way up, and running like Usain Bolt,' Todd pointed out.

'Molly is going to hate everything about this,' Kathi said.

'Except the fact that we can't put out an APB to find everyone who took stuff from that corner and she can,' I said.

'You have no idea what an APB is, do you?' said Todd.

'BOLO?' I tried.

'I'll do the talking,' said Kathi.

'Even though *I* saw the Goth gear on the medical student and *I* saw the Easter minstrel twice?' I said.

Kathi put her finger and thumb either side of the bridge of her nose and rubbed hard. I couldn't help smiling. I should have been sorry that I'd bugged her but all I could think about was the fact that she had handled Devin's car key and then touched her face. She was getting better, whether she knew it or not. 'I'll do the talking,' she repeated, once she was done. 'Let's go.'

'Are we taking the whole car as is?' I said.

'Do you mean, can you keep some of it in case you need it?' said Todd.

'My God, if bugging your pals was in the DSM-5,' I said, 'you'd be in maximum security by now. No, Todd, I meant do we transfer it to the Jeep instead.'

'The whole point was that no one else touches any of this,' Todd said. 'But "we" means you two. It was out on a street corner and God knows what crawled in around the nooks and crannies. I'm not getting in beside it. I'll meet you there.' So he was lagging behind Kathi in recovery, but he'd get there.

'And . . . we're sure about this?' said Kathi. 'Dead sure the D&D abuelos weren't randos?'

'Who paid cash for their room,' Todd said. 'By coincidence.'

'And had a load of baby stuff in the car but no baby,' I reminded him.

'Totally unrelated baby stuff to the baby stuff that was offloaded at Free Stuff corner,' Kathi added, starting to nod. She was convincing herself, and about time too. 'I'd still be happier if we could say they were *all* the same two people.'

'Instead of four,' agreed Todd. 'Thank God for the American diet, huh? If the D&D abuelos weren't chubsters we'd be taking a fairy tale to Molly.'

'Good point,' I said. 'It doesn't matter if it's not neat, so long as it's true. And I'm happy to believe it needed four people to carry this off. Let's go.'

We totally didn't see what scorn was coming our way. We should have done the spreadsheet. We had missed something.

Give her her due, she heard us out and wrote everything down. She sent a junior officer to go and look at the tree to see if a cherry-picker was needed or if a pair of telescope-handled tongs could get the evidence out of the branches, and she personally snapped on a pair of her blue gloves and lifted the baby stuff out on to a tarp she had spread on the ground beside Devin's car, battling with a monster case of static that stuck the plastic both to itself and her trousers for so long that she was puffing by the time she'd untangled it.

'You need to powder that down,' Kathi said. 'Get it sliding smoothly again.'

'Great idea,' said Molly. 'Introduce a whole load of extra dust for the guys to deal with.' She had a point, but she didn't deserve the frown – deep and dark and long – that Kathi gave to her.

'OK,' she said, when she had whistled over a couple of uniforms to deal with the equipment and snapped those blue gloves off again. 'So your idea is that these belonged to the grandparents who dressed in youthfully branded clothing and stayed at the motel the same weekend as the two people who impersonated the stand-in managers and intermittently dressed in different outlandish clothing? That all you got?'

It wasn't, of course. We also had the fact that people without kids in tow had been seen at the Mustang and referred to as 'abuelos'. But we didn't want to drop Teto in the PD's lap and Taylor had only been primed to lie about the minstrel. So I decided, for all of us, to run with it. 'You think that's a stretch,' I said, 'we nearly swallowed the idea that all six of them were the same two. Sometimes in costume and sometimes in mufti. Except they were different weights. Four skinny and two not.'

'Two things,' said Molly. 'Mufti? And,' she turned to Todd, 'I can't believe the other solution got past *you*, Santa.'

Todd's brow twitched. Kathi snorted.

'It's an army term for "out of uniform",' I said.

'Damn!' said Todd.

'Got to hand it to you Brits sometimes,' Molly said. 'That is a useful word. So's "locums".'

'Bugger it,' said Todd. I had no idea what he was using Brit slang to talk about.

'You've got "docent" and "intern",' I pointed out to Molly.

'And we don't use the same word for a sex worker and her lawyer,' said Kathi, eternally tickled by the word 'solicitor' when I used it, which I tried not to.

'Feck,' said Todd, hopping across the Irish Sea.

'But you call a "lolly" a crossing guard like he's out of *Dr Zhivago*,' I shot back at Kathi.

'Thank you for bringing me this,' Molly said. 'We'll check it for prints along with the bowtie and the belt.'

'It's probably not a bel—'

'I don't!' said Molly, holding up a hand like she was back on traffic. 'Want to know.'

'And will you be keeping this baby stuff?' said Todd. 'Afterwards? Only Lexy was saying that it might come in handy.'

'When was *this*?' I squeaked. Todd was over every line, truly.

'Is that right?' Molly said, her face softening.' Well, congratulations. Good for you.'

And whether it was the stress of the case or the grinding tension of waiting for the Millers' bodies to turn up, or the thought that I was so far north of thirty and I didn't need any of this baby clobber, actually, or that Todd was driving me demented, or that I was too hard on Molly and she was OK really, my eyes were suddenly shiny with tears.

'I'm not pregnant,' I blurted.

'Yet,' said Todd. 'But,' he added to Molly, 'they're trying.'

'You people are weird,' Molly said, and took herself off back into the building, leaving us to trail home in two cars, but on speakerphone, bickering about whether she was right. It was two against one but the one was Todd and if he had been squashable none of that would just have happened in the first place.

'Why did she call you "Santa"?' I asked him, to change the subject. Kathi snorted again.

'I can't believe we didn't think of it,' said Todd. 'We said "masters of disguise" and we knew they had costumes. And the worst thing is, Molly just *loved* reminding me.'

'Of?' I said.

'Fat suits,' said Kathi. 'We need to ask Devin for more detail. And we need to go back to the dream streets. Ask around the houses nearest that corner. See if anyone noticed them being dumped there.'

'What do fat suits look like anyway?' I said.

'Neoprene onesies,' said Todd. 'I wore one once to play Santa.'

'You–You played Santa?' I said.

'Why not?' said Todd. 'Because I'm *gay*?'

'Literally the only thing about you that doesn't matter,' said Kathi.

'Oh! Because I'm brown?'

'No one's right to be Santa should be denied or abridged on account of race or colour,' I said. 'Sorry! But this time it *is* relevant. Or else why does Molly care? Talk about over-policing.'

'Well, to be fair to Molly,' said Todd, 'she only became involved when the . . . occasion got a little out of hand.'

'What occasion was it anyway,' I asked, 'where a young, slim, brown-skinned, clean-shaven man was first choice for Santa?'

'Duh,' said Todd. 'Christmas. Let's go.'

The Miller kids were poolside when we arrived at the Ditch, each of them on a sun lounger – if you came from Seattle, I suppose the spring weather in California would strike you as pretty clement. They turned and followed us with anxious eyes as we stepped down and, while we were still a good way off, Phil shouted, 'Any news?'

'We have made some progress, actually,' Kathi said. 'We've just been to report to Sergeant Rankinson.'

'Not–Have you–Is it—?' said Jilly, sitting up and hugging her knees hard into her chest.

'You parents haven't been found,' said Todd. That's the thing about him. He drives you within an inch of your sanity and then he goes and does something as thoughtful and kind as working out what a new orphan can't bring herself to say and letting her down gently.

Jilly Miller slumped back, making the webbing of the sun lounger squeak and its legs rock. None of the Ditch's furnishings was top of the range.

'And it might be nothing,' said Kathi. 'Just elimination. Some people were seen at the Mustang while it was parked by the Patsy Denoni and we're slowly accounting for them.'

Both Miller kids looked at her with meerkatty expressions, ready to hear a whole lot more. But it was all so strange and twisted it seemed disrespectful to start in on it – minstrels and Goths and kink aids in shade trees – that in the end she just gave them each a sad smile and walked over to bug Devin again.

TWENTY-ONE

'S open!' Devin called, just like last time. 'Hey, look who it is twice in one day. I'm not giving away any more baby gear, so don't ask me.'

'It's not that,' I assured him.

My face must have been serious. He took one clamshell headphone off and let it clap against the hair behind his ear. I could tell from the way he worked his jaw that he'd been wearing them for hours. I wondered how long it had been since he last stood up. Then I reminded myself that he was an adult.

'The D&D abuelos,' Todd said. 'Can you tell us everything you remember about them?'

Kathi let out a low moan and sure enough Devin went back over every scrap of merchandise the couple had been wearing: the classic Venger hoodie, the classic fanny pack, the Tiamat hoodie, the two pairs of roll-to-win pool slides, the Mimic fanny-pack and the frankly incomprehensible baseball caps. This time, though, I noticed something.

'Why do you always hesitate when you mention their hats?' I said.

'Do I?' said Devin, unconvincingly.

'You do. You say that they wore – big pause – polywhatsit die caps. What is a *die* cap anyway?'

'It's a cap with a die on it,' said Devin. I glanced at Kathi and Todd. They were glancing at me. 'Die,' said Devin. 'One die, two dice?'

'Aren't all dice polyhedral?' Kathi said. 'That means "many-sided", right?'

Devin nodded. He stared at us for a moment or two then seemed to come to some decision. 'Look, there are seven dice in D&D,' he said. 'Tetrahedron, cube, pentagonal trapezo-hedron, octahedron, dodecahedron and icosahedron.'

'That's only si—' I tried to say.

'There are two pentagonal trapezohedrons in a set,' he said.

'Of course there are,' said Kathi. 'And?'

'And, OK, you're really going to make me say this? I saw those caps and I couldn't tell what kind of dice were on them.'

We waited. Then we realised that was it.

'That's it?' said Todd.

'I couldn't even tell if they were the same or different,' said Devin, his voice betraying real anguish.

'That's *it*?' said Todd again. He turned to Kathi and me. 'How can a man with a job, a wife and two kids have absolutely no life?'

'Dev,' I said. 'That is the best news you possibly have given us. Hallelujah!'

'Are you being kind?'

'I'm not. You really hated not being able to tell, right? Like turn in your geek badge and crawl away in shame?'

'See?' said Kathi. 'She's not being kind. Where you headed, Lexy?'

'So you probably scrutinised them?'

'Yep,' said Devin, very clipped. He still wasn't over it.

'So you'd definitely know what sort of size they were?'

'Size?' said Devin. 'They were baseball caps, Lexy. Look, I'll show you.'

He lifted his phone and started thumbing buttons.

The three of us gaped at one another. Kathi found her voice first. 'Dev,' she said, 'are you saying you took a photo of the merch?'

'Hm?' said Devin.

'Are you saying you've had a picture of these people's heads all this time and didn't tell anyone?' said Todd.

'What? No,' Devin said. 'I'm showing Lexy what size a baseball cap is.'

'Please don't,' I said. I've got an already large but steadily growing aversion to being shown photos on someone's phone in lieu of conversation or a quick sketch or, in this case, someone holding out their hands a skull's width apart. And anyway, he had completely misunderstood me. 'I know what a baseball cap is,' I said. 'I know online games manufacturers don't reproduce the hats from the horse race in *My Fair Lady*.'

'Dungeons and Dragons isn't an onl—' Devin began, but I shut him down.

'What I was asking,' I said, 'was the S, M, L or XL of it all. And even that was only a way in to asking you if these people had . . .' I didn't want to say it.

'Fat faces and bulging necks to go with their out-of-shape bods,' Todd obliged. 'Or – and this is the more interesting possibility – if they had strangely thin faces and reedy necks rising out of all that flesh.'

'Huh?' said Devin.

'We reckon they might have been wearing fat suits,' said Kathi. 'Waddaya think? And hey, you didn't happen to see discarded fat suits when you picked up the baby seats from the Free Stuff pile, did you?'

'How would I know if they were wearing fat suits?' Devin said. 'They had long-sleeve sweatshirts on, like I told you.'

'Listen to what we're saying though,' I said. 'Think of a thin person . . . Anyone.'

'Steve from Odies,' said Devin.

I sighed. Devin had picked the only skeleton with chipmunk cheeks I had ever seen. 'Well, then, think of a chubby person.'

'Belin—'

'Not Belinda from UPS!' said Kathi. Belinda, as round as a nut in her brown uniform, had cheekbones like David Bowie in his coke years.

'OK, never mind examples,' I said. 'Devin, you know how most fat people have fat faces and most thin people have thin faces?'

'Do they though?' said Devin. Why the hell he had decided he was a philosopher all of a sudden was beyond me. I decided to get my own back on him.

'Look.' I fished out my phone and called up my saved pics. 'Lean bodies, lean faces, basic jerky from head to toe,' I said, showing him the photo of the Millers in their kayak. I swiped it away and showed him the picture of the unknown brother and sister-in-law of the wrong Press Carmichael up there in

SeaTac. 'And then this pair of beachballs. From their chubby cheeks to their swollen ankles. They go together. You can tell they're not wearing fat suits, right? Right, Devin? You see?'

'That's not the D&D abuelos,' Devin said.

'Yeah, I know, but—'

'So . . . why did you want me to tell you what size *their* heads were?'

Kathi was massaging in between her brows again, 'To gauge whether it was nuts to think they had fat suits on,' she said. 'Like we've just been *saying* to you.'

'The abuelos?'

'Yes, Devin, the abuelos,' I said. 'The people we've been talking about since the early fourteenth century when we came in here.'

'But, even hypothetically,' Devin said, as Kathi made a small moaning noise, 'why did you think they were fat?'

'Because you told us their clothes were XXL,' I said.

'The abuelos?'

'God give me strength,' I said. Devin had turned me into my own granny. 'Yes!'

'Wait,' Devin said. 'Is that why you asked me what size their clothes were? Like you asked about hats instead of heads?'

'In the name of the risen Christ,' said Todd. He didn't go to Catholic school and so didn't have Kathi's early training, but he had all three seasons of *Derry Girls*, and Devin had turned him into Sister Michael.

'Cos like . . .' Devin said, opening his hands at his sides.

It took me a minute to twig what he was showing us, and when I did I groaned. That's how I knew that all three of us had got it at more or less the same moment: our three groans made a chord of anguish. Because, of course, no one who wears D&D merch has it tailored to fit. Devin himself, as he had just indicated by opening his arms like St Francis waiting for sparrows to alight on them, was built like Ichabod Crane and was dressed in John Goodman's cast-offs. Before he lost all the weight.

'Devin,' I said, and the effort to stay calm was making my voice tremble, 'we have been trying to work out whether the

Goth and the minstrel – it's not fucking racist, Kathi! There have been minstrels since they invented the fucking *lute*! – and the locums and the D&D abuelos were all the same people. Twatting on about fat suits! And now you reveal . . .' Words failed me.

'Why are you yelling and swearing at Kathi?' said Devin.

'Because I won't kill Kathi with my own two bare hands. And if I start in on you I just might. I am having some very seditious thoughts right now, Devin. Green-card-shredding thoughts about punishments both cruel and unusual but not excessive.'

'Wow,' said Devin. 'That's not what sedition is, Lexy. You mean generally un-American. And like I said – wow. It was you guys who kept on about the abuelos instead of . . . you know.'

'Pretend we don't,' Todd said.

'And anyway,' Devin said. 'Why were you asking me when it turns out you already know?' he said. 'I'm confused.'

'When we already know what?' said Todd. 'I'm confused too.'

'That they were really and truly kinda chunky,' Devin said. 'Not just bundled up in bodysuits.'

'Who was?' said Kathi.

'The locums weren't fat,' I said. 'Della said so.'

'And the abuelos weren't fat,' said Kathi. 'Despite their shirt sizes.'

'And the Goth and minstrel,' said Todd. 'So who are *you* talking about, Devin?'

'Them,' Devin said, holding my phone out to me. 'I'm not trying to be a dick here, but what is it you want, you know?'

'Devin,' I said, 'the people in that pic on my phone are just examples of chubby people. I'm not trying to say they were here that weekend.'

'Sure they were,' Devin said. 'They were here the same weekend as the fake locums. The weekend everyone was coming and going. *I* saw them, Lexy. Not you.'

Aware that my eyes were so wide and unblinking that they had started to dry out, I leaned forward to take my phone out of his hand. 'You're telling me,' I said, 'that these two people stayed at the motel the weekend of the murder?'

'Yup,' said Devin. 'I thought you knew that. What with the pic and all.'

'But they weren't the locums? Or the D&D abuelos? Or anyone else we've been talking about?'

'Nope,' said Devin. 'Who are they?'

'They are the Millers of Tacoma, Washington,' I said.

Devin practically threw my phone back at me and then wiped his hand on his jeans as if he was eating Cheez-Its. 'No way,' he said. 'I thought they were killed on Friday. They were here till Sunday? They can't have been. I'm wrong. I'm no good with faces. Sorry.'

'Devin, this is serious,' Todd said. He's so obsessed with staying youthful that he rarely if ever acts as much older than Devin as he is. Right now, he was making an exception.

'What about Taylor?' said Kathi. 'He saw the chubby rando in boring clothes too, didn't he?'

'The chubby *not* rando,' said Todd. 'Has Taylor seen the pic you got from . . . What kind of name is "Press"?'

I was clicking buttons. 'Texting it to him right now,' I said. 'Of course, he might not remember. If the guy had had a pigeon on his head, we'd be in business, but you know Taylor.'

'I thought I knew us,' said Kathi. 'But we're not firing on even half our cylinders.'

'We were distracted by distractions,' said Todd. 'Don't beat yourself up.'

'It's OK for you,' said Kathi. 'I'm the one with the licence here. I'm the one who signed the contract. I'm not just rubbing feet and stroking egos.'

'That's not . . .' said Todd. 'We need to reset and not waste a moment feeling dumb. We need to talk! Now!'

'Before you go though,' Devin said. 'Can I just ask you this one thing? If *they're* the Millers, like who is that in the canoe?'

TWENTY-TWO

'Who *is* that in the canoe?' I said. It was my turn. Todd had said it first, once we were in the Jeep with the windows closed where no one could overhear us. Kathi had said it next, as we pulled out of the forecourt, headed God knows where. I was the one who got an answer.

'It's the Millers,' Kathi said.

And then a very strange thing happened. I ducked. I didn't decide to duck; my brain wasn't involved in the process at any stage. I simply found myself doubled over in the passenger seat below the level of the windows. Expecting to hear the start of some extensive wind-up from the other two, I turned my head to the side and saw Todd, still driving but scooched all the way down in his seat too, knees round the steering wheel and just about strangling himself with the chest bit of the seatbelt. I twisted round. Kathi was owl-eyed but not within a million miles of laughing.

'What's up?' she said.

'I thought you meant . . .' said Todd. He braked and pulled over. It's a back road but it's still not a great idea to drive when you can't see over the steering wheel.

'What?' said Kathi.

'I thought . . .' said Todd. But again he ran dry. He checked all his mirrors, then signalled to the empty road stretching as far as the underpass in one direction and as far as the eye could see in the other, pulled out again and drove sedately towards the downtown, hands at ten and two, speedometer on twenty.

'What?' said Kathi again. I didn't blame her for being confused. Todd had never had an unexpressed thought in his life. He had clearly just experienced the same phenomenon as me: his body had reacted and his brain was playing catch-up.

'When you said, "It's the Millers",' I began, 'you meant the couple in the kayak, right?'

'I think so,' said Kathi. 'Even though that makes no sense at all. Did you think I was saying, "Oh there they are, lying by the side of the road. I wonder why we didn't notice them before?"'

'No,' I said.

'Why'd you duck?' said Kathi.

'Why *would* someone duck to not see a two-week-old corpse?' said Todd. 'You'd shut your eyes surely?'

'If you were driving?' said Kathi. 'Say that ain't true or get out right now and let me take over.'

'You duck,' I said, slowly, 'so that someone can't see *you*.'

'Right,' said Todd. 'What . . .?'

'And,' I said, even slower if anything, 'the picture in the kayak must be the Millers, like Kathi just said, because it was their kids who gave it to the cops and the *Voyager*.'

'Shit,' said Todd. 'I just realised why I ducked.'

'Me too,' I said.

'Cool,' said Kathi. 'Nice for you both. Any chance you're gonna tell me?'

'We thought you meant you'd seen the Miller kids,' I said. Todd hissed a soft *yes* under his breath. 'And we didn't want them to see us. On account of how . . . they handed over a fake picture of their parents.'

'After,' said Todd, 'they killed them.'

We were at the police station by now and, in total, bone-chilling silence, Todd signalled, turned in and parked.

'Yes,' Kathi said, calmly enough considering. 'That's right. They killed their parents. In our motel. On a tarp that Jilly Miller shouldn't have known all about. That single mistake has been bugging me since the moment I heard her blowing what she should have kept quiet. It was like a shred of barbecue stuck in my molars.'

'Lovely image,' I said. 'What's been bugging me is their other single mistake: dropping one tiny little buckle-collar spike under the bed.'

'And trying really hard to get it back again,' Todd said,

stealing my point and making it for me. 'Got to hand it to them. But those aren't their only single mistakes, in my book.'

He paused. If I had known what he was going to say I'd have stolen his point right back.

'There's no way in hell they should have wanted to stay at the Ditch,' Kathi said, doing it for me. 'There's no way in hell they should have wanted to be within a hundred miles of the place.'

'And no bloody wonder Jilly thought Phil might wring her neck for mentioning Auntie Press,' I said. 'God almighty, if I'd let it slip that I'd been in touch! Christ, if they knew I had a photo of their real parents! I need to text Taylor back and tell him not to say a word to anyone about anything. And get him to delete that fat Millers pic from his phone too.'

'And now, finally, we hand everything over to Molly,' Kathi said. 'Right? Right. That's what we're doing, Todd? Yeah, that's what we're doing.'

'Once we get our story straight,' said Todd. 'Don't look at me like that and stop having both halves of the conversation. It's freaky. I don't mean story straight like *that*. I mean, ducks in a row, pages collated, loins girded, you know.'

'OK, but we better be quick,' Kathi said. 'And we better be chill.'

'Neither one of you two has ever been chill in your—' I tried to say.

'OK! We better *look* chill,' said Todd. 'God knows who's watching.'

We shut ourselves in Kathi and Noleen's owners' apartment. That's how freaked out we were. The boat – our usual meeting place – was too open; too many doors and windows and the porch too. And Todd's room was a place the Miller kids had been in and out of getting pampered and cared for; there was too much chance they'd come knocking, looking for more. But no one would think of coming to the owners' flat if they couldn't find Kathi in the Skweek. It was testament to how flabbergasted she was by this development that she let Todd and me across the threshold.

She gave us over-booties and hairnets just inside the door but she didn't try to make us put on paper suits. I thought that was progress until she explained that, because she did our laundry, she knew our clothes were clean. 'If you'd been wearing those jeans you think you can get four days out of, Lexy,' she said, 'you would be sitting on a roll of butcher paper. I wish you would just put them in the hamper at the end of each day. It's not as if the laundromat is a long way off. You know what? This might be displacement. Ignore me.'

'So,' Todd said, 'the Miller kids killed their parents. Is that a thing people actually do, Lexy?'

'Why the hell are you asking me?' I said. 'It's not a Scottish tradition, no.'

'I meant psychologically,' said Todd.

'Oh. OK. Um, patricide and matricide? Not really. Mercy killings of the elderly do happen but usually one at a time and even the really twisted murders tend to be single kids in tight co-dependency with single parents. Two siblings whacking both parents at once isn't something I've ever heard of outside fiction. Are they rich? Were they? The Millers. The Mustang was swanky but it was only a hire car. And the kids don't look rich, do they?'

'Maybe that's the point,' Kathi said. 'Rich parents and greedy, broke kids.'

'I suppose there's no reason to doubt that those two *are* the Miller kids, is there?' Todd said. 'They're "very close". What if they're a couple and not siblings at all?'

'What if they're both,' I said. 'I would find the rest of it easier to believe if it was twisted dysfunction all the way down.'

'OK, Virginia Andrews,' said Kathi.

'Who?'

'Lucky you,' said Todd. 'Don't google her. And stop adding garnish. It's bad enough without you making stuff up. So. How are we going to sell this to Molly without her ordering a psych eval for the three of us?'

I drew in a breath to start composing an answer but before I could speak, someone hammered on the owners' apartment's front door. For the second time in an hour and my life, I ducked. Once again, I wasn't alone.

'It's them!' breathed Todd.

'They must have been watching,' Kathi whispered.

'And they must have worked out that we're on to them,' I whispered back.

'How?' Todd mouthed.

'It doesn't matter,' Kathi murmured. In her panic, her voice was less soft than it had been.

'Sssshhhh!' I said and, as is so often the case, it whistled out louder than anything else preceding it.

The pounding on the door came again.

'Maybe they just want a chat,' Todd whispered. His face was as desperate as his voice would have been if his voice had been loud enough to express desperation.

'No way,' I said, soft again. 'That's a copper's knock.'

'Oh for God's sake!' said Kathi at full volume. 'Yes, it is. The mountain has come to Mohammad.'

She threw open the door to reveal Molly on the doorstep. 'Come in,' she said, relief making her giddy.

Molly strolled in, unaware of what a huge deal this was. She threw a look at Todd's and my hairnets and bootees and frowned. 'Are you tampering with evidence again?'

'Again?' said Todd. 'We brought you the baby stuff in the car where we found it and we didn't even try to get the tie and strap out of that tree. How did that go by the way?'

'We've got them both.'

'The strap and the tie?' I said, because for one wild moment the way she said it had made me hope that she meant the Miller kids were both clapped in irons in the back seat of a cop car.

'You've really got to grips with pronouns there, Lexy,' Molly said. 'Yes, the strap and the tie. But what I came to tell you was that the baby equipment might be very useful.'

'Oh?' I said.

'It's clean,' said Molly. 'I mean it's brand-new. It has never had a baby's butt anywhere near it. No drool, no juice, no Triscuit crumbs, no puke, no poop, no pee.' Kathi was breathing hard. 'And only two sets of fingerprints. One of which I assume belongs to Mr Muelenbelt. Which is why I'm here. To persuade him to give us a set for comparison. I thought you could help with that.'

Kathi made a noise that sounded like a town in Wales.

'Exactly,' Molly said. 'He'd give his right arm to defund the entire department but he won't give a smudge of ink to help us nail a killer.'

'We'll make up for him,' Todd said. 'We think we know who did it. We were on our way to tell you when you arrived.'

'What did you hear me say?' said Molly. 'Did I say I needed help to work out whodunnit?'

'You won't turn it down though, right?' I asked her.

'If you've got any corroborating evidence,' said Molly. 'Lay it on me.'

'Corroborating?' I said. 'What do you mean?'

'We know who killed the Millers,' Molly said. 'We've been building a case. We're hoping the prints on the baby seats are going to help with that.'

'You know who killed the Millers?' said Kathi. 'Are you sure? Can you listen to an alternate theory for five minutes? And then I can give you Devin's fingerprints. If latents are OK.' She saw my frown. 'He touched one of the high stools in Reception two days ago, after I'd just cleaned them all. But I didn't notice which one it was – because I'd moved them to clean them all – and I didn't have time to do the whole lot again, so I just moved the two potentials into the back room until I could inspect them.'

Oh, Kathi.

'You've got five minutes exactly,' Molly said. 'And yes, latents will do. It's just that we don't usually rely on them because we can't usually get them because most people are normal. Outside of this motel, I mean. Obviously.'

Cautiously, then, we set out what we knew, building a case that even Molly couldn't dismiss without at least a bit of consideration. I argued that Jilly Miller's obsession with the spike meant she knew about the buckle collar and that she also knew about new tarp, for no reason. Todd, the body fascist, pointed out that Phil and Jilly shared a common general frame with the Goth, the Minstrel, the fake locums and the D&D abuelos. Kathi spoke of the weirdness in them being happy to stay at the Ditch where their parents were supposed to have died. Then I took a second shot and told Molly I'd been in touch with Press Carmichael of Tacoma, Washington, to ask about her relatives, and she had sent me the picture that Devin had only just confirmed was of motel guests on the fateful weekend and I thought Taylor had seen one of them too.

'And you see what this means, don't you?' I said. 'Phil and Jilly gave a fake photo of their parents to the *Voyager* and to you.'

'Yep,' said Molly. Laconic to a fault as she might be, this was still a stupendous lack of reaction.

'Also,' said Todd after sharing a quick frown with the other two of us, 'the time of the murder might have changed. Depending on when Taylor and Devin saw who they saw. Even though the Mustang was at the Patsy Denoni on Friday.' He sighed. 'If only one of the people who looked in the car window had been legit, we could—'

'What's this now?' Molly said.

'Oh,' said Todd. 'Right. Huh.'

'Lexy?' Molly said.

'Er,' I said. 'So. Um.'

'Mrs Muntz?'

'Well,' said Kathi. 'Yeah. No.'

'Or,' said Todd, just as Molly was about to blow her top, and who could have blamed her. 'Think of it this way. Yes, we didn't tell you something. But we knew it all along and it didn't help identify the culprits, so no harm done. And, of course, we just identified the culprits for you. So there's that too.'

'Right,' Molly said. 'You just identified the culprits for me. Because we got a photograph of the victims from the newspaper who got it from close relatives and we ran with it. No need to check anything. No need for any formal documentation. We looked at the obviously faked ID in the car and we just opened wide and swallowed whole. Maybe it's because we were so bamboozled by why on earth a suspect would try to take evidence from the crime scene. Is that why we didn't try to find out anything about these Millers for ourselves? Jimin-*ee* Christmas! How dumb do you think we are over there? How dumb do you think I am sitting here?'

'Wait,' Kathi said. 'Are you saying you already knew the Miller kids killed their parents?'

Molly said nothing, only raised and lowered one eyebrow and then the other, before settling both in a stern frown.

'And you left them here in our motel?' said Todd, pressing a hand against his chest. 'Without telling us?'

'While we built a case,' said Molly.

'Knowing that they had employed us to look into the killing for them?'

Molly straightened out her eyebrows and did a classic double-take, possibly even a triple. 'What?' she said, in voice that could have refrozen the melting icecaps from right here in California, no need to journey northwards.

'They said they weren't sure you were really on top of it and wanted us to help,' I explained. 'Help with counselling and pampering as well as—' I was trying to soften it. I was failing.

'As well as interfering in the case and undermining our work?' said Molly.

'When all along our only place in their unfolding story should be if we get picked to serve on their jury in accordance with—'

'Can it, Lexy,' Todd said. Then he turned on Molly. 'Why are *you* giving *us* a hard time? We got lied to. We got duped. We'll probably never get paid.'

'*And* we were in danger,' said Kathi. 'What happened to protect and serve? Because obviously, the Miller kids *didn't* hire us to do what they feared you wouldn't. They hired us to shadow what you *did* do, to find out whether they were going to get away with it. If we had got too close to the truth, God knows what might have happened.'

'More murders,' said Molly, a bit too cheerfully for my liking. I didn't think she was actually buoyed up by us having had a narrow squeak; she's not a psychopath. I think it was more that she knew we were in trouble and that had reset her mood to sunny across the board.

'Have we committed a crime?' I said.

'And could we get immunity if we help you nail them?' said Kathi.

'Immunity is a lawyer word,' Molly said. 'Not a cop word.' She worked her jaw for a minute or two. 'What help?'

'What's the cop word?' said Kathi.

'Phrase,' said Molly. 'Not word. A bunch of phrases: looking the other way, selective memory, keeping it real . . . What help?'

'The Millers' fingerprints,' Kathi said. 'If it would be useful for you to have them without having to ask for them. I take it you're hoping that the other set on the baby stuff is theirs?'

'Where?' said Molly.

'What exactly would this "looking the other way" entail?' Kathi said.

'It would entail us deciding we don't really care too much about who looked in the Mustang and when,' said Molly, which was a very good point. 'We didn't ever have a time of death anyway, seeing as how it was so stinking hot in there. And, even if we find the bodies, we're talking ballpark now. So we haven't been focussing on Friday and neglecting the rest of the weekend.'

'They touched pool recliners,' Kathi said. 'One each. Metal rims and plastic webbing.'

'And no one touched them since?' said Molly.

'Nope.'

'How can you be sure?'

'Because I set them aside for cleaning,' said Kathi, the "duh" only just silent.

'So *you* touched them?' said Molly.

'But I didn't put my hands where they had put their hands,' said Kathi and this time she said it out loud. 'Duh.'

'And what exactly did the Millers do on the recliners that made them so filthy?' Molly said, setting off echoes of the notion that they weren't siblings at all, or not only siblings. Who *was* Virginia Andrews? A tennis player brought down by a family scandal?

'They're bereaved,' Kathi said. 'So they cried. Tears, snot, sweat if they really got going.'

'Well, they might have cried,' Molly reminded us. 'But if so, it was as much part of the act as the stilts and the bowtie. They sure ain't grieving.'

TWENTY-THREE

'So . . . what?' said Todd, once Molly had gone and Kathi was busy lint-rolling the chair back she had leaned against. 'Now we just sit here knowing what we know, pretending we don't, waiting to see if the Millers exsanguinate us and leave us all somewhere in a tie-dye Camaro?'

'I gotta go and put the recliners in the back office,' Kathi said. Molly and she had arranged that the Miller kids be summoned to the police station first thing in the morning to be re-interviewed about something or other; meanwhile a uniform would pick up the poolside seats and the Reception high stools for latent-print-getting purposes. 'But I guess so. Will you be able to?'

'Puh-lease,' said Todd. 'I worked for five years with the biggest homophobe this side of the Rockies and the day I left the guy was convinced that he had hidden it from me and I adored him.'

'*Adored* him?' I asked.

'Yeah,' said Todd. 'He was definitely hiding something and I messed with him a little for my own entertainment. Shoot me. How about you, Kathi?'

'That's the good thing about not being a gusher,' Kathi said. 'No offence.'

'None taken,' I said. 'And you're right. It took me two years to decide you liked me. If I ever work out what Noleen thinks, I'll let you know. I should manage it too, by the way.'

'Of course, *you'll* manage it,' said Todd. 'You have to hide your feelings about your whiny clients all day every day, and you deal with maniacs on the regular.'

'You are sounding more and more like your mother,' I told him.

'That,' he said, gravely, 'is a terrible thing to say, Lexy. Even in jest.'

He swept out and didn't hear me say, 'Who's jesting?' I loved Todd's mom, but in successive editions of the pictorial dictionary she was there as 'high maintenance', 'a lot' and 'extra', and no doubt we'd find out that 'extra' had been replaced by something else again when someone said it of Barb.

I texted Taylor as I left the owners' apartment, feeling the need for connection. Feeling, actually, exposed and vulnerable and close to terrified walking across the expanse of the fore-court, expecting the Millers to appear at any moment.

I felt a bit safer once I was along the side of the motel, which was completely nuts: out of earshot of all the windows and passing thick vegetation that could hide any number of murderers is actually a much dodgier spot. I felt safest of all back on the boat, gently rocking, surrounded by my belong-ings, lighting a fire in the woodstove, picking some comfort viewing. As the evening unfolded and wrapped its arms around me – well, it was mostly Taylor's arms – I finally relaxed. The trouble and confusion all seemed far away and not quite real.

So it was that, on Saturday morning, I left my phone by my bedside while I went to the kitchen to make coffee. Which is how come Phil and Jilly could walk right onboard and see through the open door clear to the other end of the corridor, where I was standing, with nothing more than a kettle full of scalding water to protect me.

'Come in,' I said, trying not to sound too wild. 'How *are* you? Stupid question. How are *you*? That's not better. Argh, Sorry. I've had a rough . . . Never mind me. Come in.'

Jesus Christ, right?

'We're just back from the police station. Again,' said Jilly, laying herself down into a chair. That's the only way to describe how she sat.

'Have they arrested someone?' I asked. 'Have they found your parents?'

'No and no,' said Phil. He took the footstool near his sister and leaned towards her, clasping his hands in between his knees. Now that I knew, everything about their whole demeanour struck me as ludicrously off-beam. Although I supposed the stress was real enough.

'Ugh,' I said. 'I'm so sorry you're going through all this.'

It was true. I wished they hadn't killed their parents and weren't going through any of it.

'It's just . . . everything,' Jilly said. 'It's grief like it would be however and whenever they died. But it's trauma too. And it's not as if any of that takes away the rest of it. There's still all the admin, except we can't get started on any of it. And there's still the decision to be made about a funeral or a memorial, except we can't get going on that either.'

'Because they haven't been found yet?' I said. For some reason that word that Todd used was going round and round my head: *exsanguinated*.

'I thought the authorities would declare them dead and at least we could begin to deal with things,' said Phil. 'But, even though the police are rock-solid sure there's no hope, it's not that straightforward. We're in limbo. You'd think it would be better than having it nailed right down. But it's not.'

'No one would think that,' I said, 'who has ever been through it. Not through exactly what you're going through, I mean.' *Exsanguinated*. 'But missing persons, or loved ones lost at sea. Mountaineers and what have you.'

'We're really struggling,' said Jilly.

Exsanguinated.

'Practically, as well as emotionally,' said Phil.

Exsang— Wait. All of a sudden, I thought I could see a motive and I thought I could see a way to start poking around in it too. 'When you say practically,' I began, 'do you mean you're having financial problems?'

Yeek. That was far too bald. Both Millers reared back, pulling their chins into their necks and narrowing their eyes. Oh, they were definitely siblings, whatever else they might be lying about. I mean, I was hoping Taylor and I would be married long enough to start looking like each other but not to this degree. That would be creepy.

'What I mean is . . .' I said, buying time as I cast around for a fix. What had I learned about lying from my most manipulative clients? Aha! 'Sorry,' I said. 'I'm being a bad immigrant. I'm very happy to be here and I'm actually studying for my citizenship test right now, but sometimes some bits of your culture still strike me as weird.'

Their eyes went back to factory settings, all of four of them. And both their chins poked forward in a normal fashion again. It worked every time. Pretend you're reluctantly saying something bad about yourself and no one thinks you're still messing with them.

'Like?' said Phil.

Shit.

Luckily, my studying saved me. 'Like the fact that everyone gets two senators,' I said. 'Whether it's us – fifth biggest economy in the world – or some patch of dirt where the governor's got a dry-cleaning franchise plus an Uber-eats gig at the weekend.'

'Yeah, but that wasn't what you meant,' said Jilly.

No, but I had bought myself some thinking time and used it. 'You're under twenty-six, right?' I said. I hadn't even noticed that their shoulders had hunched along with the other bits of physical squinching but they dropped too now, as the Millers worked out what I was talking about. Or thought so anyway. Coverage on their parents' Obamacare.

'It's not actually medical,' said Jilly.

'But I mean – sorry, I know this must be offensive,' I said, 'but tuition fees? Utterly bonkers. And even a cell-phone plan! The cost of a phone in this country will never stop astonishing me. So if everything's frozen? You poor things having to deal with money worries on top of everything else.'

'It's not just the day to day,' said Jilly.

Ding! Ding! Ding! Ding! The winning bell at the top of the high striker went off so loud inside my head I was amazed none of the noise leaked out my ears. There it was: the motive confirmed. They had killed their parents for money and they couldn't get their mitts on it. Whether it was insurance or inheritance I had no clue, but it was one or the other. Why else would grieving orphans be thinking beyond the 'day to day' before the bodies had been found and the case closed? They'd have been ghouls to have dollar signs in their eyes this early if they hadn't bumped off Mom and Pop. As it was, they were just rubbish murderers: great at the shell game of costumes and fakery, inspired about Free Stuff Corner, bold regarding the Mustang. But, when it came to holding their nerve, they were crumbling.

Or Jilly was crumbling. Phil seemed to realise she had misstepped. He waded in to distract me. 'So, is tuition cheaper in Ireland?' he said.

'Scotland,' I replied with the usual rueful smile, as if it pains me to correct a person when it doesn't really matter. 'It's free.'

'Oh,' he said. 'I meant college. Not high school.'

'Yeah,' I replied. 'It's free.' I truly believe that for one second they both forgot they were trying to get away with murder. 'And you probably know that the healthcare's free, right? And prescriptions. Care homes. Social care *at* home. Childcare.' Then I took pity on them. Or pretended to. 'Well, twenty hours a week of childcare and it doesn't start till they're three.' Then I really stuck it to them. 'And maternity leave ends when they're one. So there's a whole year when you're completely stuffed.' I beamed. 'But that's not going to get me naturalised, is it?' I let my face fall. 'Sorry for the levity.'

'Please don't be,' said Phil.

'It's welcome,' said Jilly.

They each gave me a brave smile.

Fuckers.

'So how can I help you?' I said. *Get arrested soon*, I thought. 'What brings you to me?' *When I'm determined to bring* you *down so very hard*, I thought.

'We were wondering if you would be willing to talk to someone who's kind of bugging us and get them to stand down,' said Phil. 'It's so insane you won't believe it but we can't get through to them.'

Nope, I thought. *Good. Nope. Good. Great.* 'Of course,' I said. 'Who is it who's clueless enough to be pestering you at a time like this?'

'Fern,' said Jilly. It's a soft word especially in an American accent with no trill on the R, but she managed to spit it. Fern, Fern, Fern, I thought, trying to haul a face up into view. 'And Yuzula.'

'From the gallery,' I said. There's only one Yuzula. 'Museum, I mean?'

'You'd totally think it was a gallery,' Phil said. 'What with all the hustle. They want us to help them with a "piece" inspired by what happened to our parents. There's some guy from Oakland involved too.'

'Oh, I just bet there is,' I said. 'Help them how, though? You're not artists. Do they need your permission? I say, withhold it.'

'No, they need our—' Jilly said.

'We don't want to go into details,' said Phil.

Jilly shrank at the tone of his voice. 'Right,' she said. 'We agreed. It's all so awful. But could you try to explain to them that our parents' murder wasn't art. And shouldn't be the inspiration for art. Would you be willing to?'

And you know what? Even though it would help a couple of murderers get peace while they waited for their scheme to pay out, I would. And I said so. What I didn't say was why: because I was pretty sure I could find out from Fern whatever it was Phil had just stopped Jilly from telling me.

They went away happy and I set off looking for Todd and Kathi to regale them with my courage and my discovery and the news that I had volunteered all of us for a return trip to the Patsy Denoni.

TWENTY-FOUR

We never got there, or not until later anyway. And I didn't have to search hard for the other two. I ran straight into Todd firing round the side of the motel coming to find me. Banged right into him so completely I could tell what belly-button ring he was wearing under his shirt today.

'Ooft,' he said. 'You look soft like a marshmallow, Lexy. But you almost winded me.'

'We've been summoned,' said Kathi, over his shoulder as he bent to get his breath back. 'Carmela called and said she needs to come clean.'

'Who?' I asked.

'From the Best Western,' Kathi said. 'I *knew* something about her was bugging me. I should have been round there leaning on her long before now. Still. Better late than never, huh?'

'Unless we're wrong and "come clean" means what it usually means,' I said. 'And we're going to go there and turn into her next three victims. But we're not wrong.' I dropped my voice. 'I just found something out that more or less proves it. I was coming to tell you.'

'Tell us in the car,' Todd said, before peeking round the corner of the building Pink Panther style and scuttling over to the Jeep like a cockroach when the strip light comes on.

Back at the Best Western again, after I had filled them in during the short journey, we clambered out feeling stunned. Insurance or inheritance, neither Todd nor Kathi could call it either but they were gratifyingly certain it was one or the other.

Winebox Winnie both did and didn't deserve the nickname today. On the one hand, she was sober as a judge. But she was trembling and had a slack, sweaty look on her face.

'Are you OK?' I asked, as we followed her from Reception into a little meeting room by the business centre, as the Best

Western chain no doubt called it on the website. It was a windowless room eight feet square with a table and six chairs and then there was a photocopier outside. The point is Carmela had to steady herself with one hand on the photocopier lid as she unlocked the door with the other, and the way she crossed the carpet to the table looked like a steep ascent.

'Not even nearly,' she said, sinking down. 'I've stopped drinking.'

'How much have you *been* drinking?' I asked.

'Don't judge me,' Carmela said. 'You haven't lived my life.'

'I'm not judging you,' I told her, putting my hand on top of her clammy, shaking fist where it sat on the table-top. 'I'm worried about you. How much did you drink yesterday?'

'Two bottles of red wine,' said Carmela.

'And the day before that?'

'Two bottles of red wine.'

'And the day before that?'

Todd stood up. 'When was the last time you didn't drink two bottles of red wine in a day, hon?'

'Weekend before Easter,' said Carmela. 'I told you before. That musta been more like three. Where you going?'

Todd had gone.

'He's gone to get you a drink,' Kathi said. 'You need to tail off, Carmela. You can't go from all that to nothing overnight. Have you never heard of the DTs?'

'I was going to tough it out,' Carmela said. 'I still think I should. One day at a time, right?'

'In about a week,' I said. 'Absolutely. But if you stopped dead right now you'd be having seizures after a day or two. And stopping dead might be exactly what happened.'

I didn't think Carmela was going to react at first. She stared for a moment or two, but then a tear brimmed in one eye and spilled, rolling down her cheek. 'How'd it get this bad?' she whispered.

'Girl,' said Todd, coming back in the door, 'this world is full of people ready to hack you to pieces. Do not help them.' He plonked an open bottle of white wine down on the table and set a plastic cup beside it.

'I prefer red,' Carmela said. 'And I always use a stem glass. Even on my worst day.'

'Uh huh,' said Todd. 'Well, this is medicine, not a party. Capiche?'

Carmela poured a good glug into the beaker, only spilling a little on the table-top due to her shaking hand. She downed it in one, shuddering. Todd was a genius.

'So,' I said, once she'd got another cupful over her back teeth, 'I'm assuming you called us to start apologising?'

Carmela frowned. 'I wanted to come clean, like I said.'

'Step nine, isn't it? Admit and amend?' said Kathi. I made a mental note to ask her sometime how she had that particular little nugget so readily to hand.

'Oh no!' Carlmela said. 'Is that who you are? Twelve-steppers? No way, José. I'm not interested.'

'Uhhhh, Carmela,' said Todd. 'You called us. We didn't barge in here. And you *know* who we are. Trinity Investigations. Looking into the Miller murder for the—'

Before he could say "kids", fail to sound normal and make Carmela suspicious, she interrupted him. She didn't actually say anything, but she burst into noisy sobs, complete with snot bubbles and a string of drool. Kathi had been near the door anyway but now she went and stood where the handle must be pressing into her back.

'See?' Carmela wailed. 'See what I mean? This is why I knew I had to stop drinking. I'm losing it. I forgot why you were here. I thought you were trying to suck me into a cult!'

'AA don't do house calls,' I said. 'I don't think. And they definitely don't give you wine. Come on, eh? Deep breaths. In and out. In and out. There you go. That's better.'

'It is,' Carmela agreed. 'It is. You're always hearing how great breathing is. It might be true.' Kathi, in a staggering display of generosity, took out one of her personal supply of paper hankies and pushed it halfway across the table. I pushed it the rest of the way and Carmela dabbed her eyes, blew her nose and did some more breathing, before smiling, pouring another glass of wine, sipping it and sitting back in her chair.

'I'm just going to say it,' she said. 'Soup to nuts. Hear me out, OK?'

Kathi sat down on the edge of the farthest away chair and took out her notebook.

'I'm a drunk,' said Carmela. 'Two bottles a day. And incidentals. Now, on my regular two bottles, I'm high-functioning. Once I add a little sumpin sumpin on top, I'm not so much functioning as passing. You know?'

We nodded.

'So likes of the day those Millers were going all over town looking for a room? There had been a reception here in the afternoon.'

'Yeah,' said Kathi. 'You told us.'

'I did?' said Carmela. 'See this is what I'm talking about. I didn't remember telling you that.'

Even though she had referred to telling us, two and half plastic cups of warm white wine ago? I hoped we were doing the right thing.

'You finished off the booze since it was already opened,' said Todd.

She took another sip of her wine. 'Yeah, well, that wasn't the half of it. I also went around and drank up all the poured glasses and finished the glasses that people had left half-drunk. And there were a lot of those, let me tell you. It was *terrible* wine.'

'You drank out of everyone's glasses they'd been drinking out of?' said Kathi. She had her arms folded across her chest trying to comfort herself. 'How many people?'

'Forty,' said Carmela. 'And I know what you're thinking. You're wearing it on your face.' She probably had no idea what Kathi was thinking, but that hardly mattered. 'Anyway, I was slaughtered by the evening. I was . . . I don't even know the word.'

'Blootered, trolleyed, paralytic, steaming, wrecked and stocious,' said Todd, sounding like some kind of X-rated Mary Poppins and leaving Carmela blinking. 'Lexy here is Scottish,' he explained. 'Most Scottish adjectives mean "drunk".'

'So I didn't want to be the only innkeeper in the whole of

Cuento who didn't remember the Millers,' Carmela went on. 'What the hell does "stow-shuss" mean?'

'Drunk,' said Todd. 'Are you saying they didn't stop here after all?'

'They must have, right?' said Carmela. 'Why wouldn't they? I'm sure they did. But it wasn't them I remembered. You know how I said it was the woman and not the man? That wasn't the case. I've stared and stared at that picture in the *Voyager* and I've never seen that woman in my life. Kayak or no kayak.'

I started to interrupt, but Kathi quelled me.

'And when I asked my friend,' Carmela went on, looking as if she might cry again, 'my friend, Sylvia, over at the Hampton Inn and Suites? I'm calling her my friend but she's more of a drinking buddy. I'm going to have to not see so much of Sylvia. After this last week you've given me.'

'This isn't the last week of your drinking, Carmela,' said Todd sternly. 'This is a transitional week of gradual detox, to be followed by the first week of you not drinking.' I was beginning to wonder how hard he tried over the years to get his mom off the sauce. He certainly seemed to have an action plan all ready to go. 'But anyway, when you asked Sylvia . . .?'

'She said it was surprising that someone so outdoorsy would wear as much make-up as Mrs Miller was wearing when she stopped off there. And she said – Sylvia can be pretty judgemental, you understand; she was born pretty and so she really thinks looks matter – she said it wasn't even as if the make-up made Mrs Miller look younger. She said it was almost as if Mrs Miller was wearing a ton of make-up expressly to look *older*. If that wasn't insane.'

All three of us sat up straight like schoolkids hearing the home bell.

'Oh my gossamer thread of explanation at long, long last!' said Todd. 'Of course! Of *course*! Of course. The whole story of the migraine and Mary and Joseph looking for a room at the inn bullshit was . . .'

'Bullshit?' I suggested.

'Exactly,' said Todd. 'Of *course* the actual Millers didn't do that. It was the kids! Disguised! Again!'

'So this is helpful to you?' said Carmela. 'Already? Before I've even—?'

'Helpful?' said Kathi. 'Carmela, you have cracked the case wide open. When you tell the cops what you've just told us your friend Sylvia told *you*, you'll be a local hero. Both of you.'

'Before you've even what, though?' I asked her.

'Before I've even told you what I was going to tell you,' said Carmela. 'Well, the rest of it anyway. Half of it is that I had never seen that canoe lady. The other half was that the lady I saw whose husband stayed in the car while I told her the hotel was full was a total nother one. Of course, I had forgotten all this or nearly anyway. It was lost in a fog of booze, you know? But anyway, it was definitely the woman who came in, not the man. I get pretty maudlin when I'm really . . . did you say "bladdered" in the middle of all that?'

'He didn't,' I said. 'But, as it happens, "bladdered", in Scottish, means "drunk". You were saying?'

'Yeah, I get pretty maudlin. I can sit and cry myself a river. Do you know, I once got turned away from a blood drive because my O-positive was ninety proof and I sat in my car feeling sorry for myself and blubbing for a half-hour before I drove home.'

I felt a sudden prickling sensation, without knowing why.

'*Drove* home?' said Kathi.

Was that it? I didn't think so. *Exsanguinated.*

'And that Friday night,' said Carmela, 'I thought what a shame it was for that poor woman – like I said, I'd forgotten all of this till I remembered – but I thought what a shame, when she had such a lovely head of hair, that she must have had a serious injury and she had probably had a big patch of it shaved right off and when it was healed and she lost the bandage she'd have to comb it really carefully over the bald spot or take the whole lot down into a pixie cut. Sorry. I'm rambling. But that's how I know it was the wife. And that's how I know it wasn't the canoe lady. Her hair wasn't any kind of crowning glory at all. Shut up.'

After a minute or so of our stunned silence, she added, 'I meant me. Yakking on and on.'

Exsanguinated.

'Carmela,' I said. 'Your yakking has just done what three detectives and a whole PD couldn't accomplish in two weeks. You have nothing to be sorry for.'

'One detective,' said Kathi. 'And two assistants.'

'They're still alive, aren't they?' said Todd.

'Oh, that's fantastic!' said Carmela. 'The canoe people? I brought them back to life? I'm so glad my memory got jogged! Their kids are going to be so happy!'

'Their kids are going to be so incarcerated,' said Kathi. 'For fraud.'

'Exsanguinated!' I said. 'I should have listened to myself!'

'Tourette's,' said Todd to Carmela, as he hustled Kathi and me out of the little meeting room. 'Only when she gets excited. And what you've just told us is very, very exciting.'

We were halfway to the front door when I stopped and turned back. Carmela was just slipping behind the Reception desk, with another full glass in her hand.

'Why did you remember?' I said. 'What was it that jogged your memory nearly two weeks later?'

'About Sylvia and the too much make-up and the lady in the kayak?'

'About the other lady. The one with the bandaged head.'

'Oh,' Carmela said. 'Yeah. I saw her again. Smaller bandage now but definitely the same woman.'

'Y–You–You saw her?' I said. 'When? Where?'

'Here,' said Carmela. 'Well, the back road to that weird new artsy place at the edge of the campus. Must have been nearly an hour ago.'

'Great. Thanks. Got to dash,' I said. 'Don't tell anyone else. Don't drink more than that one bottle. Call us again tomorrow, eh? Don't talk about the canoe lady's make-up. Don't— Look, is there any chance you could just lock the door until we call you back?'

'Seriously?'

'Maybe,' I said. 'Or even better. Dial nine-nine-nine and tell them what you told us.'

'Nine-nine-nine?' said Carmela, drawing back. 'Is that the number for AA? I told you I'm not interested. What are you playing at?'

I didn't have a cat's chance on that test. I might know why elections intervene before laws varying compensation take effect, but I could still fall on my arse over the small things. 'Nine-one-one,' I said. 'Trust me.'

TWENTY-FIVE

The Jeep was on two wheels as we peeled out of there.
'Wheeeeee!' said Todd. 'Only, where are we going?
To Molly? We're an hour too late to start a thrilling
chase sequence.'

'Molly for sure,' I said. 'Scenic route though, past the Patsy
D. Because I bet I know what twisted art installation Fern and
Mr Oakland want the Miller kids to *donate* to.'

'You think Yuzula and her minions were after a donation?'
said Kathi. 'Isn't a memorial usually funded by someone else?
Or if the family choose to fund one, then OK. But it's weird
to ask for money from grieving relatives because *you've* decided
on a statue or whatever.'

'I don't think the museum asked the Miller kids for money,'
I said. 'Not that kind of donation at all. I think they asked
them for something much more intimate, for their artwork
inspired by the Miller Mustang and I think the kids realised
– quite rightly – that it was far too likely to get people
thinking. That's why Phil shut Jilly down before she could
say the word.'

'What word?' said Todd. To give him his due he was concentrating on the traffic too.

'Blood,' I said.

'Is *that* why you keep saying "exsanguinated"?' said Kathi.
'I said it twice.'

'You said it out loud twice, but you muttered it three times
more,' said Kathi. 'Twice in the car and once in front of
Carmela.'

'And finally it all shook loose,' I pointed out.

'Walk us through it,' said Todd.

'With pleasure.' Smug, to be sure, but this hardly ever
happened. 'So the plan was this. Take blood, over time, like
blood donors do. Keep it in a freezer, stockpile it. Then take

a bit of scalp too to make sure no one doubts it. Fake a murder, scoop the insurance, skip off into the sunset.'

'But why the hell did they do all the crap with the disguises and the fake locums and the tarps and the . . . It's so over-the-top,' said Todd.

'*Where's Wally?*' I said.

'Waldo,' said Kathi, 'but you're right otherwise. Like flecked carpeting in the letting rooms of dirty, nasty motels,' she added, predictably. 'So no one can see the crumbs.'

'And ruched shirts for middle-aged women,' said Todd even more predictably.

'And the two-term limit.'

'Huh?' said Kathi.

'How is *Where's Waldo* anything like the two-term limit?' said Todd.

'It's the one I can never remember when I'm running through them all, even though it's right there.'

'That is noth— Never mind,' said Todd, changing tack when Kathi moaned low in her throat.

We drove in silence for a minute or two.

'Also, why oh why oh why did they give out a fake photo?' Todd said, at last. We were pulling into the Patsy Denoni car park and slowing. The tiny little tomato plants in the field at the far end were visibly bigger already, thanks to the California sun. The museum wasn't going as well as the agriculture, though. There was only one car in the public spaces, as well as one more plus a locked bike in the staff parking zone at the side.

'That's a really good question,' I said. 'Having the canoe couple lodged in the minds of the public did mean that the real, semi-scalped, much-exsanguinated Millers could go cutting about town on the fateful weekend, but it would have been a far better idea for them to hide far, far away and then change their appearance before their eventual re-entry into society with new names and more money. The kayak photo and them at the motel makes absolutely no sense to me.'

We climbed the steps of the museum and let the big doors swish open to admit us, expecting a reverent hush that I was planning to destroy with loudly delivered thoughts on Fern and Yuzula's clueless badgering of the innocent bereaved. As far as they knew.

Instead, what met us in the atrium was the unmistakable sound of argy-bargy already in progress. Yuzula was posed with her hands on her hips so her biceps sprang out, her power stance setting her stilettoed feet so far apart I feared that she might find herself doing the splits if she wasn't careful. Fern cowered half behind her but still with a pretty belligerent look on her face. They seemed to be in an altercation with a couple of punters, mightily displeased about something or other.

As we entered, the lady half of the couple wheeled round to face the three of us and we all saw four things: the bandage on the side of her head, the unmistakable stain of unhinged rage on her face, the echo of Jilly Miller's cheekbones and, standing beside her, exactly what Phil Miller was going to look like in another thirty years.

For one moment, we were all frozen. Then Trinity Investigations, in its finest moment since Kathi hung her shingle, surged forward as one, grabbing Fern and Yuzula and dragging them along the marble corridor to the back office before either Mr or Mrs Miller could stop us.

I locked the door and, with Kathi, started dragging furniture across it while Todd put Yuzula down and steadied her. I was right about the combination of those heels and that floor; he had had to fireman's lift her the second half of the way.

'Call nine-one-one,' I said, like a native.

'So *that's* why they faked a photo and came hanging around Cuento,' said Todd.

'Because they're so cocky they thought their kids' word would be enough, if there weren't bodies?' said Kathi.

'Or because they knew it wasn't a serious crime until the moment they tried for the life insurance?' I said.

'No,' said Todd. 'Because they're certifiably out of their drooling gourds!'

'Do you *know* those people?' said Yuzula. 'They just turned up and started bleating and whining about our curation practices. Poor Fern held them off for a while, but there was no dealing with them. I still don't know what it was that upset them so. They don't look like art patrons. Or aficionados. Or even—'

'They're fraudsters,' I said. 'They're grifters, swindlers, scammers. They're a con couple.'

'Well, it's a long con then,' Yuzula said, 'because today all they were doing was— Jesus!'

This last was in answer to the blow on the outside of her office door. She winced as a second one came and a third. Fern, on the phone, said, 'They're trying to break in! Five of us. No we don't have *guns*. Guns are what's wrong with this count— Look, I have no idea who these people even ar— Oh you do? Oh. Did they? The Best West—? When was this? *What?* Huh. Wait. Yeah, I think I hear them now.'

She did. We all did. All of five of us – huddled in Yuzula's office, with the mad Millers, unmurdered and unbowed, banging to get in – heaved a massive communal sigh of relief at the sound of police sirens outside, slamming doors, raised voices, a scuffle from the corridor, and finally a loud voice saying, 'It's all under control, folks, you can come out now.'

We could have lived off Yuzula's cold leftover pizza for a day or two, but we did as we were told and emerged shaking our heads and stretching our limbs as if we'd been in a bunker for days.

'Good old Carmela,' Kathi said. 'My God, if she hadn't had that warm white wine this morning she'd never have been able to explain what was happening. We had a close call there.'

'I found it invigorating,' said Fern.

'Very stimulating indeed,' Yuzula chimed in.

'It's given me an idea for a—'

We walked away.

MEMORIAL DAY

It took Kathi eight days to rid the motel of the Millers'
presence, the memory of the Millers' presence, the echo of
the memory, the ghost of the echo, and every trace of the
ghost. She was so busy cleaning she had to shut the Skweek,
which did her business a power of good since, after all her
regulars had to let other, lesser Cuento laundromats dab their
spills and fold their shirts for a while they came back asking
Kathi why there was no tip screen on the card reader.

Eventually, however, when all four Millers were processed,
arraigned and awaiting trial in Madding jail, and the *Voyager*
had reverse-image-searched the canoe couple and run a double-
page-spread (whole lot of scrolling) lifestyle piece on their
energetic outdoorsy retirement, and the medical student and
one-time minstrel had both sold the story of their costumes
to the *Chronicle*, and all the kids who'd scooped the D&D
merch had listed it on eBay, and the dream-streets residents
had smudged the short-lived Free Stuff corner with sage and
then decided to instigate one for real – that's Cuento for you
– we found ourselves, as we so often do, at the long trestle
table on the forecourt, with more food than you'd think the
table legs could deal with, never mind our stomachs. Our ranks
were swollen by Carmela, sipping Diet Coke, and Sylvia, also
sipping Diet Coke, inspired by the new sobriety of her friend
and promising to be as good a buddy on the journey as she'd
been during the party.

Fern and Yuzula weren't invited.

We weren't talking about the case, on account of Diego and
Hiro's little ears. Instead, we were doing what we do. Devin
was talking to Diego about their stuff: could have been video-
games; could have been last night's dreams. Hiro was filling
Gramma Kathi in on the important news of the week at pre-
school. Della was listening, ready to cut her daughter off swiftly

if she bored a grown-up or looked like turning whiny. Noleen was complaining about the City, the County, the state, the country and the world. Roger was listening to Sylvia telling him about a health complaint, like he usually does when he meets someone for the first time. Taylor was telling Carmela about migrating waterbirds, which I'd have to deal with soon, since I could see on Carmela's face that she was wondering if all parties would be this boring now she didn't drink any more. Todd, unusually enough, was silent. And he was staring at me.

'What?' I said at last. 'Have I got something in my teeth?'

'Would it matter if you did?' Todd said. He never gives up believing he could get me an American smile; could persuade me to file down my strong, healthy, cream-coloured, barely crooked teeth and snap expensive fakes over them.

'It's not on the test,' I said. 'They don't just say open wide and then either faint or ask you to raise your right hand and face the flag, you know.'

'They could do,' said Todd. 'Not the dumbest idea they ever had.' Then he went back to staring.

'What?' I said.

'This driving me nuts!'

'I'm just sitting here eating my dinner,' I told him.

'Exactly!'

We were starting to attract attention.

'I have no idea what you're talking about,' I said.

'I know! It's shredding my last nerve.'

'Give me one clue,' I said. 'I'm not messing with you, Todd. I just can't work out what you're on about.'

'Clue about what?' said Kathi.

'I don't know!' I said.

'What's he on about?' said Taylor.

'I. Don't. Know! What did I just say?'

'What's going on?' said Sylvia, distracted from Roger at last.

'Dunno,' said Noleen. 'Ask Lexy.'

'Which one's Lexy?' said Sylvia. She dropped her voice. 'The crabby one?'

'Jeez, Sylv,' said Carmela. 'I always assumed you had no tact because you were blootered. Is that just how you are?'

'Because I was *what*?' said Sylvia.

'I'm not crabby,' I said.

'No,' said Todd. 'You're not, are you?' His eyes were so wide I could see the whites all around the brown bit.

'Was that supposed to be my clue?'

'No,' said Todd. 'Here's your clue.' He paused to make sure everyone was listening. 'How are you feeling, Lexy?'

'Huh?' I said. 'Fine. That's a rubbish clue.'

'Lex,' said Taylor. 'I think I got it.'

'And?' I said. 'What's with the long pause?'

'Oh come on!' said Todd. 'What's another way to say "*long* pause"? You *are* messing with me, aren't you?'

'What?' I said.

'A hiatus?' said Diego. His mum and dad beamed.

'I ate us!' said Hiro. 'Monster! Warrggghhhh!'

'She's only two,' Diego explained to Sylvia and Carmela, not unkindly.

'Yes,' said Roger. 'She's still a . . . Finish this sentence . . . Fill in the blank . . .'

'Toddler?' I said.

'For fu— For crying out loud, Lexy,' said Noleen. 'Even I got it now.'

'Good for you,' I said. 'Do I *have* to get it? If I'm not fussed one way or the other? Is it obligatory? You know I never bothered learning how to do Magic Eye pictures. Remember them? I used to think: I've seen dinosaurs before. It's not worth giving myself a headache over.'

'Do you *have* a headache?' said Todd. I didn't answer. 'No headache, huh? And you're not crabby. And you're just sitting there eating your dinner, without a thought in your head. After everything you put us through.'

'That's not fair, said Taylor. 'Lexy didn't put you through anything. You volunteered. She certainly didn't put me through anything I wasn't happy to be put through.' He waggled his eyebrows at me.

'Niños!' said Della, in the voice she always uses to tell us not to swear or talk smut in front of the children. She really is a devoted—

'There she goes!' said Noleen, raising a glass as she watched it break over me like an egg smashed on my skull.

'I forgot!' I said. 'I actually forgot! Ahhhhhhh! How long has it been?'

'Three weeks,' said Taylor. 'You're a week late, babe!'

'Who's sober enough to drive to CVS?' said Todd.

'Hon?' said Roger. 'Calm down and step back. I mean it.'

I gave him a smile of bottomless gratitude. He was a brilliant doctor, even off duty. Thinking about doctors reminded me of my own.

'Aw, man,' I said. 'I've got to learn to bake muffins now.'

'You know what?' said Carmela. 'Apart from all the birds,' she threw Taylor a look, 'sober life is exactly as freaky as drunk life. Unless it's you guys. Is it you guys?'

It probably is. And I wouldn't have it any other way.

FACTS AND FICTIONS

I've given up denying that Cuento, CA, where Lexy lives, is Davis, where I live. There are Easter eggs in all the Last Ditch novels – go to their pages at www.catrionamcpherson.com for the evolving 'Schmavis Quiz'. But there are some more general Easter eggs in this one too. If you care to look, you'll see that Lexy refers to twenty-six of the twenty-seven constitutional amendments. I had to miss one out. It was quite easy.